BLACK

Russell Blake

First Edition

ISBN: 978-1492124016

Published by

Reprobatio Limited

CHAPTER 1

A harsh wind tore at the scrub along the edge of the rural road, the gusts assaulting the hills with startling ferocity. Electricity crackled across the elephant-hide sky as the Ford Econoline's tires shrieked in smoking alarm. The heavy vehicle lumbered around a hairpin turn, far in excess of any sane speed, engine roaring as it labored toward the summit. The Ferrari California 30 convertible ahead of it negotiated the curves like an Olympic skier, its red taillights winking at the van like a taunt, the deceptive twists a slim challenge for its driver, even after more than a few drinks.

It was late afternoon and a front had moved in, one of the freak storms that could come out of nowhere and disrupt the late spring warmth that was the birthright of Southern California's privileged. Flashes of light pulsed within the blanket of dark clouds brooding over the hills, threatening a downpour at any moment, but for now the heavens' growling was the harmless protest of a caged bear.

Another curve, another screeching drift as tortured rubber fought to grip the asphalt and the huge motor propelled the cargo vehicle closer to its elusive quarry. Inside, a hirsute young man with two days' growth dusting his swarthy features gripped the black lens of a Canon EOS 5D camera and gritted his teeth as the driver gave the van everything he had, pushing the ungainly conveyance to its limits.

"Damn. Slow down, would you? It's not worth getting us killed," he complained.

"Relax, Omar, I've got it under control," the driver snarled, his furrowed brow betraying the lie in his assurance. An old Chevrolet pickup truck swung around the bend and narrowly missed the van's front fender, causing them to lose a few precious seconds as the Italian car pulled over the rise and began its descent down Malibu Canyon Road, the sheer drop to the rocks hundreds of feet below a slim deterrent to its increasing speed.

"Crap. We're DOA if we can't catch up," Omar said. "DOA pays lousy."

"I intend to get paid," the driver muttered, and tromped on the gas as the Ferrari disappeared from view around another curve.

~∞~

The Ferrari driver wiped her face with the palm of her hand and shifted into third gear, increasing the engine revs to buy traction as she crested the summit. The clouds roiling over the ocean pulled her attention toward the water, a slate mirror stretching to the horizon, calm before the heavens let loose. Snoop Dogg's hypnotic atonal delivery wove its serpentine spell over a booming bass groove pulsing from the stereo, and after twisting the volume louder she tapped her fingers on the steering wheel in time with the rap beat. She glanced at the van in her rearview mirror and allowed herself a small smirk before her eyes drifted back to the road. Another hairpin was coming up, one she knew well from having almost lost it there the last time she'd had a few too many at one of her Valley hangouts, and she downshifted with a sloppy stab at the transmission paddle.

The high-performance eight-cylinder thoroughbred racing engine whined as the RPMs hit the ceiling, the tachometer needle pegging into the red, and then the car began to gradually but reluctantly fight gravity, enough so that she could keep it mostly in her lane. A rush of adrenaline surged through her system as she guided the vehicle along a knife's edge, the painted divider line the only thing between her and oblivion, her dilated pupils taking in the panoramic tableau of Malibu laid out before her. Her stomach seemed to float for a brief second, as it did on the first drop of a roller coaster, and then her eyes saucered as she saw her future approach from around the treacherous turn, offering no time to react.

~∞~

Omar's face blanched as they picked up speed, and he noticed the Italian car's brake lights remained dark as it headed for one of the dead man's curves on the drop to sea level.

"Come on, man. Be careful. She's whacked out of her mind. No way should she be moving that fast on this stretch," he said, trying to steady the

2

camera's telephoto lens and get some shots of the car hurtling at breakneck speed in front of them.

"Maybe she'll get it wrong and we'll have an exclusive on the biggest story of the month," the driver said, an ugly grin twisting his features. "You getting anything?"

"We're bouncing around too much. Holy shit. Look out!"

The Ferrari struck a glancing blow to a red Mercury Montego straining up the hill in the outside lane and then careened against the steep rock face, slammed onto its side, and plunged through the guardrail into the chasm beyond.

Time seemed to compress as both men found themselves staring at the Mercury's grill partially in their lane, the car overcompensating from grazing the Ferrari a few seconds before, instinctively trying to inch away from the ravine edge as it fought for stability. The middle-aged woman's face was framed for a split second by her windshield, dried insect smudges a testament to the rural road's unspoiled allure, and then the van driver wrenched the wheel to the right and stood on the brakes as Omar wedged his legs against the dash in an effort to brace against the impact.

But the pedal felt mushier than usual, and after a token resistance it dropped uselessly to the floorboard with a soft clunk.

The van's high center of gravity and inadvisable speed carried it into a sideways drift, the back end swinging around as its rear wheels lost traction in a slow-motion pirouette. The screech of smoking brakes echoed through the canyon as the Mercury rolled to a stop just in time to see the van flipping in a series of cartwheels, drawn inexorably to the precipice.

It smashed into the guardrail and seemed to hesitate for a brief eternity before executing its final somersault into the void. The fireball that followed its drop to the distant rocks could be seen as far away as Malibu, and by the time the shaken driver in the Mercury had stopped her car and was digging in her purse for her cell phone, a local squad car was already wending its way up the hill from town, lights flashing and siren keening as the pregnant clouds finally let loose their deluge with a rumble.

CHAPTER 2

Orange and red streaked the sky as the sun shimmered through the smog layer that hung across Los Angeles like a beige blanket, a perennial part of life in the big city, as tenacious as a divorce lawyer and equally pleasant. The storm had blown through and exhausted itself the prior night, and not a cloud now marred the balmy spring day.

A convertible white 1973 Cadillac Eldorado, the top down, growled its way through traffic on the gridlocked streets leading into downtown, consuming enough gas to power a cruise ship, its red leather upholstery faded from the years but still garish enough to turn heads. AC/DC blared from the crackling speakers, the singer's shrieking caterwauling a lewd promise over the driving guitars and thumping drums, drawing stares from a few of the surrounding cars' occupants – those not on the phone making deals or excuses or promises they had no intentions of keeping.

The light on La Cienega turned red and the big car rolled to a stop as Artemus Black punched the button on his cell phone and listened to the warbling ring on his earpiece. He was running late, and hoped that his office manager, Roxie, had made it in before him – he hated to set a poor example by being tardy, but hadn't accounted for the pileup that had put a twenty-minute dent into his well-oiled plans.

He considered his reflection in the rearview mirror as he waited for her to pick up, noting that his gleaming black hair, cut like mid-career Elvis, could use a trim. His piercing blue eyes radiated intelligence and a sincerity he rarely felt, although he would certainly pretend to care if he thought it was important to a case or could gain him an advantage. And he looked sharp in his choice of lightweight gray vintage-cut suit – very Bogey, he thought with satisfaction, straightening the skinny oxblood tie, also vintage, and in keeping with his preferred style of Elmore Leonard-era noir. At least that was *his* perception.

"Black Investigations – er, crap, I mean, Solutions. Black Solutions. May I help you?" Roxie answered on the fifth ring, sounding frazzled.

"Nice. Very professional, Roxie," Black chided. The name change had been his latest idea for increasing business and being able to charge more per hour. *Investigations* sounded lower-end, whereas *Solutions*…well, who wouldn't pay a few bucks more for a solution to their problem, whatever it was? It had come to him about midway through a self-help and motivational program he'd been listening to, taught by a self-declared success guru and celebrity flim-flam seminar speaker whose claim to fame was hosting fire-walk programs and group stadium gropes of orgiastic affirmation.

"Whatever. It's a stupid name. I don't see what was wrong with the old one," Roxie responded.

"It didn't reflect our scope."

"What does that even *mean*?"

Black had been working with Roxie on improving her attitude, but some days it seemed like a losing battle. It was a pity she was so good at what she did – running the office, juggling administrative duties and research that made the FBI look like neophytes.

"It means I think we can improve our brand, Roxie."

"Our…*brand*. I see. Have you been drinking?"

"Branding is very important."

"Maybe if you're a cowboy or a steer. Wait – did you mix up your meds again?" Roxie asked.

"Please at least try to answer the phone professionally. Is that too much?"

"I don't know. I'm getting confused about our brand. Are we not a private detective agency named after that Brad Pitt movie?"

"We're a solutions enterprise group. We provide security and investigation solutions. Brad Pitt has nothing to do with it."

"And here I was sticking around because I thought I had a chance at him. I hear he likes to smoky-smoky. Angelina goes berserk on his ass because all he wants to do is party hearty."

"I could pretend I have any idea what you're talking about, but I know better."

"What's that noise? A leaf blower? Seagull fight?"

Black turned down the stereo. "There. Better?"

"Are we at the part where you tell me what you want?"

"I wanted to let you know there was an accident *en route*."

"*En route?* So we're going to start speaking French to each other now? Like some kind of Euro-trash secret agent code?"

"A fender bender. I'll be a little late."

"I'll alert the media."

"Is that your subtle way of telling me there are no calls?"

"Oh, wait," Roxie said, her voice quickening with excitement, before returning to her usual dry delivery. "Hmm. Never mind. No, no calls. Does that mean I won't get paid this week? I'm starting to worry now that Brad's off the table."

"Brad was never on the table. Come on, Roxie, I've never stiffed you. Relax. Money's in the bank."

"I do the books, remember? The account's emptier than a Kardashian's head."

"Don't worry about it. Something will come up. It always does. I haven't let you down yet."

Roxie let out an exasperated sigh. "Was there something else, Mister *En Route* Solutions?"

"No, I just wanted to let you know I'd be in soon."

"Did you quit smoking?" she asked, skepticism dripping from every syllable. "Wasn't this the weekend you were going to?"

"Soon. Roxie, why do you always bust my chops? Why can't we ever have a simple, normal interaction?"

"Besides that you're delusional and have a Bogart fetish, you mean?"

"See? That's what I'm talking about. You can never stay on track."

"Hold on. The other line's ringing," she said.

"No, it isn't. I don't hear anything."

"Hmm. Maybe it's going to. I've been thinking I might be psychic."

"You aren't psychic. There's no such thing."

"I so totally knew you were going to say that." Roxie paused dramatically. "Is there anything else?"

"I don't suppose there's any way I could get you to make some coffee, is there?"

"You know I don't drink coffee. It's poison."

"I was thinking more for me, Roxie."

"It's poison for you, too."

"Roxie. Please?"

"Starbucks is just around the corner. Oh, here comes the call!"

"Do you not realize I can hear everything, including that the phone isn't ringing?"

"Pick me up a vente chai."

The line went dead, and Black shook his head as if to clear it. Roxie was brilliant, but hard to deal with when she got her back up, which was early and often. An aspiring singer in an indie art rock band, her instinct was to flout authority, which he more than understood from his youth – but it wasn't so great when it was his ass getting flouted. The problem was that she ran his company, so he had to suck it up and take whatever she was dishing out. Which, today, appeared to be a heaping helping of screw with Black. A regular menu item with her.

A lowered BMW seven-series sedan eased up beside him at the next light. The tinted windows rolled down, revealing three laughing homeboys whose gangsta rap was vibrating the street. Black looked over at them and nodded, and they exploded in peals of mockery at his flimsy white-boy suburban cool. He was afraid it was going to escalate until a motorcycle cop pulled to the crosswalk between them. The BMW's windows whined closed and the music dropped to earthquake level, and the impassive policeman eyed the big sedan without comment before turning to glance at Black's pimpmobile. Black tried his nod again, and the cop shook his head disgustedly before gunning the throttle and pulling away as the light changed. Black wasn't sure which was worse – being dissed by the homeboys or the five-oh. Obviously, L.A. was a town singularly lacking in good taste.

Then again, it always had been. He still remembered moving here over twenty years ago, fresh out of the army, having exchanged his M16 rifle for a Gibson Les Paul guitar, determined to make a splash in the music scene and become a star. Seven months of living at home with his crazy parents after his discharge had been enough to drive him three hundred and fifty miles south of Berkeley, California, to Hollywood, where the music scene was vital, and miracles could occur seemingly overnight. Guns N' Roses had broken big the year before, and the whole Seattle grunge thing hadn't really caught on yet, so if you were a rock guitarist with aspirations of hitting it big, Los Angeles was the epicenter of the music industry.

Black goosed the gas and lurched forward, enjoying the feel of the hazy sun on his skin. It seemed like only yesterday he'd rented the fleabag apartment three blocks off the Sunset strip, relieved to be free of his parents' hippy lifestyle. They'd already done enough damage to his psyche, starting with his name: Artemus, an idiotic homage to a crappy seventies-era TV show – *The Wild Wild West* – whose number two character, Artemus Gordon, had somehow cut through his father's drug fog around the time of Black's birth and seemed like a brilliant namesake for his only son.

He hadn't even named Black after the star of the show. No, that would have been too fortunate. His moniker was drawn from the little weasel guy who dressed up in funny costumes every week while the star, James West, kicked serious ass and took names. So instead of James Black, he was Artemus. A name he despised, as he had since he'd been old enough to realize how badly screwed he'd gotten in the name department. His parents had neglected to give him a middle name, so as soon as he hit his teens, he took the one he wished he'd been given, and went by James, shortened by his friends to Jim.

Black swung onto Pico and nosed the Cadillac east toward his office, the recollections infuriating him even twenty-plus years later. He took a few deep, calming breaths, as he'd been counseled to do by Dr. Kelso, his therapist, and willed the agitation away. An old woman in a Camaro almost sideswiped him when she pulled from the curb without looking, and he flipped her off while standing on his horn. He knew it was childish, but he felt strangely better.

Black circled his block, looking for a parking space, and cursed his circumstances for the thousandth time. Living in an apartment that was only slightly nicer than the one he'd had when he hit town, perpetually on the financial rocks, making it job-to-job with no consistency to any of it. Anyone else might have turned to introspection, but the only thing that bubbled to Black's surface was more rage – at being thoroughly boned by the cosmic powers that be, butt-rammed at whim by a bombastic deity who'd singled him out for persecution, raising him up just enough to give him hope for the future and then slamming him to the canvas, crushing his dreams, leaving him empty and broken inside.

At least my positive thinking tapes are paying dividends, he thought morosely. Then again, it was easy for his doctor to counsel harmony. *He* hadn't written an album of hit songs, met the love of his life – who also had pipes like Joplin and the sex appeal of Shakira – and then been screwed out of both at the last minute, just as things were taking off, preparing for a world tour opening for Nirvana to support the release of the record that would go on to become one of the biggest sellers of the nineties. Easy for his quack to say, "Take a few deep breaths" and dismiss his rage as a personal failing. *He* hadn't climbed to the top of the mountain only to be thrown off its sheerest face.

A spot opened up on his right and he signaled as he slowed, earning an angry honk from the car behind him. Black offered another middle finger and then swung into the space, all thoughts of his past banished in favor of controlling his focus, just as his MP3s soothingly advised. He was a winner. Everything leading up to this point had made him one. It was his time now. He was master of his destiny and everything was possible, each new day the start of a powerful, compelling beginning.

A tidy enough mantra, indeed, though with a delicate hint of pure BS, he decided as he shut off the engine. But it was all he had. That, cigarettes he had to quit smoking soon, and anger. Always anger, as familiar to him as his favorite underwear.

Succumbing to his base motivations, he cracked the glove compartment open and extracted a hard pack of Marlboro reds, and after a moment's hesitation, withdrew one and lit it with the car lighter. Black greedily sucked the smoke into his lungs, despising his weakness even as the rush of nicotine into his constricting vascular system dampened his annoyance at the world, if only momentarily. The cigarette didn't last long, and he considered having another one, then checked the time and swore under his breath.

When he pushed through the door to his "suite," as the small antechamber and postage stamp office was referred to by the landlord, Roxie was on the line with someone. She glowered at him as he inched past her desk, which faced the dilapidated black faux-leather couch he'd bought from the prior occupant for a hundred bucks. He pretended not to notice her disapproving gaze and ignored the fact that, even though he'd asked her a hundred times to dress appropriately, she was again wearing a tight ebony concert T-shirt with the sleeves cut off, the better to display her tattooed arms. She brushed an errant dyed black lock aside and put the call on hold.

"About time. Where's the chai?"

"Damn. I forgot. Running too far behind. Who are you talking to?"

"A potential client. Says she knows you."

A furry, rotund form approached from beneath her desk and rubbed against Black's leg before stalking away, leaving a trail of cat hair on his suit trousers, which drove him nuts. Mugsy was a stray that had figured Black for a soft touch the day after he'd moved in, and had promptly taken up residence in the office, doted upon and spoiled rotten by Roxie, whom he adored.

"Really? Who?"

"Have you been smoking? You smell like a big fleshy ashtray."

"I resent the fleshy crack. Uncalled for."

"If it fits, own it."

"Who's the client, Roxie?" Black tried again.

"Crap. I could think better if I had a refreshing chai in front of me. I get all forgetful if I don't have my fix."

"Roxie. Who?"

"Says her name's Colleen. Sounds kind of whack. A little *loco*, if you know what I mean."

Black searched his memory banks. "Colleen Fleishman?"

"That's it. She wants to talk to you. Line one." Mugsy resumed his position under Roxie's desk after gracing Black with a wide-mouthed yawn and a look of complete disdain.

"What did you two talk about?" Black asked as he moved into his office and plopped down into his worn executive chair.

"She wanted my advice on currency hedge derivative contracts. What do you think we talked about? Ask her yourself," Roxie said with an exaggerated eye roll and her trademark sneer, then turned to face the sofa again, her part in the discussion at an end, annoyed because he'd forgotten her drink.

Black hit the call button and lifted the handset to his ear. Colleen was a friend from way back, although he hadn't talked to her in months…no, make that years. At one time she'd been a heavy hitter gossip columnist, but the business hadn't been kind to her of late, and as the industry had shifted from paper to online, she'd fallen on hard times. But she still knew a lot of people. A lot.

"Black Solutions, may I help you?"

"Solutions? What the hell does that mean?"

"Colleen?"

"Maybe I should say, Colleen Solutions?"

"Colleen. Nice to hear from you. Been a while."

"Your receptionist is a hoot. You banging her?"

"Colleen. Come on. I'm not going to dignify that with a reply. Really."

"You should never bang the help. That's a good rule to live by."

"Thanks for the tip. You should write greeting cards – you have a gift. But concern over my love life aside, what's up? Everything okay?"

"With me? Never better. I can't get anyone in this stinking berg to answer my calls, but other than that, can't complain."

"I answered."

"I meant anyone that mattered."

Black was beginning to wonder whether he was wearing his "I'm an asshole" shirt today, or if perhaps this was the new normal for his interactions with the opposite sex.

Colleen's tone softened. "Sweetie, it was a little joke, okay? You know I love you. I'm just bitter because you won't jump my bones. Probably worn out from your twenty-something hottie answering the phone, am I right? Men are all pigs."

"Maybe you could do fortune cookies, too. Greeting cards and fortune cookies. We'll be rich," he said, and then tried one more run at it. "What can I do for you today, Colleen? I'm kind of busy…"

"Yeah, your receptionist told me. Sounds like LAX over there. You've got a lot on your plate."

He waited a beat, refusing to be drawn in. He knew her, and he knew that she'd get to her point when she was good and ready. This was all just foreplay.

"But assuming you can push all the other big 'solutions' cases aside, I think I've got one that will pay the light bill for you. Maybe even get you a new suit."

He stopped scanning his emails and leaned back in his chair, his interest piqued. "Really? You know what a clothes horse I am. I have expensive tastes."

"It's all that retro junk you wear. You should dress like an adult."

"Again, your counsel is priceless. I'm making notes. But you mentioned a case?"

"I did. It's a friend of mine. A bigwig who's got a problem. I was trying to get some dirt about his next movie, and he let slip that he's in big trouble. So I suggested he talk to someone who's a professional. That would be you, by the way."

"A bigwig? Those are my people. Who is it, and what's the problem?"

"Not so fast. This will go a lot easier if you come out to my place. I can walk you through it. Won't take too long. Besides which, I haven't seen you for all kinds of forever."

Black groaned inwardly and then glanced at the big pile of nothing on his desk. Colleen lived in a mobile home off the highway that stretched like a ribbon through Riverside to Palm Springs and beyond. If he was lucky he could get there in forty minutes, now that rush hour was over. He knew she was emotionally blackmailing him – if he wanted the juice on the client, he had to show he cared, and in this case, caring meant visiting her even though he'd rather be vivisected by zombies.

"All right. You sold me. Give me the address and directions again. It's been a while. I can probably move some things around and make it out there in an hour or so."

"Yeah, Roxie felt you might be able to. She's a firecracker, isn't she?"

Black eyed her in the other room, now texting someone on her cell phone, swinging one black denim-clad leg slowly as she hummed to herself.

"That's the understatement of the year."

CHAPTER 3

The drive out of L.A. was a misery even in the late morning, clogged with heavy trucks steaming their way east with their bounty fresh off the docks in Long Beach and San Pedro. Black was beginning to get a sunburn by the time he rolled into the sad collection of mobile homes grouped just off the freeway in a community laughingly named The Oasis.

Colleen's singlewide was several hundred yards from the entrance, and the downtrodden vehicles he passed gave silent testament to her fall from grace. She'd been methodically downsized from her once-lofty perch as the top gossip columnist in Los Angeles until she now earned a paltry income as a stringer for the new wave of gossip websites that had cropped up. The most popular of these had been created by her old boss, Freddie Sypes, who was also the conniver responsible for her ultimate downfall as he power-grabbed and schmoozed his way to the top of the newspaper's food chain before kicking it to the curb in favor of his current enterprise. Colleen had reciprocated by starting her own site, but lacking Freddie's financial resources, it ultimately drained her savings and went under, taking what was left of her career with it.

The smog-laden air smelled like burning oil when he shut off the engine and climbed out of the car. Colleen's mobile home seemed to sag in the middle, and looked like it had last been painted around the end of the Korean War. The screen door opened and she stepped out, and he had to admit that even with all the hardship, she'd held up well. Her bronze skin was taut from her most recent face-lift, and her augmented breasts announced themselves with unapologetic rigidity, putting the tensile strength of her emerald green blouse to the test with each careful step toward him. She had to be sixty if she was a day, but she could have easily passed for a decade or two younger, and Black told her so, noting the smile his flattery brought to all of her face but her eyes.

"Come on in, darlin'. It's not Beverly Hills, but hey, I hear that's all immigrants anyway these days," she invited, after delivering a not-so-matronly kiss to Black's cheek, leaving a faint trace of knock-off perfume on his collar.

"How've you been, Colleen?"

"You know how it is. I'm on disability – my back. The painkillers help pass the time. And I do a deal here or there. It's not the old life, but I get by. How about you?" she asked as she led him to a brown tweed couch across from an entertainment center.

"Same old. Working too hard for too little money."

"I know that story. Where are my manners? Can I get you anything to drink? Soda? Water? Something stronger?"

"Water's fine, Colleen. Thanks."

She went to the kitchen and fetched two small plastic bottles from the fridge and then sat down next to him, turning coquettishly to face him. "My friend needs someone savvy to help him out of a jam, Black."

"A friend. I see. Does this friend have a name?"

"Andrew Hunter."

Black digested the name. "*The* Andrew Hunter? Actor?"

"Now director and producer, babe. Times they are a changing, and all." She paused, and sat back while fishing in the cushions for the television remote control. "Yes, *the* Andrew Hunter. And believe me – he's got a problem. If you can do anything to solve it, he's a great guy to know."

"That's what I do, right? I'm the solutions guy. PI to the stars."

"Hmm. I wouldn't put that on your cards quite yet. Anyway, I told him that you would stop by his place whenever you had some time. He said he'd be there all day." Colleen powered on the TV and pushed play on her DVD player, and an image flickered to life: Andrew Hunter at a high profile press conference several years ago, calling for a ban on the paparazzi – a campaign he'd taken on as a cause célèbre. They listened as he laid out his case, and then she muted the sound.

"You mentioned that he had a problem?" Black nudged her.

"He does. It's a security matter. Which I told him was right up your alley."

"Security? As in…?"

"I'll let him tell you about it himself. But he's pretty agitated, I'll say that much. And when rich, powerful guys get worried, that means opportunity to little people like us."

"How do you know him?"

"You forget that in my past life I knew everyone. I always treated him fairly, and a few times I softened a story that painted him in a negative light. We still talk. Since his star started fading at the box office, he's gotten way more friendly with his remaining allies. He counts me as one. Which is where you come in. I recommended you. He wants to meet as soon as possible."

"Sure. Where does he live?" Black asked.

"Where else? Bel Air." Colleen rattled off an address and he entered it into his phone.

"Will they even let me drive up there?"

"You clean up pretty good. Just don't wear any gang paraphernalia, and you should be okay."

"I'm always representing the 'hood. Peace."

Colleen didn't say anything, the silence deafening. The pause was broken by the sound of a vehicle pulling up in front of the trailer. A car door closed, and a muscular blond man in his late thirties with longish hair and a deep tan pushed through the doorway carrying a bag of groceries.

She cleared her throat and offered a fatigued introduction. "Black, this is Seth. Seth Avery."

Black rose as Seth placed the bag on the cheap dining room counter. The two men studied each other, and then Seth's face broke into a practiced grin, his handsome features instantly at ease as he reached a hand out to Black.

"Nice to meet you," Black said.

"Likewise. I'm sorry, Col didn't tell me she was having visitors."

"Seth's staying with me, helping patch the place up. He's a very talented director," Colleen volunteered, and Black surmised that there was more going on than a little handyman action around the trailer. None of his business, and good for her if she could pull off the cougar thing.

Seth smiled again. "Well, it's kind of you to say so. But that was a while ago. Now I'm a simple carpenter…"

Black and Seth stood facing each other like heavyweights who'd fought to a draw, and then Black held up his phone.

15

"I was just getting ready to hit the road." He turned to her. "Thanks for the tip, Colleen. Any wise parting words?"

She stood and moved to his side, linking her arm in his as she led him back to the door. Seth had already lost interest in him and walked into the kitchen to unpack the groceries.

"Hunter's under a lot of pressure right now, with his new movie getting ready to break. My advice would be to try to minimize the funnies with him. He's not in a very comedic mood, and he sounded, if not exactly panicky, certainly agitated. So I'd keep it professional."

"Good to know."

Colleen frowned. "Don't blow this. I don't want it to seem like I referred a loser. Hunter's an important guy, at least to what's left of my career. And I need all the friends I can get, Black."

"I won't. No wisecracks. I get it."

She escorted him to his car. Seth's big silver Dodge pickup truck was parked directly behind it.

"Let me know how it goes," she said.

"Yo. You know how I roll."

She pulled away from him and gave him a warning glare. "Black…"

"Kidding."

CHAPTER 4

"Roxie, pull up everything you can find on Andrew Hunter," Black called out as he strode into the office. Mugsy glared at him from his position on the sofa, then resumed his beauty rest, which Black had thoughtlessly interrupted.

"Yes, Bwana," Roxie replied, and Black heard a flurry of lightning key strokes begin. Ten minutes later she stuck her head in his doorway. "Check your email. Does this mean I get paid on Friday? I'll be able to eat for another week?"

Black looked up from the periodical he was reading – *Billboard* – at Roxie standing there, ebony hair aggressively tamed in an edgy cut, the tips dyed blue, the obligatory nose stud complementing her tattoos, displayed like badges of courage. She gave him a smug glance, then sauntered back to her station like an extra from *Road Warrior*, her pants so tight they looked like she'd dipped her lower body in ink, heavy biker boots clumping on the cheap linoleum as she moved. He watched her departure and felt a stirring, but forced it away – Roxie was only a little more than half his age, and a freak. The last thing he needed was to ruin their working relationship with some kind of a…thing. Not that there was much chance of that.

He turned his attention to his computer screen and pulled up the message, which contained about a dozen URLs – and not just Wiki links. Roxie's morose attitude was more than compensated for by her research skills, which were stellar, and one of the primary reasons he tolerated her barbs.

The first was an article about Hunter starting his own production company a decade ago, when his acting career had been winding down. The forty-something action star had faded from the public eye as his films drew increasingly smaller crowds even as their budgets inflated like the national debt. Next was an older interview from his heyday, talking about the release of *Kill Club Love*, which had set box office records and spawned five sequels, each more sophomoric and unwatchable than the last. The third was more interesting to Black – a recent article about the new film he was directing and starring in, which was expected to revitalize his flagging career and establish him as more than an also-ran director with marginal skills.

Next was a clip about Hunter's messy and expensive divorce – his second – and a short piece about his daughter, a common Hollywood story: in and out of rehab a half dozen times, arrested for possession more often than she'd changed her hair color, a downward party spiral culminating in an ugly incident outside a club where she'd been injured. Nothing else on it; more an afterthought to fill up space.

The last bunch chronicled Hunter's vocal anti-paparazzi campaign, where he'd used his influence to get a bill floated in the California legislature to impose restrictions limiting their access and delineating what they could and couldn't do. Hunter had made it his mission to single-handedly gut the annoying photogs who swarmed like blackflies around the bloated celebrity carcass that was Hollywood, and had made considerable headway before the bill was voted down. In response he'd redoubled his efforts, making enemies out of most of the local press in the process.

The final link was to that morning's *Los Angeles Times*, about a tragic fatal accident in Malibu Canyon the prior day involving the female star of Hunter's new film, as well as a van with paparazzi in it. The coverage was short on specifics, but a witness said the Italian sports car that the star – Melody Cambridge – had been driving lost control due to high speed, and the van was unable to evade the ensuing chaos and also crashed.

Black scrutinized the photo of Cambridge and shook his head. Gorgeous twenty-something, a hot career on the ascent, dating one of the more eligible eye candy actors in town, a blockbuster about to be released…and now she was being scraped off the rocks at the bottom of the gulch. A final line in the article said that the police were testing for the presence of drugs or alcohol, and he wondered how they did that after a car ignited following a ten-story drop.

He pushed back from his desk, stood, and stretched, deciding to stop for coffee on the way to Bel Air, the most expensive real estate in L.A. He'd spent plenty of time in the area operating the last failed business he'd tried before starting the P.I. firm: discreet private limousine service to the stars, which had been one of the ways he'd gotten so connected in town.

During its two-year operation, he'd driven just about every celebrity and mogul worth mentioning. He'd gotten referrals from his friend Bobby Sorell, an entertainment attorney who'd gone from being his worst enemy to an unexpected ally, after structuring the deal where Black had foregone any claim on the songs he'd written in return for a lousy hundred grand. That had been bad enough, but then the bastard had begun sleeping with Nina, his nineteen-year old wife, and had helped her divorce him when she'd become the hottest female singer of her era, eclipsed only by Beyoncé when Destiny's Child had bounced and shimmied onto the scene.

Be that as it may, Sorell had done his best to make amends, and Black believed that he really felt bad about how it had played out. Black had moved from his customary blind rage to a cautious truce that had developed into a real friendship, as his ex had moved on from Sorell to a string of high-profile flings that had culminated in two disastrous marriages to A-list celebs – bad boy actors with big careers and even bigger egos, probably overcompensating for other shortcomings.

"I'm headed out," Black announced as he strode through Roxie's reception area. She didn't look up from her furious text messaging, thumbs punching and stabbing her little cell phone with rapid dexterity as she listened to music on her computer speakers. "What's that you're listening to?"

"A band."

Black nodded. "Yeah, I got that. What band?"

"You wouldn't know them. They're hip and cool."

"I know hip and cool things."

She eyed him scornfully. "Sure you do."

"I'm serious. I do. I've got game."

"Uh huh. Nobody says that anymore."

She turned the music up, and the chorus of the driving, psychedelic-tinged melody filled the office:

When you see yourself in a crowded room
Do your fingers itch, are you pistol-whipped?
Will you step in line or release the glitch?
Can you fall asleep with a panic switch?

She lowered the volume. "I love these guys. They're called Silversun Pickups. I think they're slathered in awesome sauce."

"I swear I've heard of them."

"No, you haven't. Don't lie."

"No, really, I have. Don't they do that Fox song that's gone viral?"

She rolled her eyes. "You are so not being remotely truthful. It's okay. Once you're over your 'best if used by' date, you can't be expected to know what's cool anymore. No need to pretend you do in some pathetic bid for approval."

"Roxie, I'll have you know not long ago I was a player in the music business."

"Is this where you start crying?"

"I was. I wrote all the songs for Nina's first album. You know, the biggest album of the decade?"

"I wasn't born yet." She hesitated. "Is that the phone?"

"I'm standing right here. I can hear that the phone's not ringing."

"Right." She stared at him.

"I'm leaving now."

"Okay," she said, without a trace of interest. "I guess that means I'm screwed on the chai for today, huh? Thanks for nothing." She returned to texting.

"I've got a big case here. Sorry I can't be your beverage boy."

She looked up from her engrossing communiqué. "Are you really going to go dressed like that?"

"What's wrong with my outfit?"

"You look like you fought your way out of a thrift store by putting on clothes. Somebody probably died in that suit," she commented dryly, peering at the forties-cut lightweight gray two-piece. "Just promise me you aren't going to wear one of your hats."

"What's wrong with my hats?" he asked, bristling.

"Nothing, if you're a Seattle hipster trying for angst in a café. But frankly, a fedora on an adult male who's…" – she paused – "not a spring chicken anymore, makes him look like a sad old douche."

Black gawped at her, speechless.

"Maybe that's too harsh. More a twat. Yes, I think that's what I was looking for. The hat, combined with that outfit, says twat all over it. Without the hat, maybe the client will think you're poor and had to wear Dad's suit. But the hat kicks it to five-alarm clueless," she concluded, and then sat back with a sweet smile that reminded Black of a python looking at a baby chick.

"I don't know what to be more offended by…" he sputtered.

"Well, take your time. I understand you slow down as you get older." Another beaming flash of perfect white teeth.

"Roxie, I don't pay you for fashion tips," he began, annoyed.

"You hardly pay me for anything. And judging by your threads, it shows. Don't worry, this is for free. I'd just hate for you to not get the gig because the client thought you should be wearing a red nose and clown shoes along with your throwback wardrobe." She eyed him scornfully. "Hey, I know. Why don't you lose the Cadiboat and drive one of those little cars like they have at the circus? Then when you get out at his house, you can throw confetti in the air and honk a little horn as you do a pratfall."

He studied her, alternating between rising to the bait and appreciating the humor in her dead-pan delivery. She batted her violet eyes twice, the heavy black mascara around them giving her the appearance of a bipolar raccoon, and returned to her texting, his presence now ignored.

"What's up your butt today?" he asked.

She exhaled noisily and set the phone down. "It's Eric. I think he's cheating on me."

Eric – her deadbeat boyfriend who operated a tattoo parlor up on Sunset, catering to a clientele of wannabe musicians and bored suburban teens. Black had met him twice, and both times thought he was a slimy jerk that looked like Pitbull's untalented ugly brother. Roxie and he had been together for two and a half years, and this was a regular occurrence – probably because ol' Eric was in fact a lying, cheating scumbag.

"Haven't you been down that road before?"

"This time I think I busted him. One of my friends saw him with some slut yesterday when he was supposed to be at the shop. They were having coffee."

"Maybe they were drinking chai."

"Very funny, funny man. I'm serious. I think he's banging her."

"Not that I don't love Eric like a brother, but he does come across as a sneaky shit rat who'll jump anything with a central nervous system. No offense. The last time you caught him red-handed, he first lied, then denied everything, then apologized and swore it meant nothing and he'd never do it again. In my experience, a guy who would never do it again would never have done it in the first place. Which I've told you."

"I know, I know. You're right, even if you do dress like a minor character in some bad British mod movie."

Black took a step toward her, and then stopped himself. "What are you going to do?" he asked.

"I don't know. But I'll think of something. Sorry to dump my crap on you. But you asked."

"That'll teach me." Their eyes locked. "I'll bring you back a chai."

Her customary tough chick demeanor returned, and she returned to her texting. "Gee. Thanks. Remember. Lose the *chapeau*. Or print 'douche' on your business card. 'Douche Solutions.' That actually has a better ring, come to think of it."

"I wish you wouldn't use that word. It's offensive."

"Solutions?"

He shook his head and let out an exasperated sigh. He would never win. She'd been with him now for over a year, and he had yet to prevail in any argument with her. Rather than bashing his head into the wall over and over, he elected to make a graceful retreat, and barely heard Roxie's words as the door shut behind him.

"Good luck."

❧

Hunter's palatial home in Bel Air was a mini-estate on a half acre, the house a garish ten-thousand-square-foot pseudo-White House that had been designed for a prominent Iranian millionaire before he'd moved up to fifteen thousand square feet of French Revival down the street. The heavy wrought iron security gates were open, and Black eased the Cadillac up the long half-moon drive, cursing the engine's sputtering. His maintenance ethos for cars was in accord with his physical fitness regime – a combination of procrastination and denial. But perhaps it was time for a service. His brow scrunched as he tried to remember the last time he'd done anything but put gas in the Eldo, and nothing popped up. Every morning, he gave it the old Texas tune-up – started the motor and revved it until the lumpiness generally subsided. He made a mental note. Perhaps it was time to have a professional look at it.

He shut off the motor and glanced at his hat, beside him on the seat, and then opted to leave it there, Roxie's words still ringing in his ears. The car door creaked as he pushed it open, and cracked like a rifle shot when he slammed it closed. He adjusted his jacket and tie before walking up the flagstone path to the overblown entry doors. His attention was pulled to the right side near a tall hedge, where a young woman stood watching him, supported by two aluminum crutches. He removed his Ray Ban Wayfarer sunglasses and peered at her, noting the nasty scar tissue on her right cheek and temple.

"Hello," he said, offering a wan smile.

"You delivering food or something?" she asked, a slight slur in her voice.

"That might pay better. No, I'm here to see the man of the house. Andrew Hunter."

"You can't be a cop, unless they're hiring out of central casting rejects. What do you want him for?"

Perhaps Roxie had a point about his retro style. He'd taken a lot of incoming over it lately. Maybe the forties look had played out.

"I have a meeting with him."

"No shit, Sherlock. Who are you?"

Black realized she was drunk, even though it was only lunchtime.

"An acquaintance. I'll just ring the doorbell, if you don't mind." Black turned and mounted the three steps to the stone-tiled porch and thumbed the button.

"Suit yourself, loser," the girl muttered just loud enough for him to hear. He ignored it and waited for someone to answer. He was studying the ornate carving of the three-inch-thick mahogany slabs when the right one opened and he found himself facing an incredibly beautiful strawberry-blonde woman in her early thirties, he guessed, before re-appraising her up to mid-thirties. She was wearing a red silk dress that clung to her curves like a shipwrecked man to flotsam, and her frank green eyes met his without flinching.

"Yes?" she asked, her voice as musical as a Yo-Yo Ma solo.

"Look out. He's probably a process server," the girl called from the hedges, and the woman at the door gave her a sidelong glance that would have frozen lava before returning her gaze to Black.

"Hello. I'm Jim Black. I called earlier. Mr. Hunter is expecting me."

She gave him a long appraising look, taking him in, and he had the uncanny sensation that he was standing there naked, with his parents, teachers, dead relatives, and everyone he knew pointing at him and laughing. She finished her assessment and held out a perfectly manicured hand.

"Meagan. Meagan Hunter."

"Pleased to meet you, Mrs. Hunter," he said, taking her hand and shaking it delicately.

"Don't worry. I don't break easily. And you can call me Meagan. Mrs. Hunter sounds so…formal."

A soft breeze stirred the tops of the mature oak trees that dotted the property perimeter, and for a split second Black felt a shiver run up his spine. The way she was regarding him was definitely not…formal. She eventually released his hand and spun gracefully, her long, tanned dancer's legs gliding easily across the Versailles-patterned travertine floor. "He's out in back by the pool. Close the door behind you, please," she called over her shoulder, leaving a lingering fragrance of fresh-cut flowers in her wake.

Black did as instructed, then hurried to catch up, admiring the way her dress moved with her, like some kind of erotically charged sheath. The garment looked expensive, and so did the woman. Life at the top had its perks, obviously.

They walked through a great room to a row of French doors. She pulled one open and held it for him, blocking a portion of the opening, so that Black had to squeeze uncomfortably close to her in order to exit to the rear patio. Okay, perhaps not uncomfortably close. But close, anyway.

"Pleasure meeting you, Mr. Black," she murmured to him as he edged by. "Don't take Nicole's attitude as reflective of ours. She's just having a difficult time adjusting today. Truthfully, every day." He sensed her appraising him again. She wet her lips with the tip of a pink tongue and then beamed at him. "I hope we see more of you around here. It gets so…boring, sometimes."

Black kept his expression neutral and averted his eyes. His potential client's trophy wife was coming on to him. Which could have been nothing, just a habit she had, the kind of thing bored, hot women did instinctively to any male within range. He knew the type, and while she was definitely exuding sex appeal like a Rainbird sprayed water, he got the feeling that it was equally unfocused, and he just happened to be the nearest target.

"Thanks. Nice meeting you," he mumbled, stepping out onto a flagstone deck that stretched for about a football field. A seated man wearing a bright orange Hawaiian shirt reclined near the azure pool, talking on the telephone, and when he saw Black he motioned him closer. Black squinted against the sun's glare and put his glasses back on as he approached. The man's features were familiar to him from countless action films, though as he drew near, he could see that while the trademark smirk was the same, the surrounding flesh was a little more worn than onscreen, with a tell-tale smoothness around the eyes that hinted at exorbitant well-performed surgery.

Hunter waved at a chair on the other side of the stone table and continued his phone call.

"I don't give a damn, you moron. This is a terrible day, blah blah blah, but the truth is we couldn't buy the kind of publicity we're getting. Move up the damned premiere date to this Friday, while the accident's still in the news. Don't argue with me. Just do it. And set up the press conference. We got handed a break. I want to capitalize on this."

Hunter hung up abruptly and tossed the phone onto the table, then held out a surprisingly small hand in greeting. In fact, Black's first impression of Hunter was of a small man – nothing like what he'd been expecting from the movies. He couldn't have been over five-seven, if that, with a barrel chest covered with tufts of graying curly hair. Black tried to reconcile the reality with the storied bad boy of brawls and volatile misbehavior, but it didn't come easily, looking at the flip-flop-wearing aging surfer before him.

Black shook, noting the crushing alpha-grip Hunter delivered like a vise.

"So you're Colleen's friend? The gumshoe? They still call 'em that?" Hunter barked, his voice gruff from years of hard living.

"You can if you like. Jim Black. Of Black Solutions."

"Solutions? That's a crummy name. No sizzle. I'd change it to something salient, like 'Black Investigations.' That's got way more sex to it, you know? In this business, it's all about sexy. A PI – now that's got some snap."

"I've been thinking exactly the same thing."

Hunter leaned over and reached for a glass of juice next to his chair. He didn't offer Black anything. "Well, Joe, I have a problem. How much did Colleen tell you?"

"Not much. Just said you needed some help with something. She's good people, so if I can do anything, I'm all ears…and you can call me Black. Everyone does."

"The problem's the frigging paparazzi. They're like locusts. A menace. Like ticks on a dog. I hate the miserable bastards."

Black nodded, waiting for him to continue.

"I'm looking for someone to head up my security while I'm preparing to launch my latest movie – *Nine Hard Lives*. It's epic, stomp-you-in-the-face action, but with some romance and a message of tolerance, and it's going to do big, big things. But I'm being very selective about how I market it. I like to have complete control over the ads, the interviews, publicity, everything. And I don't want the paparazzi anywhere near it. I don't need those maggots, and I want to keep 'em at bay."

"I'm aware of your lack of love for them."

"You know why, right?"

"I don't have all the details. That you do is enough for me."

Hunter sighed. "My daughter Nicole has problems. Issues. Likes her booze a little more than is healthy. She's also no stranger to chemical stimulants, OK? Whatever. None of us is perfect. A few years ago, she was outside of a club at two a.m. Got hassled by some paparazzi. Her story is that one of them got overly pushy and the next thing she knew she'd gone face down on the street. Face planted. A car struck her a glancing blow and broke her hip, her leg in a couple of places, tore half her face off, broke her cheekbone and jaw. The cops wouldn't press charges against the paparazzi – they claimed she was wasted and fell."

"I presume they ran a toxicology report."

"No question she was over the line. Blood alcohol through the roof. But she claims she was pushed, and I believe her."

"I think I met her earlier out front. No witnesses?"

"Just the two paparazzi. Who just happen to work for the company run by my nemesis – Franklin-Sypes Associates. FSA."

"Your nemesis?"

"I got into it with the owner. Freddie Sypes. A bona-fide fecal stain. Used to work at the *Times*, and he was worthless then, too."

"Got into it," Black echoed.

"You might have read about it. Cost him seven figures. I sued him over the incident with my daughter, and he wound up settling because his attorneys knew he would lose if it went to trial. Ever since then, he's made it his personal mission to make my life miserable." Hunter cleared his throat. "It was that incident with my daughter that convinced me to start my anti-paparazzi campaign."

"His website's one of the most popular in the country, isn't it?" Black asked.

"Yeah, but it's pure garbage. Guy's a dirt bag. I heard he had to sell off most of the company to raise money for the settlement, and he's still pissy about that. Screw the little bastard, I say."

"So, aside from needing some security, what's your problem, Mr. Hunter? What do you need me for?"

"Look…this movie I've got coming out – it's not really a comeback, because it's not like I ever faded, you know what I mean? But it's my big one. Been working on it for years. You seen the news on my female lead?"

"Went canyon diving yesterday, didn't she?"

"She was being chased. The witness confirmed it. The van that also crashed had Freddie's shitbirds in it. I hope they took a long time to roast. They caused the accident."

"I…some of the early reports say that she hit the witness first, *then* the van lost it."

"I'm telling you, she was being chased. She was panicked."

"How do you know?"

"Melody and I were…close. I knew her better than she knew herself – you get that way if you're a good director. She hated the paparazzi almost as much as I do. From what I hear, they cornered her outside of one of her hangouts and chased her from the valley. That's been confirmed by witnesses at the restaurant."

"No offense, but the stuff I read said she'd had four margaritas in two hours."

"Hey, I'm not saying she was Mother Theresa, all right? But have a little respect. She was a brilliant actress and a beautiful woman, and now she's dead because those bastards drove her over the edge."

Black chose not to argue the point. Hunter was clearly upset, and he remembered the actor's history of volatility.

"Right. Which brings us back to why I'm here."

"I…I've heard from some of my contacts that I'm being eyeballed by LAPD because of the recent deaths of some of FSA's paparazzi scum. It started last month with the photographer who got flattened in a hit-and-run while he was staking out my condo in Santa Monica. Then two weeks ago there was a fire at FSA's headquarters. Arson, with two people hurt. And now there's the van that went over the cliff. I had a couple of homicide yuck yucks here this morning asking about my whereabouts over the last twenty-four hours. Like I had something to do with the crash."

"Sounds like you need a lawyer, not an investigator."

"I got lawyers crawling out my ass. What I need is someone on my side to figure out why I'm being singled out."

"You're pretty vocal about the paparazzi being the devil's henchmen."

"So what? They are. But that doesn't mean I'm going around killing them. Someone's trying to frame me, and because of my visibility taking on FSA, I'm the natural fall guy, at least if you're not thinking very clearly."

"Did you get the names of the LAPD suits?"

"I have their cards somewhere inside. Oh, and besides the investigative work, I need someone to run my security for this premiere. Someone from the outside. I let my security chief go yesterday, and I need someone now."

"I see. Why did you let him go?"

"Freddie's parasites have been showing up at convenient times – to them, anyway – and there's no way they could be doing so without inside information. Someone's feeding them. It was either him, or someone working for him. Either way, his job was to prevent that from happening. He wasn't able to, so end of story."

"You want me to run security for you at the same time I'm trying to mount an investigation? How exactly would you see that working?"

"We meet once or twice a day, go over what you have planned for the various events, and then we work together to modify anything I think needs changing. And I'll need daily reports on your investigation, as well as what progress you're making on figuring out who's leaking info to Freddie."

Black leaned back in his chair. "I see. Do you have a lot of experience in security work? Investigations?"

Hunter's eyes narrowed and he studied Black more carefully. "It's not rocket science, from what I can see."

"I'm sure making a movie seems that way to someone from the outside. You just give the actors the script, set up the cameras and make sure the lighting's okay, and let 'em roll. Piece of cake, right?"

"Not really. And frankly, I don't like your tone."

"Mr. Hunter, I could probably help on the investigation side, but I don't work the way you want. I take a job, I check in when I have something material, and I require *carte blanche* and full access or I can't guarantee any kind of results. But as to running security and investigating leaks, and further trying to mount a parallel investigation into who, if anyone, could be framing you…I'm afraid I'm not your man. Anyone who took that on and promised more than failure would be lying to you."

"There are dozens of guys who would give their left nut to have this opportunity."

"Then maybe you should call one of them. Because all I could do is one of the three jobs you just described. I won't bite off more than I can chew."

The two men stared at each other for a few beats, the sun dancing on the surface of the pool as the tension hung like an insult between them.

"Seems like Colleen overestimated you," Hunter hissed, his tone ugly, his complexion having darkened dangerously.

Black knew his type. Spoiled, privileged, expecting to call the shots. Which was fine, except that Black couldn't be effective with a client like that. The control freaks were the worst, and Hunter had "control" painted across his chest in foot-high letters.

"Sorry I wasted your time. Good luck finding someone to help you out," Black said, rising. "I can recommend some solid security people if you need dependable help on that end."

"You're making a huge mistake. This could be a career maker for you," Hunter warned, and Black shrugged.

"Yeah. Wouldn't be the first time I've shot myself in the foot. Nothing personal, but I can't work the way you want to. Either I have complete autonomy, or it's a non-starter."

"I don't do complete autonomy in any area of my life, Black. That's how you wind up road kill."

"That's what I thought you'd say. No hard feelings. Best of luck with the cops and the paparazzi. Oh, and your movie. Don't worry, I can find my own way out."

"Thanks for nothing."

Black debated butting heads with the actor but then thought better of it. Instead, he took measured steps back to the house, Hunter's eyes boring holes in his back the entire way. Even in his dire financial straits, Black wasn't interested in being the lapdog for a Hollywood bully — and that's how Hunter had struck him. He'd been dealing with them for most of his adult life in the entertainment business, first in music, then as he'd dabbled with his entrepreneurial disasters. Life was too damned short to subject himself to the kind of abuse that would be a constant part of that job, and he knew better than to accept a position that would make him miserable.

He only saw a housekeeper busy cleaning in the kitchen as he passed through the house – no evidence of the bombshell wife or the snarling, inebriated daughter. When he opened his car door a small piece of paper, folded over, a floral aroma rising from it, quivered on his red leather seat. He picked it up and glanced at the contents, then folded it back up and dropped it into his left jacket pocket as he fished for the keys, anxious to be away from the weirdness that pervaded every cranny of the grandiose estate.

There was no way he would ever call her. Not a chance in hell.

At least that's what he told himself as he cranked over the engine and slid the column shift into gear.

He didn't need that kind of drama.

Black spent the better part of the half hour drive back to his office trying to erase from his memory her smell and the way her eyes danced in the sunlight, as well as the way a few ridiculously expensive inches of sheer red fabric hung from her impeccably molded breasts.

CHAPTER 5

"What the hell are you doing to me here, Black?" Colleen's voice crackled over his earpiece as he neared his office. The urge to have a cigarette was almost overwhelming, but Black bit back the impulse. Perhaps now would be the beginning of an entirely new phase of his life, where he eschewed boozing, smoking, chasing women…

Or maybe not. But he would wait at least ten minutes before succumbing to temptation.

"It wasn't meant to be. He didn't want me to help him – he wanted an errand boy. I don't play that," Black explained.

"You couldn't have found a way to work with him? He's really in trouble, from what I can tell."

"No disagreement there, but it wasn't in the stars. Look, I could use the money, but I'm not going to take an assignment where I have no hope of success. And this is a losing proposition the way he wants it to work. So, pass."

"He called me after you left. Not a happy man."

"He didn't strike me as happy when I got there, either, so perhaps it's more of a character trait than a response to me."

"Hunter can be difficult to deal with, but he's good to have in a clinch."

"Super. Then you cozy up to him. I'm out."

"You're making me look bad."

"That's not my intention. But the way he wants to run things, as in hyper-control-freak mode, isn't my thing, Colleen. You know that."

"Hey, it's your funeral. I was just looking out for you, thought I'd throw you some biz. Hunter knows everybody – a positive outcome would have guaranteed a thriving career."

"I hear you. Thanks for thinking of me, but this ain't my dance."

"Will you at least do me a personal favor and nose around, see if you trip over anything obvious? He really believes someone's out to get him with this whole paparazzi thing."

31

Black turned the corner and began scouting for a parking place on his block. "Sure. I can make a few calls. But other than that, there isn't much I can do without spending a lot of my time…and money I don't have."

"Anything you can do, I'd appreciate, doll face."

"You guilt-tripped me into it. I'll let you know if I hear anything."

Black spotted an opening fifty yards from his shabby office building and coaxed the Caddy to the curb like a reluctant mule. The power steering howled beneath the hood, and he made another mental note to have someone look at the belt.

Roxie looked up from her monitor when he opened the door and grinned at him winningly – always an ominous sign, he knew from experience.

"What? Did my doctor call and say the polyp was malignant?"

"Worse. Your parents are in town. They called a few minutes ago and want to get together with you."

"You're kidding. With no notice?"

"I told them you had nothing on your plate. Was that bad?"

He sighed. Of course she'd provided no cover for him. That was her way.

"No, that's perfect. And I still have the rest of my day to contend with. Maybe a piano will fall on me or something. Or a meteor strike. A man can dream."

"There's always the aneurism to hope for – I know older guys have to worry about that sort of thing." She paused and regarded him. "I'm guessing that your big meeting didn't go well? So I better stock up on ramen for dinner?"

"There was nothing I could help the nice man with. Believe me, I tried," he said as he walked into his office, shoulders slumped. "Did they leave a number?"

"I emailed you. Your mom sounded excited."

"She always sounds like that."

Black signed into his account, peered at the digits, and entered them into his phone. His mother's distinctive, trippy voice chirped at him after three rings.

"Artemus! I'm so glad we reached you. We just got to town!"

He winced at her use of his first name. "That's a nice…surprise. Did I miss where you told me you were coming?"

"You know, it came up suddenly, and your father and I decided we hadn't seen you in ages, so why not hop on a plane and visit? Mix some business with pleasure? We were hoping we could stay at your place for the night. Do you still have the same apartment?"

Black choked down the immediate anger that flashed in his mind at her assumption that she could intrude in his life whenever she felt like it. He knew how she was. This was nothing new. They could afford to stay at the Four Seasons and be chauffeured around by limo, but instead wanted to save the money and sleep on his crappy sofa bed. The resentment he felt about his parents selling their little cottage-industry hobby to a major conglomerate in the mid-nineties, pocketing a fortune, rose like sour bile. Here he was busting his hump to get by, and they'd literally fallen over a multi-million dollar deal for her hand-made organic soap. It was lunacy. And then his nice-but-dim father had decided on a whim to invest most of their newly amassed fortune in Apple – not because he'd performed any analysis, but because he'd thought the logo was cool and he liked the company's philosophy. Perhaps even more rankling for Black, after turning seven million into a hundred, he'd then sold all their stock because of an article he'd seen on Yahoo about the company mistreating some Chinese workers, and avoided a forty percent drop in its value.

For two people living in a time warp, for whom money had no importance, they'd hit the jackpot while he toiled in obscurity, scraping by with next to nothing. Of course they'd offered to lend him whatever he needed, but his pride was such that he'd rather turn tricks at the Echo Park men's room than accept a dime from them.

"Yes, Mom, still living at the Paradise Palms," he said, striving for a neutral tone. His apartment complex, a euphemistically named two-story fifties-era crackerbox boasting one- and two-bedroom dwellings grouped around a hideously maintained swimming pool, was the kind of dump that embarrassed and embittered anyone with a more promising career than fast food service. He'd been calling it home since his limousine business blew up – after he'd appeared at the Grammys with a high-profile pop starlet in the back of his car, overdosed on some powerful cocktail he'd somehow missed while regaling her about a big name music producer he'd worked with back in the day.

The sight of the young ingénue falling out of the limo onto the red carpet and then vomiting all over his pants as he stood holding the door open, face frozen in shock, had pretty much killed the business, as had the lawsuit she and her parents had filed when she'd gotten out of the hospital. Even though it had ultimately been dismissed, his "Limo to the Stars" gig had been forced to close up when the bank cut his meager credit line and repossessed his two limousines, and his trademark stretch hot pink Humvee became the punch line to every Hollywood bad joke.

"We're just around the corner, up on that Sunset Boulevard, having a late lunch – yummy salads at a cozy organic restaurant we found. Would it be too much trouble to ask you to come let us in so we can get settled? We don't have to be anywhere until tomorrow, so we put aside the whole afternoon just for you."

Black glared daggers at the back of Roxie's skull, willing it to explode for having told them that he was open for the rest of the day. Her budding psychic abilities must have been flagging, as were his telekinetic skills, because she continued reading the fashion website she favored without a hint of discomfort.

"Sure, Mom. I can be there in…half an hour."

"That's awesome! And remember – no 'mom.' It's Spring," she chided good-naturedly.

"Yes, it is, isn't it? I'll see you soon," Black said, and then hung up, eager to discontinue the interaction. For whatever reason, his parents drove him crazy, and just the sound of his mom's voice could send him into a spiral of self-loathing and anger.

"I'm going to be out the rest of the afternoon. If you read about a triple homicide-suicide, you'll know it didn't go well," he called to his second-in-command, who was captivated by a video she'd found featuring a panda stuffing its maw with bamboo leaves. Roxie didn't respond, her giggling consuming whatever slim resources she allocated to her workday chores. "I said I'm going," he repeated, then stood and brushed past her desk.

"I'm sorry. Did you say something?" Roxie asked innocently, not bothering to even minimize the video on her screen.

"I was considering giving you a generous raise for all the fine work you're doing, but then decided to spend it on therapy instead. I'll need it after a day with my parents."

"So you won't mind if I leave early? I've got a sound check on the strip at six. And a girl likes to freshen up."

"You're going to try to catch him in the act, aren't you?" Black asked from the doorway.

"Of course not. I told you, I have a sound check."

"Sure. Okay then, good luck with that," he said, and with a glance at Mugsy, who was busy clawing the leg of the coffee table to shreds, he exited his suite, shaking his head. Roxie was so damned smart, but when it came to men she had zero common sense. Not that he was anyone to talk, with his hit parade of failed relationships. But still. Eric was a complete loser, and had that perennial smirk of the punk who was always getting over on somebody – and if you didn't know what he was laughing about, it was probably you.

As luck would have it, he made it to his place faster than he'd hoped to. He was just walking up the central courtyard to the stairs when a voice rang out like a bugle call from the unit closest to the street.

"Black!"

He cringed and wondered if he could will himself invisible. His landlady, Gracie Kemper, was a hopeless alcoholic with a heart of gold who could have gone twelve rounds with Tyson and not broken a sweat. At seventy-four, she downed a bottle of scotch per day, without fail, and insisted on regaling him for hours with her stories of the film business back in her day. She'd had a career that had lasted about as long as a joint at a rock concert, but had managed to parlay it into a marriage to a nice attorney who had promptly died of a heart attack within a year of their nuptials, leaving her with the Paradise Palms and a diesel Mercedes that was older than Tarantino. She still had both, and as far as Black could tell she would take them to her grave – which in spite of her alcohol intake was probably eons away.

"Gracie. How are you this fine day?" he sang out, resigned to paying his dues. Rent wasn't owed for another eleven days, so he had no idea what she wanted, but it invariably involved something he wished he'd ducked.

"Look at you, you big stud! I swear you get younger and thinner every month," she cackled as she approached, swaying ever so slightly, a fog of whiskey fumes trailing her like a semi-rig's exhaust.

"Well, you're half right – my hair gets thinner. Listen, don't take this the wrong way, but I'm kind of in a rush, Gracie. No offense, but I've got guests arriving, and I need to clean the place up a little before they get here."

Predictably, she didn't take the hint. "Sure, Sweetie. I've just got a little teensy favor I need to ask you for. It's really nothing."

Black squared his shoulders. When Gracie led with her "it's nothing" act, he could expect a whopper.

"Who do I have to kill?"

"It's nothing like that. It's my nephew. Jared. A sweeter boy you've never met. Just arrived a couple weeks ago from Milwaukee. He's trying to break into acting. Good-looking kid, and I think he's got a shot, if anyone does these days."

"Jared. Fine. But you know I'm not in the life anymore, Gracie. I don't know what kind of help I could be…"

"It's nothing like that. It's just…well, he may have gotten mixed up with the wrong people already. It's a long story, but he came out here with five thousand dollars, and now I think he got swindled out of it by some lowlife shitgrubs he met." Gracie had the eloquence of a drill sergeant when she'd had her morning cocktail, much less her lunchtime fortification, which Black was guessing had gone down the hatch recently.

"I'll tell you what, Gracie. I'll drop in later. Right now, though, like I said, I gotta run. You and he going to be around in a few hours?"

"Sure thing. Where else would a broke-ass kid and I go? We'll be in my place, watching reruns of *24*. That Kiefer. A talent, I tell you. Not like his dad, but still. Did I ever tell you I knew Donald? Many moons ago, that was, but he could take your breath away…"

"You might have mentioned it, Gracie. I'll stop by once I'm done with my stuff, okay?" Black reassured her, trying to detach without being rude. She'd let him slide on rent more than a few times when he was short, so he owed her, although it was invariably an expensive way for him to pay her back.

"Don't forget me. Don't you dare forget me, Black,"

"Never, Gracie. Never in a million years."

The hug was unexpected, but Black returned it, Gracie's pugnacious demeanor belied by her frailty and the faint reek of perennial decay, of organs breaking down and time having its way.

The encounter depressed Black, and not only because it committed him to yet another obligation. He tried to shrug it off as he mounted the steps to his apartment, focusing on the scant few minutes he might have before his parents descended upon him, but the taint lingered like a bite of spoiled shellfish.

Dust motes performed a slow-motion aerial waltz in the beams of sunlight streaming through his guest bedroom window as he hastily changed the sheets on the sofa bed. He'd just finished folding it back up and was stuffing the cushions into place when he heard a rapping on his front door, three knocks that echoed like firecrackers in the empty rooms.

Black balled up the old sheets, tossed them into the hamper in his bedroom closet, and then answered the door. His parents stood, their overnight bags at their sides, looking lost, as they did everywhere besides Berkeley, which was the center of their universe.

"Artemus. You look wonderful!" his mother exclaimed, her face radiating a tranquility Black was convinced was chemically fortified. His dad stood slightly behind her, with the vacant expression of a deer watching an onrushing Peterbilt. Black fought to control the flicker of annoyance in his expression caused by the continued use of his legal name.

Not that it would have occurred to Spring and Chakra Skywalker, the latter AKA Ernest Black, to worry about such earthbound vagaries as Black's dislike of his name. They lived in a constant state of giddy delusion, where it was always the Summer of Love in their time-warped Berkeley eco-system and everything was groovy, baby, and consequently they had never understood why Black had refused to answer to Art, Arty, or Artemus once he'd entered his teen years. Just as they'd been unable to understand why he'd forged his father's signature on the consent form when he'd turned sixteen and joined the army. They had been completely oblivious to the simmering rage that had built in their son and how it colored his every decision. He would never forget when he'd broken the news to them, expecting an explosion of protest – his parents were typical hippie pacifists, and so everything was about positive energy and good vibes and love and peace.

"Mom, Dad, I've got news," Black had announced, standing in the small living room of their two-bedroom hovel six blocks from the university campus, the walls plastered with concert posters from the sixties featuring Creedence Clearwater Revival and Moby Grape and similarly antiquated bands he also hated with surprising intensity.

"Whoa, cool, man. But we've told you a million times, use our first names. The whole structured title thing is part of a patriarchal society's oppressive rules for keeping us subjugated," Chakra had said with the annoyingly calm voice he used no matter what the occasion.

"Whatever. I joined the army. I'm shipping out in a week."

Spring and Chakra had been taken aback, but only slightly, and then the customary veil of tranquility dropped back into place. His mother was busy with her idiotic handmade soap in the cluttered kitchen – the sale of which at local shops their meager, sole means of support. That genius had been the brainchild of Chakra, who rejected notions of conformity and material possessions in favor of a subsistence living that was one step away from panhandling.

"The army?" Chakra had managed, his preternaturally blue eyes unwavering, beaming holes of positive energy through Black as he non-judgmentally inquired, pronouncing the words as though they were alien, as strange to his tongue as Cantonese or Urdu.

"Why?" Spring had asked from her position by the steaming kettles, her long, untamed graying hair tied back with a smudged yellow ribbon.

"Because I want to kill. I want to slake my thirst for blood and become the angel of death, snuffing out innocent life on a whim – the most vicious killer the Army has ever seen."

Spring had stopped what she was doing and rounded the makeshift work area to stand behind his father, hands on the shoulders of his African Dashiki shirt. They'd exchanged a long glance, and then Chakra had nodded.

"Son, you're almost eighteen–"

"I'm sixteen. Just turned. Two days ago," Black had corrected, seething just beneath the surface.

"Yeah, you know what I mean. It's cool. Anyway, you're almost a man, and dude, while I don't agree with what you're doing, I totally support you, you know? Like, it's your right to move forward in life. If you want to be part of the establishment, answer to the man, that's your bag, you know? You need to figure it out on your own."

"I forged your signature. They wouldn't let me join if I hadn't. I committed a felony. Because I want to kill."

"Hey, you know we don't get hung up on legal stuff. It's all artificial constructs imposed on us by the oppressors. You did what you thought you had to do. We understand," Spring had said, nodding sagely like some B-movie Wiccan priestess.

"I broke the law. I lied. I cheated to get in. And now I have the power over life and death. I can't wait."

"Your mother and I support any decision you make, Artemus. You're a positive energy field, and maybe you need to work through all this to discover your higher power. We're all just ripples on the surface of the same lake, but some of us view ourselves as separate, which is an illusion. But you need to learn that yourself. We're sure you'll do the right thing. If you want to go spend time with a bunch of other young men, there's nothing wrong with that."

"You make it sound like some gay convention."

"What Chakra is saying is that we can understand that things get confusing at a certain age. And it's okay. We love you unconditionally no matter what you do."

"I'm not gay. I'm not joining the army because I'm a homosexual," Black had said through gritted teeth. "It's because I hate everyone and I want to kill them."

"It's a fine line between love and hate. Go explore however you need to. We'll send out tons of positive vibes no matter what."

"Have you heard anything I've said?"

"Of course. You're a young man, and you want to be around others like you, in a structured environment, where strong older men will organize your life for you and order you around. You want the discipline of structure. It's natural. And you have urges. It's got to be hard for you–"

"I'm not gay!"

"Those are just labels. We don't use them. They're meaningless to us. We're all just us. Spirits. Seeking enlightenment, moving toward the light. You are whatever you are, however the Cosmos made you. But we love you, and we won't judge."

Black had spun, disgusted, and spent the rest of the week in a blind fury, his final bid for help mistaken as a confession of homosexual ideation. On his last day home, Spring had presented him with a flower-power T-shirt and wished him well, assuring him that his head would get into a more positive space at some near point. Chakra had given him a battered acoustic guitar in a cracked cardboard case, assuring him that music would help him make sense of everything – even though Black had never expressed any interest in music or played a note in his life.

Three years later, having never fired a shot in combat or hurt anyone beyond his constant skirmishes in bar fights, he was dishonorably discharged for disciplinary problems after a brief stint in the stockade. Contrary to everyone's expectations, his anger management issues hadn't diminished in the army; rather, he'd quickly discovered that the one thing he hated more than his dimwit parents was his chain of command and being ordered around like a slave by sadistic pricks who could ruin his life on a bet. That hadn't worked wonders for his rage, which usually manifested as drunken brawls with civilians on lonely weekend nights off base.

All of which flashed through his consciousness as he faced his parents, the memories as vivid as fireworks going off in his head. Shaking off the moment, he plastered an artificial smile across his face.

"Mom. Dad. You look great, too!" he assured them with practiced insincerity, and then motioned them into the apartment with a gesture that would have been at home in a royal court, replete with small, self-mocking bow. If they were going to use the name they knew he hated, he'd be calling them Mom and Dad. "Come on in. What brings you to town?"

Spring put her bag down and hugged him while his father stood by, smiling like a tall, graying, Caucasian Buddha, his hair pulled back into a pony tail, his perennial beard now demoted to a goatee. Black took in his tie-dyed T-shirt, shapeless linen pants, and Birkenstock sandals, and for the thousandth time wondered that he'd sprung from his parents' loins.

"Oh, just some silly business stuff," Spring replied, releasing him and stepping aside so Chakra could shake hands.

"Business? What business? I thought you were retired?" Black asked, curious now as to what hare-brained idiocy they were planning to squander his inheritance on.

"You know your mother's always been handy. Well, it's been so boring since the soap company sold. She's been driving everyone crazy, even with the volunteer work at the shelter and the work on the house." The couple had bought a large home in the Berkeley Hills on a massive lot that was easily worth many millions by now, even if the house itself was a hodgepodge of conflicting eclectic styles Black would have described as somewhere between shipwreck and scavenger hunt. His mother was constantly adding on or fixing something, and the resultant monstrosity was uglier than a water treatment plant.

"Oh, stop it. I've always enjoyed making things, you know that, honey," she said, slapping at her husband playfully. "About six months ago I started making hand-dipped fragrant candles. Anyway, I managed to convince some of the shops in town to sell them, and then some stores in San Francisco and Marin wanted some, and, well, it got too big for me to do in the kitchen, even with a helper. So I rented some space in Emeryville, and now I'm in the candle business!"

Black listened in disbelief. "Candles? People still buy candles? I mean, what's the barrier to entry? Aren't they all made out of wax?"

"Apparently people do buy them. Who knew? I call them Spring Love Candles. 'The secret ingredient's love!' That's the marketing slogan."

"So you're investing your money in candles," Black said, his voice neutral.

"Spring has never been happier, and everyone seems to like her candles, so there are worse ways to make a living. At least we're not injecting hormones into poor helpless animals or genetically modifying food until it's poisonous. Candles don't hurt anyone, and you never know…" Chakra said, his voice still tuned with the breathless wonder of the hippie movement. Black smiled in what he hoped was an upbeat manner and nodded.

"Well, I suppose if you burn your house down, candles could hurt someone, but hey, anything can cause harm if mishandled. You can die from drinking too much water."

"You can?" Spring asked. "How?"

Black felt less sure of himself. "I read it on the internet. I don't remember all the details."

He led them down the hall to the spare bedroom and showed them their shabby sofa bed, which they greeted with the enthusiasm of a vagrant stumbling across a fifty-dollar bill. He'd cleared a small area of the closet for them that wasn't stuffed with boxes of shark cartilage – another business he'd invested in, sure it was his big chance, only to wind up with fifteen thousand dollars of worthless capsules and the newfound knowledge that sharks suffered from cancer, too.

He busied himself in the kitchen throwing away a bagful of expired items. A couple of minutes later Spring and Chakra entered the living room and sat down, exuding happiness. He eyed them as he tied the top of the green plastic trash bag closed – they looked more like street people than super-rich retirees.

The next two hours dripped by like Chinese water torture as they alternated between sharing their thoughts on life with him and asking him about his business, which even on its best months was nothing more than a lifestyle-support mechanism, unlikely to ever enable him to do much more than he was already doing – renting a fleabag, living month to month, and waiting for the next big idea to come along and make him a fortune.

When his phone rang he practically did a backflip at the interruption, and even though he felt a tingle of apprehension when he saw it was Gracie, on balance that was better than sitting in the same room as his parents.

"Sugar, I hate to bug you, but if you could tear yourself away from whatever you're doing for a few minutes, Jared really needs your advice," she said.

"No problem. I'll be there in a few. I'm sure it's important," he assured her.

He turned to his mom. "Sorry. I've got an issue I need to sort out. A client. I'd love to spend the rest of the afternoon with you, but…"

"No, no, you do what you have to do. You've already done more than we had hoped with the hospitality. Will you at least let us take you to dinner?" Spring asked, her accommodating tone making him feel guilty at the relief he felt at the prospect of getting away from them.

"I can't promise anything, but assuming that this doesn't take forever, I'd say let's plan on it."

"Cool. You can choose the restaurant, as long as they've got plenty of vegetarian fare. You know we swore off meat literally eons ago," Chakra reminded.

"Of course. So Ruth's Chris is out of the question. Listen, just make yourselves comfortable. I don't have a lot in the fridge, but there's a market three blocks away, so if you need anything…"

"We'll manage. Go fight crime," Spring said, beaming at him, and as low as he felt about his mixed emotions at seeing his parents again, he found an even lower rung at that moment. What the hell was wrong with him? They'd flown into town, taken the time to see him, were offering to take him to dinner…and all he could muster was a desire to escape that was as palpable as thirst to a man lost in the desert.

He straightened his jacket lapels as he left, despising himself even as the weight that had been suffocating him lightened with each footstep he put between himself and his shabby front door.

CHAPTER 6

Gracie greeted Black like a sailor on shore leave, threw him an eighty-proof smile, and gestured for him to come in. A twenty-something slacker with two days' growth on his thin face and fashionably unkempt hair sulked on one of the two sofas. He made no attempt to stand as Black stepped inside. Gracie's cat, Blackjack, occupied the space beside him, in typical fashion: indifferent to them all.

"Black, darling, you want a little pick-me-up? Something to keep the demons at bay?" Gracie offered, her hunger at having someone to drink with as desperate as Black's impulse to abandon his parents.

"No, thanks. I've got a lot to do. Is this Jarod?" he asked, eyeing the sullen young man.

"It's Jared. Ja-*red*, like the color," Jared corrected, his tone annoyed at Black's mispronunciation of his name. Black could relate. *Try wearing Artemus for a few days and see how you like that, you little prick.*

"That's an unusual name," Black offered, and then turned his attention to Gracie, who was at the breakfast bar mixing herself something in a highball glass that smelled like paint thinner even from across the room. The pervasive stink, coupled with the cloying, decaying smell of thousands of packages of menthol cigarettes consumed in the confined space, triggered his gag reflex, and he made one of endless mental notes that he had to quit smoking for good.

Possibly tomorrow.

"Jared, why don't you take my friend Black here through your story so he knows where you stand?" Gracie asked, taking a cautious sip of her amber liquid, two rapidly shrinking ice cubes mirroring Black's waning interest in whatever was bothering Gracie's punk-ass relation.

"You really a PI?" Jared asked, his glare radiating anger at the world – a look that for a brief moment was startlingly familiar to Black; like looking in a mirror. Something inside Black softened, and he resolved to at least try to play nice. He knew that look and that feeling, and for a second he and Jared were kindred.

"That's right. Duly licensed."

"You carry a piece?"

"I have a concealed carry permit. I didn't bring my gun to this meeting, though. Do I need it?" Black asked casually, amused by Jared's interest in his weaponry, which in truth amounted to a small Glock 17 9mm he'd bought at a gun show in Pasadena for half its new price, and a K-Mart box of ammo that was at least five years old.

"Just start at the beginning, honey. That's always the best way," Gracie chirped from her end of the room. "Take a load off, Black. Sure you won't join me for a cocktail?"

"Positive."

Jared cleared his throat and stared at the ceiling, as though gathering his thoughts. On the television, Animal Planet soundlessly broadcast a muted program about wild ponies. Black looked over at Gracie, who sat staring at her freshly lit cigarette, a Salem 100. Thick coils of serpentine smoke drifted from its tip as she stared at Jared expectantly, having gone the extra distance to drag one of her tenants from his touching family reunion to hear his story.

"I met them at a club up on Sunset. Valentino's. A lot of actors and show business people hang out there," Jared started, and Black nodded encouragingly.

"I know the place." It was filled with the detritus that inhabited the lower end of the Los Angeles wannabe TV and film crowd – aspiring starlets usually dumb as stumps and hard beyond their years, nobody actors professing to be only one meeting from their big break, writers who'd never sold a script, drug-addled porn stars and their pimps...the usual parasites and the prey they fed upon. Not Black's thing at all, but it was one of the hot places these days, so all who wanted to bask in the near-celebrity of the almost-in crowd could do so for ten dollars per watered cocktail to a cacophonous DJ.

"It was last Thursday night, and it was going off, you know? Probably about midnight, and I was hanging out, chatting up some of the talent...and then I met these two guys and a girl. Preacher, Kevin, and Shelby. Shelby's stone hot, even by Hollywood standards. I mean, a full on big screen ten. Anyway, she and I start rapping, and it turns out she's going to be in a movie the two guys are producing. Low budget, but we had some drinks, and they explained their racket – they do an action or exploitation-type flick, make it for peanuts, put in some hotties who are willing to run around in bikinis or topless in exchange for the exposure, and sell it direct to DVD in foreign markets. Costs them sixty to a hundred grand, and they make four to five hundred. Investors get their money back up front from the first dollar, and then they get fifty cents of each profit dollar."

"I guess it's possible. Anything in this town's possible."

"Anyway, Shelby is telling me all this, because she's super excited because she's going to be one of the lead girls."

"What's the movie called?"

"The working title was *Vampire Ho's from the Hood.* Apparently vampires are hot, so a flick like that's easier to sell right out of the box. Anyway, everyone knows it's cheesy, but it's all about selling it to Korea or Malaysia or wherever, not producing *Gone with the Wind.*"

"Classy. Sort of sings. Especially given that it's from the hood. Nice twist," Black deadpanned.

"Apparently since *Twilight*...look, let's not debate the merits of the movie, okay? Point is that it's a racket, and they've made something like a dozen of these films before, and they've all made a nice profit, even if they're junk."

"And you know this because...?"

"I hooked up with Shelby that night."

"Really. It was an irresistible compulsion on both your parts?" Black asked. "Or did you feel like you'd won the lottery – that she was that far out of your league?"

"I guess more the second one. I mean, she was beyond a ten."

"Fine. So young love found its way. Did you go to her place?"

"No. I rented a motel. I couldn't bring her here."

"Of course not. Trust me, the Paradise Palms doesn't get the ladies squirming when they see it." Black looked over at Gracie. "No offense."

"None taken," Gracie said with a toast of her half-drained glass, her eyes now on the TV, where the horses had given way to a honey badger on a rampage.

"Anyway, after...we got to talking some, and it turns out that they only need ten more grand to be fully funded and go into production, and they had their final investor who had committed to that, and then got hit by a car or something. So there was a slot."

"Jared. Do you have ten thousand dollars to gamble on one of the most speculative plays aside from Russian roulette?"

"Of course not. And I told her that. I told her I only had five."

"The last honest man."

"Look, it's such a sure thing that she offered to put up the other five."

"Did she. I never saw that coming," Black said. He wished he'd taken Gracie up on her offer. "Let me guess. She was able to put together a meeting with you and the boys, they had a very professional looking contract with all kinds of legal mumbo-jumbo, and you, still flush with the chance of doubling or tripling your money, maybe with an associate producer credit, and of banging Shelby like a bongo at a jazz jam, signed and handed over your cash."

Jared nodded, his look bleak.

"And now she's not taking your calls, is she?" Black prodded.

"No. She said she had to go out of town for a week or two before shooting to see her aunt. Someplace in Louisiana. She's sick. But she hasn't picked up. It just rings."

"Uh huh. And Kevin and…Preacher?"

"Like I said. They've made some movies. I went online. They're legit."

"Legit in the sense that they have their names on some also-ran flicks nobody has ever heard of?"

"Yeah. I only found out later, when I came to my senses, that they don't have an office. They work out of one of their places. Preacher explained it as keeping overhead to a minimum."

"And that made sense at the time? That two authentic players who've made a bunch of movies, and make hundreds of thousands a year from them, needed your lousy five grand and can't afford a five-hundred-dollar-a-month suite somewhere in Korea Town?"

"I told you, it was ten. Shelby was putting up five."

"Super. Then what's the problem? You'll be rich in no time."

"I…since she isn't answering her phone, I'm getting a bad feeling about this."

"No. Kind of like a really expensive night with a pro who conned you?"

Jared stared at his shoes.

"You have the contract?"

"Sure. I got a copy of it."

Black watched him processing his question.

"Oh, you want to see it?" Jared asked. Not the sharpest knife in the drawer.

"That was the general idea."

"Just a second. I'll get it."

Jared returned in a few minutes with a seven-page agreement. Black skimmed it and shook his head before standing.

"I'll make a copy of this and look into it. My rate's two hundred bucks an hour. I'll take twenty percent of anything I get back. If I don't get anything back, Gracie here will give me a five hundred dollar deduction off next month's rent."

"Two-fifty for two months, you pirate," she said, instantly as sober as a judge, which wasn't saying much.

"Deal." Black swiveled back to Jared. "How much money do you have left?"

He shifted uncomfortably on the sofa. "Maybe four hundred bucks."

"Give me two of it."

Jared's eyes widened and he looked like he'd been stomach punched. "What the fu–"

"You blew your wad being a big stud, tough guy. Now you want me to try to solve your problem for you. Two hundred will barely cover my gas."

"But how am I supposed to survive while I'm auditioning?"

"Get a job parking cars or flipping burgers or making coffee. You're not a high roller. So start acting like what you actually are – a starving actor. Two hundred will last you maybe ten days if you're careful. You aren't paying rent. What it means is that you'll have to get off your ass and stop watching TV all day and hanging at clubs at night, and actually work for your money while you're struggling to get a break. That's how it works in the real world."

"Hey, it's not like I didn't work to save that money. I put away six grand back home. It took me two years, but I did it."

"Then you know how that works. That's a start. Now cough up the money and let me get on it before the trail goes cold. Either that, or find someone who will work for free. Good luck with that."

Jared dug in the front pocket of his jeans, pulled a thin wad of bills out, and carefully counted two hundred dollars, which he placed on the coffee table. Black scooped up the money and pocketed it, then nodded at Gracie.

"I'll be in touch."

Gracie finished her libation and slid off the stool. "I'll walk you out, tiger."

Outside the apartment, she fixed him with a hard stare. "Why did you stick him for the two hundred?"

He pulled the money out and gave her half. "To keep him out of trouble. Now he's got to find a job. Here. That's for groceries and whatever. I need the other Benjamin for gas. The Caddy drinks it by the barrel."

Her face cracked with a small smile. Red lipstick had worked its way up some of her smoker's wrinkles, giving her the appearance of a demented clown who'd smeared makeup on with a paint roller.

"You're a good man, Black."

"I don't know about that. Chances of him ever seeing the money back are slim. But I'll do my best. Maybe this will serve as a wake-up call. And maybe he'll be a little wiser next time somebody tries to scam him."

"It's a tough town, ain't it, darlin'? Chew you up and spit you out."

"Ain't that the truth."

Gracie reached out and clutched his arm, and for a second he was afraid she was going to treat him to an inebriated hug. Instead, she felt his suit sleeve, evaluating the material with a practiced hand.

"They don't make 'em like that anymore, Black. You're a decent enough guy, and smart. If anyone can help Jared, it's you," she said, and then spun unsteadily and weaved her way back to her door.

Black shook his head morosely and looked up with the numb stare of a chain gang prisoner at his apartment where his parents, stuck in the sixties, were waiting. Maybe Gracie and Roxie had a point. Or maybe denial just ran in the family, and a refusal to acknowledge something as obvious as what era they were in was evidence of a deep-seated dysfunctionality that would have had Freud spinning in his grave.

He briefly considered a cigarette, but the memory of Gracie's puckered lips made him shudder and he lost the urge. A pigeon flapped overhead, another survivor in a town that ate its young and offered no quarter, and a warm gust of wind stirred an empty plastic chip bag near one of the desiccated rose bushes. For some reason the sight evoked a feeling of melancholy in Black, and for a moment he was overwhelmed, as if a great universal truth had been partially revealed. Then everything came back into focus and he reluctantly climbed the stairs, his gait that of a much older man as he went to see the only parents he would ever have and try to be civil to them while seething with resentment and blaming them for making him so imperfect, such a lost and directionless speck in a largely indifferent cosmos.

CHAPTER 7

"Cheatsheet" Leadbetter parked his beat-up Toyota Corolla two blocks from the Manchester hotel downtown and fed some quarters into the meter. He glanced around a final time, taking in the cardboard lean-to a dozen yards away and the filthy sleeping bags near it. The theater district in Lost Angeles had become a no man's land taken over by the increasingly large homeless population, and both the city and the police seemed unable to make any headway against the rising tide of the indigent. His companion, "Bones" Ortiz, shifted his backpack, which contained their cameras, anxious to get moving.

The car would probably be safe, at least for the hour it would take for him to get his shot and get the hell out of there. Cheatsheet had been working for Freddie Sypes for three years, Bones for two, and they were typical of the paparazzi brigade: twenty-to-thirty-something, male, hungry, with the morals of starved piranhas, usually dressed in drab, dark colors, the better to fade into the background. Their code of conduct could be reduced to one axiom: *Do whatever it takes to get the shot.*

It was an interesting way to make ends meet – living by one's wits, developing a circle of tipsters who could let them know when a noteworthy celebrity was going to be at an airport or restaurant, or if a starlet was drunk or high and making a fool of herself at a club. Cheatsheet's usual payday for a shot could be all over the map, anywhere from nothing to a few hundred dollars to hundreds of thousands. He'd heard all about the guy who had gotten the shots of that vampire movie star kissing her married director. Rumor was the snaps had sold for a cool quarter mil, and he believed it. Of course, that was the equivalent of the Holy Grail in his business, but the point was it could happen, and once or twice a year, it did.

Most of the time, though, he was lucky to get a few hundred here, a grand there. His employer hosted the top gossip website in the world, and it had an insatiable appetite for fresh meat – but it had to be juicy, or otherwise the work was worthless. Cheatsheet had long understood the game, and for all the uncertainty, he made over fifty grand a year basically hanging out and stalking the newsworthy. Bones made about half that, but he was an up-and-comer, and would do just about anything to get a scoop, even if it meant bending the law on occasion.

This evening's exercise was based on one of the countless tips Freddie got every day, but it had seemed legit, which is why more dependable stringers like Cheatsheet and Bones had been deployed rather than any of the hundreds of aspirants who waited like starving pups for the food dish to be set out. There was a never-ending supply of paparazzi hopefuls trying to break into the business, but the plum jobs went to those in Freddie's inner circle, into which Cheatsheet had worked his way after nearly a decade of living by his wits and selling to anyone with a checkbook.

The hotel was low profile, which was probably why it had been selected for the meeting rumored to be taking place in one of its conference rooms – a meeting with Andrew Hunter and his costar, their public relations people, their media handlers, and several trusted press contacts to coordinate the upcoming film release of Hunter's latest and to manage the spin on his female lead having gone to her reward yesterday, along with two of Cheatsheet's colleagues. Freddie was still waiting for the toxicology report on Melody, but he was willing to bet she'd been drunk and high at the time of the crash. He'd gotten a phone report from the assistant manager of the restaurant where she'd been hanging out with two friends, knocking back margaritas in the private rear courtyard, and judging by a scan of the bill, which had mysteriously arrived in Freddie's email inbox, nobody had been feeling any pain by the end of the afternoon.

Freddie had posted the bill on his site, an exclusive scoop that drove traffic through the roof, along with a lurid commentary suggesting that she'd been obviously drunk and abusive to members of the staff – an embellishment, perhaps, but non-disprovable, and it made for more interesting reading. The truth was that Melody was fairly boring by Tinsel Town standards, and was mainly newsworthy because of her upcoming role opposite Hunter. Their on-screen sizzle had been rumored to extend behind the camera, and Freddie had been giving his arch-enemy Hunter hell over it, memorializing his every move during production and hinting broadly that the over-the-hill action star was doing more than reading lines with his young co-star.

Which of course had enraged Hunter, which was the entire point. Freddie delighted in portraying him as a tired, played-out has-been desperately trying to maintain a flagging career nobody cared about, noteworthy solely as an object of ridicule and because of his dalliances with girls barely out of training bras. It didn't matter whether it was true or not, because after a year or two of his anti-Hunter campaign, spin had become reality, and all the other pubs were adopting the same tone, lumping him in with favorite whipping boys like Charlie Sheen and Mel Gibson.

Hunter had retaliated by barring any of Freddie's quislings from access to him, his co-stars, or the mega publicity machine that had begun rolling six months ago to build buzz over what the studio was hoping would be a blockbuster hit. That made Freddie's FSA appear to be out of the loop, no longer relevant – the kiss of death in the gossip business. Hence Freddie had mounted a new counter-Hunter campaign focusing on dredging up dirt on the movie, its stars, industry scuttlebutt…whatever he could find to subtly smear the release so that in his readers' minds it was a non-event before it hit the screen. So far it had worked like a charm, but with the accident, news coverage had gone ballistic, and overnight the non-event had become the most talked-about film in town.

And Freddie had sustained a major black eye. It was his paparazzi who had been in the van, and now his competitors, as well as the larger media outlets, were already rumbling about them having chased her off the cliff, causing the accident. That could cause as big a backlash as the Princess Diana thing and make it almost impossible to do his job for a while. That in turn would translate into lost revenue, which was unthinkable. He needed to get in front of the story before any more leaked, and one of the ways he could do it was by drawing the always volatile Hunter out with an unexpected photo shoot and some loaded questions about whether he'd been sleeping with his drunken co-star. If the dolt lost it and took a swing at Cheatsheet, it would be front page on every screen in the country – he'd see to that.

The tip had been a stroke of luck, and the plan was to ambush the director as he departed the press conference that had been orchestrated for just a few pet networks – reporters who were in the studio's pocket and were sympathetic to Hunter's plight. If he could goad the director into going berserk it would be gold, and could be used to kill the movie's chances in the court of public opinion before a frame of it had been screened.

"Freddie said the service door would be open, back on the alley," Cheatsheet murmured as they walked past the scrapings of humanity that congregated on the sidewalks, the sour smell of body odor and human waste lingering like a pall of untreated sewage gas.

"Let's hope we can get in and out without being swarmed by this bunch of rejects. Jesus H. Christ, when did downtown become the Tijuana slums?" Bones griped.

"Actually, last time I was in TJ it was cleaner than this."

The men rounded the corner and found the alley mouth, down which a few junkies with vacant expressions stumbled on their way to nowhere. They waited a few moments till one of the more enterprising finished digging through a dumpster, and then set out for the service entrance, a heavy steel slab painted glossy black.

The door opened as promised, and they found themselves in a refuse holding area, a large concrete chamber with double doors at the opposite end and a stairway in the far corner. The informant had included rough layout details, so they unhesitatingly descended the stairs to the lower level.

Once there, they found themselves in a hushed hallway, dotted with double doors. This was the conference center level, and their info had the meeting taking place in room C – which they could have easily spotted even without the heavy cables leading from the utility room opposite the elevators to the suite at the end of the hall.

Their plan was a simple one: They would hide inside, and when the meeting broke up, they would jump out, Bones filming as Cheatsheet went on the attack with the questions, and hopefully the outrageous tone of his interrogative would cause enough of a scene for Hunter to lose it, or at least hurl invective at them, which could be used to paint an ugly picture of an angry, out-of-control bully. It was a classic set-up, and judging by the time, they would only have to wait fifteen minutes in the small, dark equipment room.

"What's with all the cables?" Bones asked as they approached.

"Lights and whatever. Maybe they have some special presentation stuff they're using. Who cares? Get in there. The tip said it would be open, too."

Bones twisted the handle and the door swung inward, and a few seconds later they were inside, unpacking the gear from Bones' backpack. Cheatsheet had a small penlight, which he held for Bones as he retrieved the video equipment and the tape recorder and microphone.

"I hope he goes frigging nuts. Grizzly on a rampage time. It could be worth six figures, easy," Cheatsheet whispered.

Bones grinned in the darkness, his countenance that of a feral animal contemplating dinner, eyes glistening in the weak beam of the tiny light.

❧

Down the hall, a figure watched from a cracked service door as the two men skulked to the equipment room and edged their way in. After checking the time and verifying that the hall was empty, the figure made for the stairwell with a measured, unhurried gait. At the base of the steps, the figure paused, extracted a cell phone from a black windbreaker, and then stabbed the send button before whirling and tearing up the stairs.

❧

Inside the equipment room, a five-gallon plastic jerry can half-filled with gasoline hid on one of the steel rack shelves. A small burner cell phone sat next to it, a tiny wire trailing from the black plastic container's top into the little device's guts.

When the call activated the ringer, an electrical impulse sparked inside the container, igniting the gas fumes, and a nanosecond later the fuel exploded, filling the room with a fireball that instantly seared the skin off the two paparazzi. A moment later the fire alarm was triggered and the sprinkler activated, drenching the floor with water as both men collapsed in steaming heaps on the linoleum. The bare copper tip of the high-voltage cable that extended from the breaker panel sent a lethal pulse of electricity through the water on the wet floor, instantly killing both men.

All but the emergency lights shut off, the master having tripped, and the hotel plunged into gloomy chaos.

CHAPTER 8

Black was finishing dinner with his parents when his phone lit up, *Highway to Hell* sounding loud and clear from its speaker. The other diners in the restaurant glared at him as he fiddled with it, trying to turn it down before answering it. His parents watched him with curiosity as he raised it to his ear.

"Black here."

"Black. This is Hunter. We met today."

Black eyed his parents and turned away so they couldn't easily hear his words. "Yes?"

"Have you heard about the hotel?"

"I have no idea what you're talking about."

"Don't you watch the news?"

"I'm at dinner with my family. This isn't a good time."

"Guess where I just spent the last three hours? With Los Angeles' finest. They took me into custody for questioning. I just got released."

Black stood up and walked to the lobby area, signaling to Spring and Chakra that he would be right back. "For what? The accident yesterday?"

"No, I was doing a press conference downtown, and somebody fried two paparazzi."

Black swallowed hard. "Fried?"

"Some kind of a bomb is what they're saying. Killed them both."

"And why were you being questioned? Didn't you have a roomful of people with you?"

"I'd slipped out to use the restroom when it happened. My co-star was wrapping up his one-on-one with the press."

"So you have no alibi for when the bomb went off?"

"That's basically it. But they pulled security camera footage. The bathroom was upstairs one level, and there's a cam there. It shows me going into the bathroom."

"Which is why they didn't hold you."

"Correct." Hunter hesitated. "Listen, I was thinking about what you said earlier, about not being able to do everything successfully by yourself. I'd like you to come by the house again, tonight, if possible. I think we got off on the wrong foot."

Black glanced at his watch. "I'm just wrapping up dinner. I can probably be there by ten. Does that work for you?"

"I've got some crap I'm also dealing with, so that'll be perfect. See you at ten. And Black? Thanks for giving this another shot."

"No problem. But as of ten, you're on the clock."

"Fair enough. Whatever your hourly rate is, consider it paid as of this call. You're already on the clock."

Black set the phone down, shook his head, and returned to the table where he scowled at his parents. "What a weird business this is," he said, and motioned to the server for the bill.

"What is it, sweetheart?" Spring asked, concerned.

"Oh, just one of the most powerful directors in Hollywood, calling to set up a meeting later tonight. He needs my help," Black said, keeping his voice casual.

"Wow! Congratulations. That's kind of a big deal, isn't it?" Chakra asked, pulling his battered wallet from his pants and fingering carefully through it before extracting a hundred dollar bill for the check. Black didn't try to haggle with him about it.

"All in a day's work. Although nighttime meetings are a little out of the ordinary. Sounds like the man's got an urgent situation."

"I'll say."

They drove home, full of organic pasta and cheap Chianti, and Black escorted them upstairs to his apartment, bid them good night, and headed back down to the waiting Cadillac. Thankfully, Gracie's apartment was dark, so he wouldn't get hijacked. By the time her Scotch ran out it was sleepy time, and she was reliably out like a light by nine.

Bel Air loomed like royal palace grounds above the city's twinkling lights. Its pristine real estate was the most coveted in L.A., every other home owned by a star or a mogul, Bentleys and Rolls Royces and Lamborghinis prowling the hilltop lanes, while only a few short miles away street people pulled cardboard over themselves in preparation for another long night. The old Eldorado sputtered to a stop in front of Hunter's gate, and Black jabbed at the intercom button and waited for the ornate iron barrier to swing open, wishing he'd had a little less wine with dinner. Then again, it wasn't common for him to be on call at night, so he'd had no way of knowing he'd be doing his second interview by starlight.

He pulled up the circular drive and rolled to a halt in the same spot he'd occupied that afternoon and killed the big engine. A silence fell, and his ears detected the soft chirping of crickets from the surrounding trees. Off in the distance, a large dog barked halfheartedly before stillness descended again. Up here was none of the noise that was constant closer to the city, and he had to strain to make out the sound of traffic from the 405 freeway a scant mile away.

The Caddy's door groaned open and he stepped onto the cobblestones, debating for a moment whether to don his hat before dismissing the idea. He straightened his tie and smoothed his hair with a steady palm as he studied the hedges for any signs of the drunken daughter, but she must have graduated to other forms of amusement than tormenting new arrivals, and he was alone under the night sky, the house looming large in front of him.

He was mounting the stairs when the front door opened. Meagan stood backlit like a goddess, her nightgown nearly translucent in the warm glow from the interior. He wondered whether she knew that her outfit hid no secrets when the light was right, then decided that it didn't matter – this was his new client's wife, and the man was a heavyweight mover and shaker. If she had an exhibitionist thing, that was Hunter's problem, not Black's, although he couldn't help but admire her toned legs and perfectly sculpted–

"Well, hello again, Mr. Black. I didn't think we'd be seeing you so soon, but looks like it's my lucky day," she said, her voice a siren's song, every note melodious and in tune, with a feline sensuality that was undeniable.

"Mrs. Hunter…"

"Meagan, remember?" she chided, still in the doorway, barring his entry while giving him a million dollar view.

"Right. Meagan. I talked to your husband earlier, and he wanted me to meet him at the house at ten."

"Oh, he hasn't gotten in yet. But do come in and make yourself at home. I'm just having a margarita before I go to bed. Would you like one? On the rocks?" she purred, stepping back and inviting him in with a wave of her half-empty glass.

"I don't drink when I'm on the job, Meagan," he said, stepping into the foyer, keenly aware of her voluptuous figure only a few short feet away.

"Nonsense. You're not on the job right now. I insist. Besides, I hate to drink alone. It's so lonely and desperate, you know? I'm guessing you like it hard over the rocks. None of that blended stuff for you," she said, closing the door softly behind her and brushing by him. "No, I can see you're a real man. Maybe even prefer just a straight shot of tequila? Skip right to the chase?"

Black shrugged in surrender. "Maybe just a small one. Margarita, that is."

"There's a good sport. Thanks for humoring a lady," she crooned and moved to the kitchen, where an orange glass pitcher sat on the expansive granite island next to a bucket of ice. She lifted out three cubes and dropped them into a Mexican leaded glass tumbler and then poured it three quarters full of the amber fluid, taking the time to squeeze in a lime before picking up the glass and bringing it to him. "Try this. It's my special recipe. Been in the family for literally hours."

As Black took a sip, the potent nectar filled his mouth with vanilla and caramel, then citrus and orange juice, all of it held together with a massive wallop of tequila.

He nodded appreciatively and took another taste, and it felt like he'd hooked an IV bag of straight alcohol up to his feed and opened the line.

"Wow. That's...that's incredible. I mean, seriously. It's the best margarita I've ever had in my life."

"The secret is using three different *anejo* tequilas, each with its own flavor profile, and topping it off with a splash of Grand Marnier and a few drops of Chambord. I find I can't enjoy anyone else's margs now. They're highly addictive," she said, moving closer to him and holding her glass up for a toast. Mischief danced in her eyes as she clinked her glass against his, and then she took a long pull on her drink before closing them and leaning her head back in obvious invitation. "Mmm. It's like heaven, isn't it?"

Black was getting uncomfortable with what had shifted from mild flirtation to something considerably more. This was a married woman. Whose husband would be arriving at any moment. His better judgment took hold and he moved away, choosing an overstuffed chair in the living room before this thing, whatever it was, with Meagan could escalate. She followed him in, gliding on the marble floor like a jungle cat, and sat on the padded arm of the chair. He caught a glimpse of her pupils, which were dilated, and he wondered in passing what else she used to dull the jagged edges of life besides alcohol.

"So tell me, Mr. Black, what do you do for stimulation in this big, nasty ol' city?"

"Mostly just work for the rich and famous, Meagan. And the odd spouse who believes his mate is cheating on him," he said, hoping to introduce some sanity into their interaction.

"I meant when you're not working. How do you relieve your accumulated tension? Are you married? Is some lucky young lady your steady girlfriend?"

"No wife, no girlfriend. Just me and twelve cats."

She eyed him distrustfully. "You're such a liar. I bet you don't have any pets."

"I have one bitter, morbidly obese cat. But he's more the office cat. The kind who despises you even though you saved at least one of his miserable lives and feed him every day."

"That's probably because he's male. I bet all the female cats melt around you."

Black took a gulp of his drink and felt the tension seep out of him, washed away by the high-octane drink. So what if his new client's wife was sitting on the arm of his chair, smelling like jasmine and female allure and radiating thousand-watt sex appeal? Did that make him a bad man? Had he put the moves on her or in any way encouraged her? Poor thing was only human, after all. Was it his fault that he had such undeniable animal magnetism?

Such were his thoughts as a curtain of fragrant hair descended on his face and her open, full lips nipped his ear and then moved toward his mouth.

The rear French doors creaked and he opened his eyes, pulled back to reality by the small noise, and he caught a glimpse of Hunter's daughter through the glass panes, her eyes burning as she looked at him accusingly. Meagan let forth a small moan, a tiny cry of hunger and complete submission, and Black was sorely tempted to close his eyes again and let her take him to heaven – but some part of him that was still sane and sober enough to know better made him stiffen and gently push her away.

"Meagan. I…I'm here to see your husband. He'll be here any minute."

"Don't worry. We have a…an open marriage. Sort of. How much time do you need? We can use the powder room," she whispered hoarsely, her voice thick.

"That's not a bad idea. But I'm thinking I need to use it alone," he said as he rose, twisting away from her, and set his glass on the coffee table before crossing the big room. "Is it over here?"

"Getting warmer," she said, disappointment in her voice, and then she knocked back the rest of her margarita in a single swallow. "First doorway on that hall, to the right."

Black found it easily enough and flicked the lights on as he bolted himself safely in. The room was done in soft orange Venetian plaster with a rustic finish, and he studied his reflection in the ornate mirror before rinsing his face with cool water, letting it drip from his chin as he leaned forward over the onyx vessel sink. His eyes stared back like vats of dirty oil as he reached for a thick towel, the powerful glow of the tequila still warming his belly even as he fought an internal struggle against his hormones. He had zero doubt Meagan would have let him take her right there, standing up in the small space, and the thought sent an erotic charge down his spine that didn't stop till it hit his toes.

Whoa, big boy. Earth to Black. Time to put your unit back in your pants and keep it there, not work out the odds of having a quickie before your client gets home.

He took several deep breaths and shook his head. What was he thinking? This wasn't some booze-fuelled porn film. This was reality, and reality was that even if Hunter's wife was an alcoholic nympho – not that there was anything wrong with that – he was there on business. So she was off limits, even if they had an open marriage, which he took to mean that Meagan screwed everything male that crossed the threshold.

Two minutes later he emerged from the powder room, whatever madness had gripped him now banished, and as he returned to his seat he heard the noise of the garage door closing and then a slam from the end of the opposite hall. Meagan looked up from where she was refilling her glass in the kitchen and winked at him before carrying her drink across the great room. Hunter appeared and she gave him a chaste kiss on the cheek and sauntered to the stairs with a wave to Black.

"Nighty-night, Mr. Black," she said, managing to make the words sound husky and sexually charged. Hunter ignored her innuendo and lumbered to the kitchen, his gait heavy. He fixed himself a drink – single malt Scotch,

Black noted – and then seated himself across from Black, glancing at the half-empty margarita glass before knocking back two of the three fingers of The Macallan.

"She's quite a girl, isn't she? Don't let her spook you. She's a show horse, only happy when there's an appreciative audience," Hunter said. "But you want to watch those margaritas. They're pure heroin."

"Yeah, I sort of got that after a few swallows." Black sighed and crossed his legs. "Tell me what happened today. At your press conference, and with the police. Don't leave anything out."

Hunter looked up at the ceiling and then fixed Black with a level stare.

"Only a few people knew about this event. My entourage – my PR people, my agent, my manager, my co-stars, and three members of the press, all hand-selected and known to me for years. We're giving exclusive interviews to the most influential networks in preparation for the premiere on Friday. So it was hush-hush, invitation only. Apparently, a couple of paparazzi got wind of it, and snuck into the hotel. Don't ask me how this crap happens. It shouldn't have. But it did." He took another, smaller sip. "But the joke was on them. Apparently there was an explosion in the room they were hiding in, and then an electrical short that wound up electrocuting them."

"And the police don't think that was accidental."

"No, they don't. Long story short, I went to the john around the time the explosion happened, so they suspected me. They pulled the video, though, and I was clearly on my way to the can when the power went off, so there's no connection between me and the explosion. Mainly because I didn't know anything about it, and I don't go around killing people, even if they're paparazzi."

"You have to admit, it's kind of awfully coincidental that paparazzi keep turning up dead in the vicinity of you and your movie, given how vocal you've been about your dislike for them."

"It gets even worse. They believe the two that got fried are from the same group that the two chasing Melody were from – FSA, which is the company I sued. Freddie's gang." Hunter took another healthy slug of Scotch.

Black leaned forward. "What precisely do you want me to do?"

"I need someone to watch my ass, line up decent security, and make sure there are no more disasters. I've got a lot riding on this film, Black.

More than anyone knows. This has to go off without a hitch, and it seems like someone's doing their best to screw it up for me."

"I don't know about that. Any publicity is good publicity, right?"

"To a point. But not if they think that the lead actor and director is a bad guy, and that's the way it's shaping up in the only court that matters to me – the court of popular opinion."

Black nodded. "I told you how it has to be. I work alone, with no strings, and I pursue whatever lines of inquiry I see fit. In other words, I don't answer to anyone, and I don't offer daily reports. I'll contact you when I have something to report, and not until then. If you can't deal with those terms, you got the wrong man."

"Okay, okay, tough guy. I told you, I agree. We'll do it your way."

"I charge two hundred dollars an hour. Five grand retainer against a minimum twenty for me to take the case. At two grand a day, on average, that will buy you a couple of weeks, max. I cover my own expenses."

"Fine. I'll have my bookkeeper cut you a check in the morning. What do we do first?"

Black noted Hunter's amped demeanor, and thought for a brief instant that he might be on something stronger than alcohol. Maybe uppers of some sort? Whether prescribed or off the street, didn't matter. It was just another data point to tuck away, and if Black's hunch was correct, it would make Hunter even more unpredictable. Much as his wife was…

"I'll find you a decent security head. Like I said, I know some people. They're professional and highly competent. Let me make some calls *mañana*. What's your schedule like?" Black asked.

"Another marathon. I've got a meeting with a distributor for the international rights at eleven, but I'm trying to keep that out of the limelight because I'm also negotiating with his biggest competitor. That's how it's done in this town. We're going to hook up in the Valley, at a breakfast place a lot of the Harley crowd hangs out at. Stubbs. You know the joint?"

"Sure. I've been there, though years ago."

"That's my first meet tomorrow – everything before will happen over the phone. Beyond that, I have to head over to the studio to make preparations for the sneak preview on Wednesday, and then the premiere on Friday night. I can get you a full itinerary in the morning, along with the check. My production office opens at nine over at Paramount. Think you can find it?"

"I've heard of the place." Black took a final taste of his margarita and then rose. "Sounds like I've got my work cut out for me. By the way, a good security chief will run about four grand a week. You can go cheaper if you want him long term, but that's about the going rate for high end. Any problem with that?"

"No. All I ask is that he's competent and trustworthy."

"I'll put the guy I have in mind directly in touch with you tomorrow. Probably early. You up by eight?"

"I'm in my gym by five-thirty. And I'll have my phone with me."

"Then we'll talk then. I'll be at your office at nine. Copy me on the email authorizing the check. In the meantime, I'll get to work digging down and see if I can make any sense out of this."

Hunter grunted assent.

"Did you ever find the cards of the detectives that stopped by here?" Black asked, remembering the loose end.

"Yeah. Let me get them. Same pair that pulled me in for questioning," Hunter said, standing. He disappeared down the hall to his office, then returned and handed Black the two cards. Black studied them, his face blank, and passed them back to Hunter.

"You're in luck. I know one of them. I'll add touching base with them to my laundry list."

Hunter offered his hand and Black shook it, noting again the overcompensated squeeze.

"You gonna finish your drink?" Hunter asked, his gaze on Black's still half-full glass sitting on the coffee table.

"Nah. Too sweet for me."

Hunter's focus drifted to the ceiling – the upstairs, where Meagan presumably awaited his arrival, if she hadn't passed out already.

"It's an acquired taste."

"I'll take your word for it."

Black found his own way out, having left Hunter to his thoughts and his bottle. As he neared his car, he heard a scrape of leather on stone to the right. He slowed, and then stopped when he saw the daughter, Nicole, staring at him accusingly from near his fender.

"I saw you," she said, her voice dead.

"I know. It wasn't what it looked like."

"No, that's clear. A strange man kissing my father's lovely, honest young wife."

"More like her kissing him, not to be too technical."

"Just to be clear, I'm not blaming you. She's a whore."

Black took her measure. Her speech was slightly slurred, but that could have been the result of her injuries.

"I try not to judge others."

"Listen to Solomon here. I don't have any problem judging her. She's a whore, always has been, and my dad deserves way better. And he can do better. He should."

"Maybe. And maybe he loves her."

"Trust me, that died a long time ago. My money's on Dad this go 'round."

She turned and gimped away, the rubber caps of her crutches making soft thumping sounds as she went. Black watched her disappear into the dark, and wondered what sorts of demons could drive such a young thing, someone with everything – money, looks, status – to methodically destroy herself.

Which quickly turned into introspection. He'd been young once, with the world in the palm of his hand, and he'd managed to screw it up pretty badly. His problem had been rage. Hers was chemicals. Everyone found their own personal hell if they went looking, he supposed.

He cranked the ignition and coaxed the big car through the gates, wondering how many of the mansions he was passing had similar dramas playing out behind their privileged façades. Probably more than anyone could imagine, he thought sadly.

CHAPTER 9

The glimmer of overhead stars was replaced by the flare of city lights spreading endlessly before him like a neon blanket, and Black left the top down as he drove, the rarified atmosphere of Bel Air gradually replaced by the thicker, polluted smell of Los Angeles proper. His earbud trilled as he dialed his old friend Stan Colt's number – an LAPD homicide detective who had been instrumental in convincing Black to go into the PI game and had done his best to steer clients his way whenever he could. Black had known Stan for over twenty years, from way back in his band days, and their unusual friendship had survived the test of time, through all Black's ups and downs – mainly downs.

"What the hell are you doing calling this late? You get arrested?" Stan answered, his usually gruff voice like a Rottweiler's warning growl.

"Nah. Just left a meeting with my newest client, who had the pleasure of your company this evening. I was wondering if you were thirsty."

"It's Monday night. Eleven o'clock. What do you think?"

"So the Club Room in fifteen?" The Club Room was one of their usual watering holes, a dive off South Doheny that served strong drinks for fair prices.

"Make it ten. I gotta be up early tomorrow and I need my beauty rest."

"I'm on my way."

Black eased open the battered enamel door to the lounge and stepped into the gloom. The room was sparsely populated with life's trammeled and unfortunate: a pock-faced Asian bartender stood polishing glasses behind the long mahogany bar, a pair of middle-aged men took serious pulls on tall draft beers at the far end, and an aging woman sat at one of the middle stools, sipping gin, her eyes taking him in with a flicker of interest before settling back on her reflection in the mirror. He glanced around and chose one of the empty tables near the bathroom and waited for the bartender to walk over and take his order: two bottles of Anchor Steam beer, which he knew from experience would be delivered freezing cold with a plastic cup of stale pretzel sticks.

"And two shots of Jack on the side," he called after the little man, who raised a single hand in halfhearted acknowledgement as he returned to his station.

Just as the drinks arrived, Stan pushed through the door, and after a quick scan of the interior approached Black's table and sat across from him. Black considered his friend's craggy face, pummeled by years of hard duty and unmentionable images, his thick brown hair beginning to gray at the temples, a look in his eyes like a Bassett Hound that had been kicked once too often. Stan reached wordlessly over to the shot, raised it in salute, and downed it in a single swallow, then grimaced before exhaling loudly, the alcohol pungent on his breath. Black echoed the action, and they stared at each other for a few beats before Black broke the ice.

"Just took a job working for Hunter."

"Couldn't find a gig cleaning septic tanks?"

"He's not so bad. Says he's being framed."

"That's pretty much what they all say. Other than, 'I din't do it.'"

"You really think he's behind the killings?"

Stan sighed and took a thirsty gulp of his beer. "I don't know. The guy's connected to them in some way, that much I know. And he hates the head of the company all these clowns work for. What's his name, Freddie Psycho?"

"Sypes. Freddie Sypes. But from what I hear, lots of people hate the guy. It's a long line."

"I'm not arguing with you, but every one of these killings has been related to your new pal's movie. Which has been getting a fair amount of attention as a result. I mean, come on. He's over the hill, hasn't had a hit since eight-track tapes were big, and then on what's being called his big comeback flick the paparazzi start dropping like flies? Why this, why now?"

"So your theory is that this is all some kind of desperate publicity stunt?" Black asked.

"I have no theory. I'm just saying there are an awful lot of bodies down at the morgue since he wrapped filming. Seems like it's gotten hazardous to be a freelance photographer around Mr. Hunter, wouldn't you say?"

"It's too obvious, Stan. The guy's not a moron. He's got to know that he'd be the first person you'd look at, given his track record. Besides,

Hollywood bigwigs don't off lowlife photogs for publicity. Not even in this town. Not without a permit."

"Fair point. Besides which, we don't have enough to hold him. Which you know since he's out driving his Rolls or whatever instead of sitting in the joint saying 'ahh' for Bubba."

"Have you considered that he's being set up?"

"Sure. The problem is, by who? And to what end? I mean, his crappy movie is getting more press than if the President had gone skinny-dipping with a Mexican hooker, and suddenly a guy who's invisible to the media is front page news. How is any of that bad for the guy who keeps saying, 'Woe is me'?" Stan asked.

"Do you have anything on the car crash?"

"Off the record, no. They're still working it. Trust me, you don't want the crap job of trying to do a forensic exam on three bodies after a fireball gets through with 'em. Same with the mechanical evaluation. This ain't CSI Miami. We've got two vehicles that look like somebody put 'em in a car crusher, three stiffs that make beef jerky look good, and no answers."

"I probably shouldn't say this, but I get the feeling that Hunter was banging her."

"Big deal. People bang each other all the time. This is Hollywood. Banging is like ordering a latte or something, except for guys like you and me. Everyone else in this town is out banging right now – while we're sitting in this armpit talking about how your client is out banging. Did you ever see that Melody chick? She was smoking. She probably had guys crawling through broken glass to bang her. Besides which, Hunter has a rep as a lady's man, so it comes as no surprise. But it doesn't get us any closer to the hows or whys of the case."

They drank their beers in silence, then Black stretched his arms over his head and yawned. "You should see Hunter's wife. I mean, she's just raw sex appeal. I met her this afternoon, and she was trying to get me to join her for quickie in the bathroom before the man of the house got home. I'm not making this up."

"Poor you. Believe it or not, that doesn't happen to middle-aged homicide dicks with beer bellies and bad attitudes. I should have been a PI."

"It's never too late. The hours are terrible and the pay stinks."

"Right now, that doesn't sound so bad. At least you don't spend your days putting thermometers in corpses and listening to sociopaths lie to you."

"Never say never. The night is young."

"But we're not. You going to have another one, or are we hitting it?"

"I have a ton of stuff on my plate tomorrow. But listen, will you do me a favor? Would you give me a heads up if you come across anything that implicates our boy, or points you in another direction? Just so I'm on the same page and don't step on your toes."

"You mean will I knowingly reveal pertinent information in a homicide case to someone working for our prime suspect?"

"You make it sound so ugly."

"That's what I do." Stan chuckled, a dry, harsh sound.

Black wished he'd brought his cigarettes in with him. Not that he could smoke in the bar – the nanny state had made that illegal along with just about everything else that was fun or felt good. But the craving was stronger than he could have believed, and he shifted uncomfortably, silently cursing his weakness, which inevitably intensified when his blood alcohol level spiked.

"So will you keep me in the loop?" he asked, trying not to radiate desperation.

Stan leaned back in his chair and swung his leonine head around, looking for the bartender. He caught the Asian's eye and lifted the bottle of beer, then held two fingers aloft before returning his attention to Black with a humorless smile.

"Of course I will. But you're buying the drinks tonight."

Black sighed in resignation. "I may be easy, but I'm not cheap."

"We'll see about that."

CHAPTER 10

Morning light streamed through the designer blinds into the lavishly appointed offices from which Freddie Sypes operated his celebrity gossip empire, the heady aroma of freshly brewed dark-roast Costa Rican coffee pervading the suite like ambrosia. Freddie's assistant Daniela, a severe brunette Italian beauty who stood six one in her stocking feet, lightly rapped on his Honduran mahogany door with her carefully sculpted nails.

Freddie looked up from the pile of publications he was poring through, a daily ritual that started each of his days before anyone else but Daniela was in the office, her hours of 6:50 to whenever long ago tacitly agreed to as part of her continued employment.

FSA was a twenty-four-hour shop, but for the executive offices, the business day began when Freddie appeared precisely at seven each morning and ended when he left, which was usually ten to twelve hours after he arrived, six days a week, and sometimes on Sundays. One of his favorite sayings was that bad news didn't sleep, and if you didn't like the grueling treadmill that was part and parcel of his empire, you were free to go find work elsewhere.

Freddie eyed Daniela's cutting-edge outfit and cocked a carefully groomed eyebrow, his salon-tanned face looking every day of his forty-nine years.

"Yes, Daniela?"

"I'm sorry to disturb you, but we just got a tip that I knew you'd want to look at."

Freddie had a long list of celebrities whose names would generate an instant alert so he could personally decide how to handle the tip. He waved a manicured hand and pursed his lips, impatient with her. He still had a faint buzz of hangover from the party at one of his favorite haunts the night before, a casual soirée with twenty of his closest right-now friends that had gone on a little too late, as had the ensuing encounter with a twenty-something cameraman with a body like Adonis and a face to match.

Daniela placed the slip of paper on his desk and stepped away. Freddie peered through his designer tortoiseshell reading glasses at the brief message and sat bolt upright with a sharp intake of breath.

"Who have we got available?" he demanded.

"Simon and Rick are both on deck."

"Get them out to the place, but it has to be discreet. Total stealth. Maybe we can catch the old fool with his gut hanging out and a few days' growth. We can run anything they get this afternoon with the piece about him being picked up for questioning by the police. It would be nice if we could paint a picture of him being totally out of control."

Freddie was particularly pleased about the scoop from one of his contacts at LAPD headquarters. He'd had someone call Hunter's press contact about it, but all he'd gotten was the expected 'no comment,' the arrogant bastard's standard response to FSA on any topic at all. Hunter remained convinced that Freddie had somehow contrived to have his slut daughter run down, which couldn't have been less true. It still tasted like bile in Freddie's throat that he'd been forced to shell out millions to Hunter over the alleged actions of one of his lowest-end stringers, but the attorneys hadn't wanted to take it to a jury, cautioning that the public perceived his profession as ranking slightly below call girl or congressman in terms of integrity.

Not that the impression bothered him, or was necessarily wrong. He'd created an incredible entity with FSA, but its currency was dirt and innuendo and scandal, and Freddie had long ago learned that it was better to get the scoop without questioning the ethics behind the way it was obtained or who might be hurt as a result. He was in the titillation business, and fornication, overdoses, drunk driving, rehab, adultery, and scandal were his stock in trade. Nobody paid big advertising dollars to feature front and center on a site that had countless dog-bites-man articles. He needed a constant stream of juicy tidbits, star sightings, ugly mishaps, and tall tales to draw the numbers that kept him at the top of the rankings.

"I'll call them right now," she said, and gently pulled his door closed, leaving him to consider the slush pile of folly that had collected on his desk overnight to be trawled for anything tasty enough for the consumption of the idle masses.

Freddie rose, walked to his picture window, and activated the blinds. As they rotated open, slowly and obediently revealing a panoramic view of the

Pacific Ocean from his penthouse suite, he was reminded that the trappings of his lifestyle didn't make him feel as potent as they should. Sure, he had the inevitable canary-yellow convertible Porsche, invitations to all the best functions, designer drugs and clothes, unlimited sexual adventures…but in his gut, he always felt like an employee, not fully in control of his destiny. He'd had to sell majority interest in FSA to a group of investors who were professional money jockeys, and they expected performance out of him like any other hired gun – he was only as good as his next quarter. The pressure was constant, and more irritating than anything else. He hadn't changed his approach, which was charging hard 24/7, but now he felt like he had no choice in the matter, which made a huge difference in his motivation level.

And all because of that bastard Hunter.

He could trace a hundred percent of his recriminations back to the settlement.

The blackest day of his life.

Freddie turned from the view and plopped back into his Herman Miller chair and studied the pile of pubs on his desk. Years of clawing, cutting throats, backstabbing, and conniving and plotting had gotten him where he had been, and then it had all come crashing down. True, he was still a multi-millionaire, but he should have been far richer. And he lived in a town where talentless deadheads pocketed twenty million a film for showing up and phoning it in, so his money looked meager by comparison.

No, he was still an outsider, nose pressed against the glass, watching the privileged and the pretty leading dream lives while he shivered in the figurative cold. A necessary irritant to most of them, to be pandered to when it suited their purpose and ignored when it didn't.

Freddie viewed himself as one level above the reality TV stars he stalked with regularity, feeding the public's endless appetite for twaddle. Not quite legit, but known enough to get a decent table at a good restaurant on a Saturday night. In Hollywood, that was often how one could determine the pecking order – who could walk into Nobu and command a prime spot without a reservation.

He wasn't an A player, or even a B, he knew. He existed in a kind of celebrity purgatory where he was a known quantity, but despised for how he made his living. Paparazzi were like insects, swarming over the still-warm carcass of whatever object of fascination had attracted the public's interest. And he was the king roach. He didn't kid himself, and there was no self-loathing. Freddie was accepting of his station. But he'd gone from owner to towel boy overnight, and there wasn't a day that went by that he didn't curse Hunter and his bitch of a daughter for ruining his good thing.

An icon on his flat screen monitor blinked, signaling that his first virtual meeting of the day was about to start. He sighed and took a swig of coffee, then pushed his pile aside and reached for the mouse, an acrimonious aftertaste lingering as he swallowed, thoughts of Hunter having ruined even that for him.

But not for much longer.

Hunter needed this film to be big, and Freddie was putting every ounce of muscle into subtly denigrating the man and his work, planting seeds of doubt in his audience's mind.

In this business, that could be enough.

Freddie would have the last laugh.

He'd make sure of it.

CHAPTER 11

Black sat on the mocha leather sofa, fidgeting as Dr. Kelso scribbled something on his ever-present notepad. Finished, Kelso scratched his salt and pepper beard – a nervous mannerism that Black particularly disliked – and studied him like a lab specimen.

"And why do you think that you got so impatient with them? Did they do something specific?" he asked.

"No, it's more like a general irritation. It's the cumulative effect of a host of little things."

"Give me an example."

"My name. They insist on using my first name."

"Well, it is your name."

"They know I hate it. They know I use my middle name. Which I had to make up, since they neglected to give me even that."

"Maybe they forget. Or maybe they think it's a phase you're going through," Dr. Kelso suggested.

"Yeah. A phase. I mean, I'm only forty-two. I might grow out of hating my shitty first name. You know, around the time I die."

"Do you think about death a lot?" Kelso asked, instantly more interested.

"No. I mean, no more than anyone else does, I suppose."

"And how much does everyone else think about it?"

"Look, I think we're getting off topic here."

"Yes, I suppose you would."

They sat in silence for a few moments, and Black wondered for the umpteenth time why he squandered his hard-earned money on this quack. A hundred bucks twice a month, and he had seen no discernible progress in his anger issues even after two years.

"I'm still angry a lot of the time."

"But not all the time."

"No. But I was never angry all of the time."

"Would you say you're angry more often lately?"

"Not really. Just not less."

"Besides your parents, what else makes you angry?"

"We've been over this. Don't you remember any of our discussions?"

"Of course I do. Just tell me again."

"I'm broke. I got screwed over by my wife. The songs I wrote made tens of millions of dollars, and I never saw a cent of it. Just a lousy hundred grand to sign a deal I should have never agreed to."

"Ah, yessss. Now we're getting somewhere. The record deal. Let's explore that, shall we?"

"We've talked about it a dozen times."

"I sense you're making progress each time."

"How do I know you aren't just running out the clock and choosing topics you know will torment me?"

"Do you often feel persecuted by those you've selected to help you?"

"That's not what I'm saying."

"Tell me again about the record deal. It still makes you furious, doesn't it? That the renowned Nina Angel became rich and famous from your songs. But it was your idea to sign them over to her in the first place, wasn't it?"

"Of course it infuriates me. I sign over all the songwriting credits and copyrights in my new wife's name, and then the album goes quadruple platinum and I get the shaft. How would you feel?"

"But why did you sign them over? Wasn't it to cheat on taxes?"

"Not to cheat on them," Black corrected, growing annoyed. "She was a Nevada resident. Her address was still her mom's trailer in Henderson. It made no sense to pay California tax on any income from the songs if we could have them in her name. We were married, for God's sake. How was I supposed to know that the second the album started selling, she'd start screwing the attorney we'd hired and then divorce me? Who wouldn't be angry? And by the way, her real name isn't Angel. It's Gomez. She changed it."

"Interesting. So she disliked her name too."

"I don't see what that has to do with anything…"

"Back to your anger and the songs. You were trying to, mmm, minimize taxes. So you were trying to be tricky, and it backfired, and now you're resentful."

"Didn't you hear anything I just said? My nineteen-year-old wife became an international sensation singing songs I sweated blood to write, got richer than Bill Gates, and promptly dumped me to bang our attorney. And then she had him butt-hurt me by having me sign a deal nobody in the world should have taken. I really should have sued both their asses."

"Yesss. 'Should.' Sounds angry to me. Wasn't it your inability to control your rage that resulted in the whole situation?"

"I guess you *have* been paying attention," Black said sheepishly.

"You broke your hand a week before you were supposed to go on tour. How did that happen, anyway? We ran out of time the last time we were discussing this."

"I got into a bar fight."

"Ah. So one of your long string of outbursts. Is that not correct? You told me that the record company had no choice but to replace you – you couldn't play, and they weren't about to cancel the tour because you couldn't control yourself. Isn't that right?"

"They could have hired a session guy, and I could have picked up in eight weeks. But they didn't. I think my wife was screwing the attorney even at that point. Otherwise, why not hire a stand-in? The fix was in from the start."

"And you could have then had another fight on the road, and they would have been right back in the same position. So they decided to get rid of you. And you're still angry about it."

Black exhaled noisily.

"You know what the strange thing is? Not that much, anymore. I mean, the attorney? He feels terrible about the whole thing. We've actually become good friends. He helped me set up my business. He's helped me with my other businesses."

"The ones that failed. The limo company, the supplement company, the carpet cleaning company…"

"The carpet company could have happened to anyone. It was an accident. I had no idea the products would ruin a million-dollar Persian rug."

"No. Of course not. Do you feel like the 'fix was in' there, too, as you put it?"

"Look, I know I screwed up on that. I don't need to be reminded."

"Fair enough. Let's circle back to the record deal. Are you still angry at your wife?"

Black considered the question. "A little. I think I'll always be pissed that she cheated me out of millions, became a household name, and dropped me like a bad habit. Hard to get over that kind of thing."

"So you're angry at your ex-wife, and you're angry at your mother."

"And my father."

"Bear with me here. What other women do you have in your life right now? No new girlfriends since the last time we talked?"

"No. I'm broke, I told you. It's kind of hard to hook up in this town if you don't have a pot to piss in."

"Mmm, right. So those are the only two women in your life. Didn't you mention an assistant?"

"Roxie? I don't really think of her as a woman."

"Really. Interesting. Why not?"

"Because…I mean, she's twenty-five. I have socks older than that."

"So you think of her as an old sock?"

"No, you're twisting my words."

"Is she attractive?" Kelso sounded interested again – twice in one sitting, a rare event during their sessions.

"No. Yes. I mean, yes she's attractive, in a kind of punky, goth way. Or emo. Whatever that means. I can't keep up. She's got the whole black hair, black nails thing. Sings in an art rock band."

"Ah. Another female singer. Hmm. And she's a young female singer like your wife was when she dumped you."

"This really isn't helping my anger, Doctor."

"And she's attractive, yet you claim you aren't attracted to her. Tell me, are you angry at her?"

Black was stumped. How had they wound up here? "That's ridiculous. I mean, sure, sometimes I am, but that's because she can be difficult."

"Huh. I see. Do you ever think of her sexually?" Kelso asked, leaning forward, a gleam in his eye.

"What kind of question is that?"

"It's a routine question. All part of the process. Do you think of her sexually?"

"Wha – okay, Doc, I'll admit that when she parades around the office wearing next to nothing but Doc Martens, she's kind of hot, but that doesn't mean I want to have sex with my receptionist. Assistant," Black corrected.

"So you have her come to work wearing provocative outfits?"

"I don't tell her what to wear."

"I see. So she chooses to come to work wearing these sorts of sexually alluring clothes?"

"I...that's how the young chicks dress now, Doctor. I think you're making more out of it than I do."

"Do you spend a lot of time noticing what the 'young chicks' wear?"

"No. Not like that."

"How young do the chicks have to be before you stop noticing what they're wearing?"

"Christ. Now I'm a pedophile?"

"I'm not labeling you. I'm trying to get to the bottom of your rage issue. I think we're on to something."

"You say that every session."

"Which is a good sign, isn't it?"

"Look, Doctor. Okay, maybe I've had a few impure thoughts about my assistant. And yes, maybe I've been angry at all the women in my life at one point or another. But that doesn't mean–"

A tiny chime sounded. Kelso put his pad down and checked his watch, then fixed an impassive expression on his face.

"I'm sorry. I'm afraid our time is up. It's nine. Shall we pick this up the next session?"

"But I was just making a really important–"

"Yes, but you know the rules. Boundaries. Remember?"

Black gave him a dark look.

"Right. I have to respect your time, but you can intimate that I'm some kind of–"

"I think this was a productive session. Same time, two weeks from now?" Kelso asked, thumbing his Blackberry.

Black waved him away. "Sure. Great. Let me ask you something. Why do I always feel worse when I leave here than when I came in?"

"That's a great question. Let's revisit it next time, shall we? You can pay Martha on the way out," Kelso said, tapping his watch. "I'm sorry, but I have another patient scheduled."

Black stood. "I haven't even told you about how the cat I saved hates me, and how angry I am about it. I do everything for that damned cat."

"Mmm. Okay then. Next time. Sounds like we'll have a lot to explore."

CHAPTER 12

Mugsy glared out from his position by Roxie's leg as Black walked through the office door. Roxie was seated at her desk applying a layer of what looked like tar to her short fingernails.

"Well, good morning. Hard at work, I see," Black said.

She glanced at him with silent insolence, a moue of indifference her only greeting.

"How did the show go?"

"Great. I'm turning in my notice. I got signed by Capital Records and go into the studio next week."

"So, not a great turnout?"

She shrugged. "Monday night."

Black didn't ask about Eric, and Roxie didn't volunteer anything.

"Is Mugsy getting even fatter?" he asked as he passed her desk. He hesitated a few feet away and debated petting the hostile tabby, but thought better of it when Mugsy stood and arched his back, looking ready to defend his honor with claws. "I swear I don't understand why the tubby bastard dislikes me so much."

"He loves you. He just has a hard time showing it."

"Yeah. Kind of like how a bear loves a salmon. Listen, I'm only going to be in for a few minutes. I have a list of phone numbers we need to get call records for. Three cells and a landline. And I want you to run Hunter and see what comes up on his finances or liens and judgments – you know the drill. Oh, and I also have a contract with some names on it I need you to try to locate – low-end movie grifters, by the sound of it."

She turned, her chair squeaking as it pivoted. He handed her Jared's contract and one of his business cards with Hunter's phone numbers printed on the back in pencil. She took them with her free hand, the other drying, and returned to her original position to complete her cosmetology mission, frowning disapproval at having been thoughtlessly interrupted.

Black decided to stifle his complaint and play nice. "We got a job. I'm going to pick up a check this morning."

"Great. Is it enough to cover my salary?"

"And then some. Even with the lavish wages I struggle to pay you."

"Awesome," she said in the perennially bored tone that signaled she'd already drifted on to more important matters.

Black took another step toward his office and paused for an instant, then arrived at a silent decision and continued inside. He flipped the wall switch and the fluorescent lights illuminated with a flicker. He sat heavily in his chair, tapped his mouse, and waited for his computer to come to life.

Roxie would have the phone records by the end of the day, he knew. She was magic at things like pretexting, which, while illegal, was the most expedient way of obtaining them. He wanted to understand what he was getting into with Hunter, and the first step would be to figure out whether the former security chief or any of the Hunter clan had been sneaking calls to Freddie. Job number one in figuring out who was behind his woes would be isolating the leak and containing it.

He'd already contacted his friend Mitch, one of the best private security providers in town, and arranged for him to contact Hunter that morning, so he mentally checked that off his list. His email inbox popped up on the screen, and he performed a cursory scan of the messages promising to give him longer-lasting erections or an application for his phone that would enable him to see women's underwear. Tuesdays weren't a big correspondence day. Rather like the other days in the Black Solutions week.

His appointment with Kelso lingered in his psyche like toxic fumes, and he sneaked a glance at Roxie in the other room, just visible at that angle as she finished her nails. The good doctor had it all wrong. There was no way he felt any kind of meaningful attraction for her. The therapist had sex on the brain.

He again questioned why he even bothered going to him, then dismissed the thought in favor of focusing on his day's itinerary.

It would take him a while to get to Paramount to pick up the check, and then he'd have to deposit it and get to Stubbs for the meeting. It would be tight, but he could make it, the Eldorado and the god of traffic willing. He had an uneasy feeling in his stomach at the whole Hunter scenario, but dismissed it, attributing it to the second and third shots of Jack and too many late night cigarettes.

He was walking down to the street to his car when his phone rang, and he depressed the button on his earpiece.

"Black speaking."

Silence on the line for a few seconds, and then a voice that was as famous as Elvis came on the line.

"Hey, babe. Long time no talk."

That was Nina's way. His ex-wife would call out of the blue after not communicating for a year, as though finishing a discussion they'd started five minutes before.

"Do you call everyone 'babe' now? That's very show biz."

"Only you, babe."

"Nina, your ears must have been burning. I was just talking about you."

"Do I need a restraining order?"

"Very funny. What's up? Where are you?"

"At home." Nina had an estate in Red Rock Country Club in the Las Vegas foothills that was worth more than Versailles, where she spent most of her time holed up, having become increasingly reclusive as she'd aged. Her career was still vital and she toured eight months of alternating years, but she'd grown to despise it, and only agreed to continue because of her entourage's assurance that it was key to staying in the public eye. Like many performers, her biggest fear was becoming irrelevant and being forgotten by fans who had moved on to bigger, newer things.

"Are you okay?" By which he meant, was she stoned out of her mind on prescription painkillers again – as she had been the last time he'd been treated to a call – or had the latest round of rehab finally taken?

"Right as rain. Been clean and sober for six months. Boring as hell, I might add."

"That's great news, Nina. One day at a time, right?"

"I…I'm not looking forward to going back out on the road. That's always where the trouble starts."

"You can do it. Hell, you can do anything. You've always been strong."

"Says you."

A soft rattle sounded on the line, like silverware, and Nina hesitated before continuing. Black stepped into the breach.

"What's going on? Why the call? Do you need to borrow money?" he asked, unable to resist the dig.

"I actually was thinking about you yesterday, and I realized it had been forever since we talked. That's all."

"Well, we're talking."

"How are things with you?"

"So-so. Surviving. You know how it is. Nothing comes easy," he said as he opened his car door and heaved himself behind the wheel. "Was there anything specific you wanted to talk about, Nina? Not that it isn't always a delight, but I'm kind of busy…"

"Your mom called and told me she was in town."

Ah. So that was it. Spring and Nina had fallen in love with each other the first time they'd met, and even through the divorce and subsequent bad times they'd stayed in touch. Another betrayal by his mother, he thought morosely as he started the engine.

"Yeah. They've got some kind of thing today. Cheaped out and slept at my place last night. Typical."

"She was trying to get me to fly out, but I told her it probably wasn't such a hot idea."

"That's mom. Always up to something."

"She loves you a lot, Black." Nina had always called him Black, even in bed. Which he still remembered like it was yesterday. He looked over his left shoulder and swung into traffic, gunning the gas to avoid being sideswiped by a Lexus.

"Love is always in the air in Tinsel Town. Was there anything else?" he asked, irritated. Nina was just bored, and had decided to intrude in his mundane life in a bid for attention. Typically selfish and self-involved.

"No…we were just talking about how much things had changed since you and I were kids, just starting out. About what a weird trip it's been. She sounds like she misses you. Do you ever get up to Berkeley to see them?"

"I haven't had a lot of time lately," he said, wondering why Nina was playing conscience today.

"She said you weren't seeing anyone."

"I'm guessing hookers don't count."

"Funny. You never had any problems with the ladies, as I remember."

"What do you want, Nina?" Black said through clenched teeth, annoyance beginning to show in his tone.

"Nothing. I guess talking to Spring just had me nostalgic. That's all."

"We can't go back. Road only runs in one direction." Black fumbled on the seat next to him for his sunglasses and slipped them on. "What about you? How's what's-his-name?" She'd been dating a famous British actor off and on for a year, and all Black knew about it was what he read in the tabloids.

"That was over last month." Her voice lost its chipper tone.

"Sorry to hear about that. I hear Bobby's available for pinch hitting – not much going on with his law firm these days," Black sniped.

"Good to know you haven't let any of that go after, what, twenty years?"

"Everyone needs a hobby. Listen, Nina, I gotta go, okay? I hope everything goes well on tour."

"Yeah, me too. I guess calling wasn't such a great idea. Take care of yourself, Black."

The call disconnected, and he was left with a metallic taste in his mouth that only Nina could summon in him. Damn his mother. She'd probably heard that Nina was single again and had contrived some deluded fantasy where she acted as matchmaker. That was Spring for you. The only question was why Nina had gone along with it.

He rolled to a stop at a red light and shook his head. Was it possible she missed him?

After everything that had happened, everything that she'd done to him?

"Impossible," he muttered to himself, and then caught a glance from an Indian woman in the car next to him. He pointed to his ear piece and grinned. She turned her head and faced forward, eyes locked on the street in front of them.

The sun peeked out from behind the scattered clouds that had crept in overnight and warmed him as he waited for the green. He absently turned on the stereo and smiled as Angus' guitar led with the opening riff of "Thunderstruck." The new stuff wasn't as good as the classics, but few could still deliver like the Boys from Down Under. His fingers kept time on the steering wheel as the light changed, and he dismissed the thoughts of his sex-obsessed therapist, Nina, his mother, Roxie, and Meagan Hunter in favor of a kicking backbeat and mindless lyrics – as good an exchange as he was likely to make that day, he reasoned.

Hunter's bookkeeper had the actor's itinerary along with the check waiting when he arrived at the production office, and after signing for it, Black strode back to his car. Costumed extras and young production assistants hurried along the side of the building, their reality absolutely nothing like his, he was sure. He looked at his watch and did a quick calculation, figuring he could make it to the restaurant with twenty minutes to spare if all went well. The security guard at the main gate took his visitor's pass from him with a disapproving eye on the Cadillac, and then he was on the road again, wheeling his way west, over the hill to the San Fernando Valley for his first official task in Hunter's employ.

CHAPTER 13

Rows of Harleys hulked along the parking lot perimeter of Stubbs, an iconic gathering place for two-wheel enthusiasts ranging from dentists out for a weekend fantasy ride to hardcore bikers – although the latter had diminished significantly due to the criminal justice system and the rigors of time. The restaurant/bar was only half full on a weekday, and Black easily found a spot near the entrance for the big Cadillac.

He checked the time and saw that he was a couple of minutes early, so he settled in to wait after putting the fabric top up – his concession to discretion. It was cool enough out so that he didn't need to run the engine to power the vintage AC unit, and he listened to the stereo, turned low so as not to attract attention, which he quickly realized was pointless given that every new arrival felt obligated to gun their motors with an ear-splitting roar before shutting down.

Hunter arrived on his bike, a custom-shop sled that easily cost a hundred grand, and backed it into a slot near Black before ambling to the front doors. Black watched him as he entered the establishment and took a seat at a window booth where another man sat waiting.

Black's ear piece chirped and he fumbled for his phone. "Black."

"I swear you sound sexier every day, darlin'."

"Hey, Colleen. How's it going?"

"Good. Okay, that's a lie. How about, as well as can be expected?"

"Works for me."

"Hunter called me this morning and told me that you'd worked a deal with him. Congratulations."

"It might be too early. I haven't done anything but pocket his check."

"If there's anyone who can get to the bottom of whatever's going on, it's you, big boy. I've got faith in you."

"Misplaced, obviously, but appreciated nonetheless."

"I just wanted to say thank you for giving it another shot."

"Hey, I like a full stomach as much as the next guy. Hunter agreed to my terms, so we're kosher. Now all I have to do is figure out why he's being targeted, who's killing the paparazzi, and whether he's complicit himself. Piece of cake."

"What? Why would he be involved? He hired you to find out who's after him."

"True, but I can't help but notice that he's been the beneficiary of a lot of coverage since all this started. He claims it's the wrong kind of coverage, but scandal always sells, so I'm not so sure…"

"You're barking up the wrong tree. He's straight. And he certainly wouldn't be involved in murder."

Black winced as another big bike revved past, its rider a woman with more arm muscle than Schwarzenegger. "I don't think so, either, but I want to cover all the bases. And LAPD didn't pull him in because they wanted his autograph. He's a suspect, whether he likes it or not, which he knows."

"Which is why he hired you, tough guy. Don't make this more complicated than it already is. You're wasting your time looking at Hunter. If I was you, I'd be raking Freddie Sypes over the coals. He's as dirty as they get, and it's his firm that's also in the headlines."

"Wait, you think Freddie is somehow involved to generate publicity for his firm? That he's killing his own employees to generate buzz?"

"I'll bet his traffic has gone through the roof since this all started. Honey, I don't know who's doing what to whom, but all I know is that when a scumbag like Freddie is in the neighborhood, bad things start happening. I don't trust him. Never have. He's a backstabbing cockroach who would do anything to further his ambitions. That's all I'm saying."

Black leaned into his seat. "I'll be looking into him as a matter of course. At this point, everyone's a suspect. That's rule number one of investigative work: never assume anyone's innocent."

"I thought rule number one was to get paid."

"Fair point. Oops. Sorry, Colleen, but I have to go. I'm on a stakeout."

"A stakeout! Look at you, like Sam Spade or something. Take care of yourself, darlin'."

"Count on it."

Black was sliding his phone back into his jacket pocket when Hunter emerged from the double restaurant doors. Apparently his meeting had been a short one. As he stepped into the sunlight, a pair of rough-looking men in greasy denim and black leather vests were arguing with a young woman wearing a neon pink tank top and a skirt so short it was an afterthought. One of them grabbed the young woman's arm and began manhandling her. Hunter paused, stared at the two men, and then approached them, his flat black half-helmet clutched in one hand.

Black's internal alarms triggered as the actor moved toward them, and he hastily swung his door open as Hunter engaged. Within a few seconds the altercation had turned ugly, and one of the bikers took a swing at the actor. Hunter ducked the clumsy punch and swung his helmet, striking the big man in the head with it, and he went down, hard. His partner released the girl and moved on Hunter, his stance unmistakably menacing. Black was ten yards away and sprinting when the second assailant's blow went wide and Hunter punched him, following the blow with one to the solar plexus. The second man fell to the ground clutching his stomach, and for a brief second Hunter stood in the bright sunlight looking for all the world like one of his action film heroes, his bare biceps rippling beneath his vest and tank top.

The girl ran to Hunter and was thanking him just as Black arrived. A small crowd had gathered as the pair of miscreants struggled to get up. Camera shutters clicked behind Black, and he positioned himself between the men and his client.

"All right, boys. Show's over. I saw everything. You threw the first punch. That's assault. This man was just defending himself," Black said loudly, hoping that his declaration would make a suitable impression on the bystanders. More importantly, he hoped that these two didn't have another dozen buddies inside Stubbs.

"I won't press charges if they get the hell out of here and leave her alone," Hunter said, his tone dangerous, gripping his helmet like he was ready to go another round.

"You heard him. Scram, or you can explain to the police why you assaulted a respected actor," Black said, realizing that the crowd had now recognized Hunter. He hoped common sense would kick in and they'd want no part of an escalation that would undoubtedly have them both behind bars for a long time.

The men clawed their way upright, holding their faces, and snarled at Hunter before retreating to their motorcycles and pulling their helmets on. Exhausts rumbled across the lot as Hunter stood, one arm protectively around the girl, until the bikes roared off with a contemptuous growl as they tore onto the street and sped south.

"Are you okay?" Black asked Hunter, eyeing the girl, who seemed somewhat in awe of the actor.

"Sure. Just a couple of two-bit punks." Hunter turned to consider his new companion. "You going to be all right?"

"Yeah. Thank you. I just want to get out of here," she said, nervously scanning the growing crowd.

"Black, would you get her a cab or something?" Hunter asked. The girl pulled away from him, the moment past, and as Black escorted her to the street he dialed his office. When Roxie answered, he quickly told her what he wanted and where the cab needed to go.

"Yes, master. Should I pick up your dry cleaning while I'm at it?"

"Roxie, please just do it. Now."

The line went dead, and Black debated calling back but decided not to. Roxie would call. She might be insolent, but she was highly competent.

"A taxi's on its way. Do you need anything?" Black asked the girl.

"Nah, I'm cool. Thanks. That whole thing just freaked me out. Creeps."

"Do you know them?"

"Sort of," she said, and Black took the hint. It was none of his business.

"Wait here. The car should be around shortly," he said, and she sat down on a concrete bus stop bench, resigned to her aborted day on the town.

Black returned to where Hunter was pulling on his helmet, having signed a dozen autographs for his fans. Hunter looked over his shoulder after swinging a leg over the motorcycle's seat and flipping off a car that two men with cameras were piling into. Black watched them pull out of the lot and Hunter grinned.

"Who was that?" Black asked.

"Paparazzi."

"Kind of convenient that they were here for that little scuffle, wasn't it?" Black asked, his expression betraying nothing.

"I'm not sure what you mean," Hunter said. He hit the ignition and gunned the throttle, ending the conversation. "You've got my itinerary. See you when I see you, big man," he called as he pulled away, and then he accelerated across the lot and edged into the sparse late-morning traffic.

Black watched him go, uneasy butterflies flittering in his stomach, and then he turned and walked back to his car, wondering what had really just happened.

CHAPTER 14

"Did you call the taxi?" Black asked as he navigated back towards Los Angeles, over the ridge of hills that separated the San Fernando Valley from the city.

"Damn. I knew I was supposed to do something…" Roxie said, and put the phone down. Black was used to it – it was her way of signaling that she was annoyed at a question. He waited a few seconds and then she picked it back up. "Of course I did."

"Great. And have you got anything on the numbers I gave you?"

"Not yet. But I did get a hit on one of your movie dirtbags. Seems like he's got a rap sheet for petty crimes. Reads more like a con man and a dope fiend than anything. Typical Sunset Strip bottom feeder."

Black sighed. He'd already forgotten about Jared. "What have you got?"

"Looks like a home address. Actually, not that far from your place. Maybe eight blocks away. Like minds…"

"Spare me the insults before lunchtime. Which one is it, and what's the address?"

"Reginald Calper. The one you scribbled 'Preacher' next to." Roxie gave him the address.

"Okay, got it. I'll go by and pay him a visit."

"So no chai for me today, either. No wonder Mugsy hates you."

"What does me not getting you chai have to do with Mugsy? And I thought you said he doesn't hate me."

"I just said that so you wouldn't hold it against him. He's protective of me, and knows when you're subjugating me."

"Subjugating?"

"Oppressing. Keeping me down."

"I'm not subjugating you."

"Classic misogynist. In denial."

"I'm not a misogynist, although you certainly have me thinking about becoming one…"

"At least you're open to accepting it. They say that admitting you have a problem is the first step."

"I'm not admitting anything. You're inventing this. I'm not a misogynist."

"He said angrily," Roxie quipped.

Black took a deep breath. "I'm not angry."

"Sure thing, Mr. Hothead. Just don't come into the office and hit me."

"I've never hit you."

"Yet."

"Roxie? I'm going to hang up now. Is there anything else?"

"Misogynist, violent and angry, and now dismissive. Why am I not surprised?"

"Will you call me when you get something on the phone records?"

"Your mom and dad stopped by."

Black pulled onto the freeway, having to fight his way on after being blocked by an older woman in a Buick, the Eldorado stuttering as it strained up the incline of the hill.

"Are you just trying to ruin my day?"

"They really did. I thought they were sweet."

"How did they find my office?"

"Uh, you *are* in the book."

"Damn."

"Spring and I had a lovely time. Although she's worried because you're not dating."

"Roxie…"

"She wanted to know if I thought you were gay."

"Roxie…"

"She mentioned the wardrobe, and also the no girlfriend… I wish I'd had something more positive to tell the poor woman. Although she seemed accepting, if resigned…"

"I think this is where I hang up for real."

"That's okay. I don't mind if you like men, Black. To each his–"

Black listened as the engine labored and prayed they'd make it to the summit of the hill, much as he did every day, on every grade he encountered. He absolutely had to take it in and get it looked at. Just as soon as the check cleared the bank.

Which reminded him to stop at the bank. Thereby solving his maintenance problem.

Small miracles were showering from the heavens like manna, he thought as he crested the hill and started down the long winding grade, the city sprawling before him. The Cadillac stopped misfiring and returned to purring quietly, and Black resolved that this time he wouldn't put off seeing his mechanic any longer.

The bank run took twenty minutes, by which time his stomach was signaling that it was time to eat. He considered something healthy, then opted for a big, greasy double burger slathered in down-home Island barbeque sauce with triple cheese, bacon, and a deep fried onion ring from a Hawaiian burger joint close to his apartment run by a constantly bickering Korean family who were about as Aloha as they were Irish. His nutritional needs met, he considered possible approaches to take with Reginald, AKA Preacher. As he burped up a rancid stew of teriyaki and pork byproduct, he decided that the direct approach was probably the best.

Roxie was correct that the neighborhood was nearby, but the proximity didn't prepare him for how run-down the building was – it made the Paradise Palms seem like Buckingham Palace. He found a parking place down the block and took his time locking the car, eyes roving over the deserted street, more out of habit than from a sense of any impending threat. Satisfied that he wasn't going to be robbed of his trusty steed, he ambled along the sidewalk until he was in front of the building, which like his, was a horseshoe built around a pool – only this one had been paved over long ago, and the exterior could best be described as prison chic.

An ancient Vietnamese man sat in the courtyard, wearing soiled brown elastic-waist slacks and a T-shirt that looked like someone had been buried in it. He watched, stone-faced, as Black eyeballed the structure. Black nodded to him, but the man gave no response, and merely continued to rock back and forth on his cheap lawn chair, seemingly oblivious to the world.

Black climbed the stairs unhurriedly and moved along the second floor landing until he arrived at Reginald's apartment – number thirty-two. He stood outside, listening for any signs of life, and after twenty seconds of silence, rapped on the door.

Nothing.

A sparrow alighted on the rusting iron railing five yards away from him and searched the area for food, then hopped away, having determined that there was nothing promising from Black's direction. *Smart bird*, he thought, and knocked on the door a second time in the futile hope of a response.

The old Asian was still staring blankly into space when he returned, and Black stopped near him and tried his most inviting nice-guy tone.

"Hello. Do you live here?"

The man looked at him like he was insane, and returned to whatever reverie was playing on infinite repeat in his brain. Black was just turning to leave when the man rasped out in a surprisingly high-pitched voice, almost feminine in timbre.

"Whatchou wan?"

Black hesitated, considering the best way to describe what he wanted. "I'm looking for Reggie. I'm a friend," Black said with what he hoped was a warm grin.

"Reggie?"

"In number thirty-two. Reggie." Black didn't see any recognition in the man's eyes. "Preacher?"

The old man spit to the side in disgust. "Piece a shit," he declared with startling precision, then folded his arms, as if convinced that Black was crafted from the same imperfect clay as his friend.

"Yes, he is, isn't he?" Black agreed, wondering how to keep the man engaged long enough to get more information out of him than his global perspective on Reginald's character.

"No good. Boy no good."

While Black certainly couldn't mount a spirited defense of Reginald in his absence, he sensed that the old man wasn't likely to be forthcoming with much more information. Still, Black was a professional, so he gave it one last try.

"When does he usually get home?"

The man's eyes narrowed to slits, and he waved a gnarled hand dismissively at Black. "You go way or I caw porice."

"But—"

"You go now. *Mao. Didi mao!*"

Black didn't need to brush up on his Vietnamese to get the gist of the old man's exclamation, and held his hands up in what he hoped was a non-threatening way as he backed slowly from the railing he'd been standing near.

"Okay, Grandfather. No disrespect intended. I'm going."

"*Mao! MAO!!!*"

That went well, he thought as he exited the complex, the old man's screams echoing off the walls in a parting serenade. Maybe next time he could just start shooting through the door instead of knocking. About as inconspicuous.

He returned to the car and slid behind the wheel, wishing he'd never agreed to do this for Gracie. Yet another example of him knuckling under, a pushover for the women in his life. The thought ignited a flare of annoyance, and as he settled in to wait for Reginald to show, he wondered whether there might not be something to Kelso's ideas about females and his rage after all.

CHAPTER 15

Lorenzo yawned as he watched the sun set over Santa Monica, the warm orange fading across the ocean and transitioning to red as its last lambent trace sank into the horizon. It had been another long day in the FSA offices, sorting through countless rumors, tips, articles, and whispers, sifting for the gold amidst the pyrite.

His love for his job was still strong even after four years, in spite of the brutal hours and the workload and the relentless expectation of perfection and dedication from Freddie, who sat like a spider in the center of his information collection web, making decisions about how to present the tidbits he deemed worthy of the company's attention. Lorenzo was the first line filter; if it made it past him, then it got passed up the line to his boss, Serena, who made the call whether to bump it up to Freddie or kill it.

It was a pecking order that worked well, and Lorenzo, one of the company's first employees, had watched with thrilled amazement as the company had gone from just a few trusted staff to an organization with hundreds, working round the clock. The website had become synonymous with celebrity news, which in reality was nothing more than the latest dirt. But for FSA, it was paydirt, and Freddie always shared the wealth – to a point.

Lorenzo continued plowing through the endless stream of information and lost track of time, as he often did. It seemed like only minutes had passed, but when he glanced at his watch, he saw that it was pushing nine p.m. – a thirteen-hour day, one of many he'd devoted to the greater good of getting the juice on the stars FSA followed like a pack of hungry wolves.

"*Ciao*, sweeties. Be back in the swamp with y'all tomorrow," he called out, adjusting his fitted jacket as he exited his cubicle. A few tired faces looked up at him, but most of the day staff had gone home already, leaving only a handful of the night shift settling in. Now that was a gig nobody in their right mind wanted. Everyone who worked the graveyard shift was doing so in the hopes of moving up to a day job at some point, figuring they had to pay their dues. Lorenzo knew that Freddie encouraged the rumor that it was a sure way into the big leagues. He also knew that only one person had ever made the leap – the rest of the story was to encourage misguided dreaming that convinced the young and the foolish to work all night for lousy pay.

He stopped in the restroom on the way out and checked his look – cropped black hair gleaming in the artificial light, stylish horn-rimmed glasses for a brooding intellectual edge, swarthy good looks still firmly in place, if a little shopworn. If he hurried, he could grab a quick dinner near his apartment and then take a shower before spending a few hours trolling the West Hollywood clubs.

Downstairs, he pushed through the heavy glass security door and ensured it locked behind him before starting down the sidewalk toward the parking lot. He knew that traffic would still be heavy on Santa Monica Boulevard headed down to Pacific Coast Highway and the beach, and he thanked Providence that he'd be going in the opposite direction, east into Los Angeles. If things worked out smoothly he could be eating at the café a few blocks from his house in no more than half an hour and out on the town by eleven at the latest. That would work.

He rounded the corner and nearly collided with a laughing couple, the woman a stunning blonde in her thirties, the man not so fetching, in his fifties. Love always managed to find a way in L.A., he'd found – popular grist for the company's mill. Even better when the honeymoon was over and the accusations started flying, which was a regrettable byproduct of the lifestyle.

A homeless person shambled along near the parking lot, incongruent with the meticulously sculpted trees that lined the street and yet also an indelible part of the landscape. The down and out, the addicted and the deranged seemed to gravitate to Los Angeles as if it were the Promised Land, and one quickly grew inured to their shabby parade in even the swankiest areas of town. Something about the beach, coupled with the concentration of wealth, acted as a magnet for lowlifes, and Lorenzo didn't even grant them a second glance nowadays – he'd come a long way since moving there seventeen years earlier with aspirations of being an actor, only to become hardened by the town, as everyone eventually did. The endless empty promises and broken dreams seasoned even the most generously predisposed inhabitants, and compassion was perceived as weakness in the city's cutthroat environment.

He was approaching his Ford Festiva when he heard the rustling behind him, and he'd just begun to spin to face whoever was there when the first icy lance of pain shrieked through his chest, his lung punctured instantly by a wickedly sharp blade. He tried to scream but found he couldn't breathe, and when the second blow landed, slicing through his carotid artery and most of the side of his neck, all he could muster was a groan of agony as he sank to the ground, his blood streaming through his hand, which clawed in futility to stem its flow.

His eyes began losing focus as his brain starved for oxygen, but even so he could make out the silhouette of his attacker, who stood silently, watching him die, occasionally glancing around to confirm that they were alone.

The 'vagrant' knelt next to his corpse once he'd bled out and methodically went through Lorenzo's pockets until locating his wallet. Inside were a hundred and seven dollars, five credit cards, an ATM card, and his security card for the building. The killer also took his keys and then moved along the structure's brick wall to the far street to disappear around a corner, leaving Lorenzo to be found by the security company that would occasionally swing by to police the lot several times each night.

CHAPTER 16

"Wow. You look terrible. Did you sleep in your car or something?" Roxie asked the following morning.

"Close enough. I was up late on a stakeout," Black said, placing a cup of chai on her desk before plopping down on the couch across from her. Mugsy stalked over on stiff legs and then leapt onto his lap, as if he knew that he could get the maximum amount of hair on Black's suit with the maneuver. Black rubbed his plump belly. Mugsy purred, and then hooked a needle-sharp claw into his trouser fabric and pulled on it. Black leapt up like he'd been scalded, and Mugsy flipped to the side, landing feet-first on the floor and scurrying off.

"Jesus. That damned cat!"

"I told you he loves you. He only does that to people he really loves."

"How come he doesn't do it to you, then?"

"I guess he loves you more," she said, batting her eyes at him. She was wearing her usual black top and black jeans, today with red Converse All-Stars. Black had to admit that it wasn't a bad combination – she had a way of filling it out nicely.

"And now I've got the scars to prove it. The fat bastard ruined my slacks."

"Ruined them? Come on. Don't be a whiny bitch, boss. They're fine. Oh. Wait. Is that blood?"

Black's hand shot to his crotch area, where everything felt intact, at least.

"Is this really appropriate behavior for a male business owner? I mean, in front of his only female employee?" Roxie asked innocently.

"You said you saw blood."

"No, I asked whether that was blood. I was mistaken. But that doesn't excuse your standing there fondling yourself in front of me. It's kind of icky. I'm just saying..."

"Roxie, I was not fondling myself."

"All right, this is getting really uncomfortable in here. Can we please just stick to being professional?"

"The cat clawed my pants."

"You mean your slacks."

"Whatever. Mugsy started it, not me..."

"Aren't you going to ask me what I've learned about your newest client?" Roxie asked in her typical abrupt manner, having lost interest in tormenting him, at least for the time being.

"After I finish bleeding out."

"Your boy Hunter's a deadbeat," Roxie said, savoring the final word with the relish of a wine connoisseur quaffing a glass of '95 Petrus.

Black did a double take. "Come again?"

She gave him an insulted look. "I'll ignore that. I got his credit report, and he's a late pay on everything but his cars. And get this – he's got tax liens on the house, in addition to the large mortgage, which he hasn't paid for five months. Credit card debt is over a quarter mil, owes the IRS a small fortune, stiffed his private jet company to the tune of a hundred grand..."

"You're kidding."

She regarded him deadpan, without blinking. "Because that's how I kid."

"So you're not kidding..."

"Nope. He's broke. Or he's stretched so thin that he's had to put it all on black. Pardon the pun."

She handed him the report. He took it and began pacing as he read.

"He's broke, all right. I don't suppose you got anything from the banks listed on here?"

"No. I don't feel like committing more than one felony per hour, thanks."

"Damn. I hope the check he gave me doesn't bounce."

"I don't get the sense from the report that he's ready to start selling his furniture yet. But the point is that he's not fat, like you'd expect."

"Looks like he took out a big second on the house...mmm, maybe five years ago. Couple million."

"And then the market tanked."

"The good news is that it's coming back," Black said.

"Not in time to save his ass from the IRS."

"Looks like he owes them over a mil."

"Ouch."

Black handed her back the report and glared at Mugsy, who was busy licking himself clean from his usual position by her desk. "Keep that bloodthirsty animal away from me. He's a menace."

"He's a big, furry ball of love with your name on it."

"You know how much this suit cost?"

"I thought you were wearing it because you lost a bet."

Black knew better than to continue.

"Did you see your parents before they left?"

"No. I told you I was on a stakeout. Why?"

"No reason."

Black looked her over. "Want to tell me what's going on, Roxie?"

"It's just that Spring seemed so...fragile. I think you're too hard on them. I thought they were sweet."

"She's about as delicate as a fighting dog."

"No, she's not. She's what, seventy or something?"

"Something like that," Black said, his voice betraying the uncertainty.

"Don't tell me you don't know how old your mother is..." she said, her voice damning.

Mugsy looked up from his ablutions and peered at Black through hooded feline peepers.

"I do. I just lose track sometimes. Seventy's about right. Maybe seventy-one."

"You should try to be nicer to her. She's the only mother you'll ever have. In fact, you should be nice to both of them."

"Yes, ma'am."

"I mean it, Black. Don't be a dick. They care about you. You should make a point of going up and visiting them at least twice a year. I would if my parents were still alive."

"I thought your mother was."

"Don't try to evade the issue."

"Can I go do some work now that the counseling session is over?"

"Suit yourself," Roxie said, and returned to whatever she'd been doing on her computer, which looked to Black like shopping at an online clothing site.

He stepped across the threshold into his office and stopped, then leaned back and looked at Roxie.

"You're right, you know. I get that."

"When have I ever been wrong?" she asked.

"There's such a thing as a graceful winner, you know."

"Not here, there isn't."

Chastened and contrite, Black closed his door and took off his suit jacket and hung it on the back of the visitor chair. He sat behind his desk and stared at the ceiling for a few moments, then picked up his cell phone with a sigh and dialed a number he still knew by heart.

"Hello?" Spring's voice was chirpy, even long distance.

"Hi, Spring."

"Hello?"

"Can you hear me?"

"Hello…"

"Mom?"

"Damn. Whoever this is, hang on. My headset's acting funky."

Black winced as a loud crackling nearly deafened him, followed by several blasts that sounded like his mother was in the middle of a hurricane, and then her voice returned.

"Hello?" she tried again.

"Mom. Is this better?"

"Artemus! What a lovely surprise. Sorry we missed you yesterday. We stopped by…"

"I know. I was out on business."

"Is…is everything all right? Do you need money?"

Black sighed. "No, Mom—"

"Spring," she corrected.

"Right. Spring. No, I don't need money, and I'm fine. I was just calling to see if you got home safely."

"Why, that's so…so sweet, honey! Yes, we had our meeting and were back home by dinner time."

"How did that go?" Black asked, feigning interest.

"Oh, you know. I'm just not sure I want all the responsibility. It's so much work, I remember from before…"

"What is?"

"Growing the company to meet these people's production demand."

"Production demand. On candles?"

"I know! Isn't that a trip? Anyway, they wanted so many over the course of each year…"

"Who was it you were meeting with, Spring?" Black asked, keeping his voice even.

"The folks that own Trader Nick's. They must really like my candles."

"Wait. Trader Nick's wants to carry your candles?"

"They actually wanted an exclusive. But the part that bothered me was that I'd have to quadruple output to meet their minimums, and…well, that's just a big hassle. Plus, I sell them through Ruthie's down on Telegraph, and she's been a good friend ever since the soap days…"

"So you're turning down Trader Nick's volume commitment to sell a handful of candles to Ruthie?" Black echoed disbelievingly.

"No, fortunately they were willing to let me have a waiver for the stores in Berkeley."

"Then what's the problem?"

"I don't want to run a big company."

Black swallowed hard. Even if the profit on candles wasn't that great, it had to be a lot of money his mother was dismissing. Then again, she already had a lot of money.

"I can totally appreciate that."

"Which is why we're meeting with some nice people the Trader Nick's folks introduced us to. They make some other products for them, and they're interested in buying my candle business, or doing some kind of a license deal."

Black's mouth tasted like glue. "A license deal. For Trader Nick's."

"Anyway, your dad and I have been discussing it. Nothing's been decided. But enough about us. That must be so exciting, working on a big case."

Black nodded, thinking about the paltry five grand retainer and how quickly that would get used up. "Oh, it is."

They chatted for a few more minutes and then Black signed off just as his door swung open, pushed by Mugsy, who looked ready for round two with his slacks.

His frail mother was swinging multi-million dollar business deals over breakfast, and he was in a battle of wills with an obese ingrate of a tabby and an assistant who thought he liked going to discos with men. He was just thinking that it couldn't get much worse when his office line buzzed and Roxie's voice rang out like a klaxon.

"Line one. Somebody named Stan. Says it's urgent."

CHAPTER 17

Black stared at the phone like it was a live snake, then raised the handset to his ear. "Hey, big guy. If it's advice you're looking for, four words: The butler did it," he quipped.

"Inside my heart soars like eagle at your pithy wit. Outside, not so much," Stan said, his voice typically dry and matter-of-fact.

"What's going on, chief?"

"You watch the news this morning?"

"No. Why? Did I win the lottery?"

"Another paparazzo bit the dust last night."

Black sat up, his mood no longer playful. "What?"

"Sliced up a block from FSA headquarters. Ugly. Lots of blood."

"Why are you telling me?"

"Why do you think? We're looking at your client as a possible. I just came from his house. His alibi sucks."

"Really? What was it?"

"That he was home, in his office. Problem is no witnesses. He claims he was reading scripts, so no computer history to verify he was there."

"Where was his wife?"

"Apparently she got the tequila flu and retired early."

"Daughter?"

"Wasn't there."

"Alarm system? Housekeepers?"

"Alarm wasn't on. Only the family at home. Or not."

"You're right. That's not a great alibi."

"Nope. Then again, we don't have anything linking him. No traffic cams of one of his vehicles in Santa Monica, no witnesses…"

Roxie's voice sounded from the front office again.

"What?" Black demanded, irritated at being interrupted.

"Your new client is on line two."

Black cupped his hand over the phone. "Shit. Really?" he asked her.

"You want me to tell him you're too busy to talk? Or you're in the bathroom or something?"

"No." Black returned his attention to Stan. "Are we done?"

"For now."

"Thanks for calling, buddy. Sorry you got another one thrown at you."

"Hey, at least it's job security, right?"

Black jabbed at the phone until line two lit up. "Black," he answered.

"Black. Hunter. The cops were just over here. Another scumbag got whacked, and they've got a hard-on for me."

"But all they did was question you?"

"Some bull about where was I last night. Like now I'm Jack the Ripper. I can't tell you how pissed off I am right now."

"Do you have an alibi?"

"Yeah, but I don't think they bought it."

"What was it?"

"That I was jerking off at the precise time they're curious about. Who the hell cares what it was? The point is I'm being raked over the coals. Have you made any progress?"

"Not really. It's only been one day. Remember our discussion…"

"Yeah, yeah. I got it the first time. You're a maverick. Work alone. Blah blah blah. Listen, that wasn't the main reason I called. You've got my schedule. Tonight's the sneak preview showing of the movie. I want you there."

"Why? Did you hire the security guy I put in touch with you?"

"Yes, but I want you, too. Because I can sense you're a film aficionado. You give off that vibe, with the clothes and all."

"The clothes?"

"Hey, I got nothing against you guys. To each his own, you know?" Someone in the background spoke to Hunter, and then he returned. "Listen, I don't have a lot of time to yak. Be there at 8:00. Show starts at 8:15."

Black found himself staring at the phone, a dial tone humming from the earpiece.

He glanced at his forties-cut retro suit jacket absently, wondering why everyone thought that such a classic look was the province of those celebrating alternative lifestyles, and then Roxie was standing at the door.

"You need to see this. FSA has a piece on Hunter from yesterday where he got into some kind of a fight."

Black stood and accompanied her back to her desk, where a photo of the actor from the worst possible angle managed to make him look paunchy, even though he didn't have an ounce of fat on him that Black could tell. He read the short blurb beneath it and whistled softly.

"Nothing like unbiased journalism. This makes it read like he went berserk and attacked some innocent bystanders for no reason."

"Isn't that what happened?" Roxie asked, and Black noticed that she smelled good – like vanilla and floral shampoo.

"Not at all. Some thugs were picking on a damsel in distress, and he came to her aid. I saw the whole thing. This is nothing more than a smear job."

"That's about what I'd expect from these guys. I checked the other big sites, and a few of them have photos, too. Probably taken with cell phones, but not bad. Their accounts more match your description of what went down."

"No question that FSA has it out for Hunter. Obviously, they hate his guts. I bet if he saved a basket of kitties, they'd spin it so it looked like he was trying to drown them."

"Hey, at least he's all over the news again. That can't hurt his new movie's chances, can it?"

Black eyed her profile thoughtfully. "Any publicity is good publicity – as they say?"

"I wouldn't know, given that my band has never managed to get noticed enough to worry about it."

"That's life in the big city." Black paused. "How did things work out with Eric?"

"I confronted him, and he swears on a stack of Bibles that he didn't do anything. I know he's a liar, but I kind of believe him." She looked away. "I'm a weak woman."

Black's hand instinctively moved to her shoulder to comfort her, but then stopped, hovering just behind it. A vision of Dr. Kelso popped into mind, staring at him like a stuffed boar's head. He lowered his arm and straightened.

"Hey. Nobody's perfect, right?"

"I guess not. I wish I had the cash to hire you to shadow him for a few days so I could know for sure."

"If you did, you wouldn't be working here, and that would be my loss. And think how it would impact Mugsy – the fat little shit would have to be nice to me so I'd feed him. I think it would kill him."

"He's probably rolling around on your jacket as we speak. Or using it as a scratching post or something."

Black's eyes widened and he darted back into his office. Mugsy was lying on the seat of his executive chair, methodically shredding the leather.

"Mugsy! Get off that right now!" Black screamed. Mugsy glanced up at him with a look of studied feline insouciance and then plopped down onto the floor with his trademark expression of disdain. Black watched as he stalked past on stiff legs, took up position by Roxie, and closed his eyes, exhausted from the exertion of destroying yet more of Black's meager possessions.

Black sighed and called out to her. "Let me know when you have the phone stuff on Hunter. That may give us a direction to pursue, because right now we've got squat, and the paparazzi are heading the endangered species list. And Hunter's a prime suspect, which is bad for us, especially if he's been naughty."

"Naughty might be a little tame for serial killing."

"Man's innocent until proven guilty."

"Aren't we all…"

CHAPTER 18

The private screening theater at Paramount held a hundred people, and the crowd gathered in the outer reception room, swigging cocktails and telling each other lies about their careers and projects. It was a mixed bag – some critics, a few sympathetic reporters, studio execs, the actors and their dates, friends, business associates, agents, and managers…and Black, who blended in like a sumo wrestler at a fashion show. Everyone had the glow of money and fame and power, even the press, who seemed to bask in it and reflect the aura like multi-level marketers at a big sales convention.

Black's gaze roved over the throng, grouped in threes and fours, sipping champagne and martinis as they tittered at each other's witticisms, until it landed on the small bar that had been set up in the far corner. He made a beeline for it, feeling like he'd caught a touchdown pass and was fighting his way downfield. Meagan Hunter appeared out of nowhere in a glittery black dress that looked like it had been glued on, and slipped her arm into his.

"Why, Mr. Black. What a delightful surprise. I'm so glad you could make it. Can I talk you into a cocktail before the festivities begin?" she purred, the aroma of expensive perfume mixing with alcohol fumes as she murmured in his ear like a lover.

"Mrs. Hunger. Nice to see you again," he said, then flushed as he realized his slip. "*Hunter*. Mrs. *Hunter*. Sorry."

"No offense taken – you're a very perceptive man, aren't you?"

"Or a really stupid one."

"I never took you for dumb. Although I've got nothing against all looks and no brains, if that's supposed to warn me off. And I told you the last time – call me Meagan. We're practically family at this point."

"Jack and coke," Black told the bartender, anxious to end the flirtation there. The last thing he needed was Hunter's inebriated wife coming on to him in a roomful of movers and shakers. He was still squirming inwardly at the idea when Hunter appeared in an Italian suit that probably cost more than Black's car and clasped one hand on his shoulder as he moved alongside him and set his wine glass down on the bar.

"So you're here. Anything new come up?" he asked, his voice low, strictly business as he pointed at his goblet, signaling a refill to the bartender.

"Not yet. I talked to LAPD about the killing. I wish you had a stronger alibi, but even so, I don't think there's going to be any more trouble from that end. There's no 'there' there."

"I think I'll have another greyhound. Extra tequila, Maestro!" Meagan said, her voice a little too loud.

"Don't you think you've had enough? Maybe you should hit the brakes for a while," Hunter said, his eyes flashing anger.

"Oh. I'm sorry. Heaven forbid that I actually enjoy myself a little. I'll just walk ten steps behind you and bow to whoever greets you. Will that work?" she asked, her voice sweet as honey.

"Don't bust my balls, Meagan. Just this once. Do me this favor, would you?" Hunter replied, offering his dazzling professional smile as he waved at two newcomers by the entry.

"Fine. I have to go to the powder room anyway. Try not to fuck any of your co-stars while I'm there, would you?" she whispered before teetering off on impossibly high heels that showcased her dancer's legs.

Hunter shook his head, a look of fatigue crinkling the corners of his eyes.

"Women, huh? What are you going to do with 'em? I thought the newer models would be easier to operate, but not at all. Can't live with 'em, can't keep 'em in a cage in the cellar…I never said that, by the way. The feminists would have a field day with it."

Hunter's prior two marriages had ended in sensational divorces, with an ugly and extremely public battle on the second one. His daughter from that marriage, Nicole, had been used as a pawn by the newly ex-Mrs. Hunter, and Black vaguely recalled the acrimonious bickering the press had reported in excruciating detail.

Black chose to remain silent, praying his drink would arrive before the surrealistic situation got any more uncomfortable. Hunter took that as camaraderie or agreement, because he drew closer, and Black realized the actor was pretty close to being drunk himself.

"Don't read too much into her, Black. We've been going through a rough patch, that's all. It happens."

Black nodded as the bartender set his drink down in front of him and then reached for a bottle of cabernet for Hunter. "None of my business."

"Speaking of which, I really could use some good news. Tell me you're making progress. Please."

"It's still first inning. I'm gathering information. Looking for connections. Patterns. Motive. Speaking of which, can you think of anyone else who would have it in for you?"

Hunter laughed, a dry humorless bark.

"Half of Hollywood would like to skin me alive and then dance on my grave, the other half would prefer to piss on it. It goes with the territory. This business is all white sharks. You never have any friends in this town, only allies, and then only until it would benefit them to move in for a kill shot."

"What about FSA? There's a common thread here. Whoever is killing the paparazzi is probably doing it for their own reasons. But why link it to you?"

Hunter lifted his brimming wine glass in a mock toast and then drained a third of it in one swallow. "Who the hell knows? There are psychos everywhere. Maybe somebody wants to become famous. Or thinks they're doing me a favor by eradicating the world of cockroaches. Maybe they're trying to send a message – that they agree with my dislike of the paparazzi, and they're going to somehow help with my crusade by killing them in my proximity? I could invent a hundred different scenarios, but the truth is that I have no idea why whoever is doing this has singled me out. Just lucky, I guess."

Black took a sip of his cocktail and noticed the security man he'd recommended to Hunter standing in a corner, watching the crowd. Black made eye contact and the man nodded, stone-faced, then returned to his nonstop scanning of the privileged few.

Meagan returned looking like a fashion model and beamed a megawatt smile at Black before throwing Hunter a patently fake one. "I'm back, darling. I hope you didn't miss me too much."

"Always, Meagan, always. Now, if you'll excuse me, I think we need to get this show on the road. It's movie time!" Hunter declared, clapping his hands together theatrically before moving off towards the screening room doors to have the announcement made.

Meagan edged close to Black again and pressed one haunch against his. "You know, we have some unfinished business, you and me. Maybe you can sneak out halfway through the movie and meet me in the ladies' room?"

"Don't take this the wrong way, Meagan, but I'm on the job tonight. And you're my client's wife."

"More like his bathmat. Trust me, big boy, you have no idea what you're missing."

His eyes roamed down her gym-toned body and he swallowed hard. "I'm sure I don't. But that's the way it has to be."

She pulled away from him. "Have you made any progress on the case?"

The sudden changing of gears threw him, and then he recovered. "No, not yet. There's not a lot to go on, frankly. It's a weird one."

"You should look at his bitch daughter at some point. I could see her doing something psychotic, and she hates the paparazzi more than Hunter does."

"I gather there's no love lost there."

"She hates me because her father dumped her mom to marry me. And since the accident, she's taken her condition as an excuse to be an abusive little fecal speck every chance she gets. So no, we don't have the very best relationship," Meagan said, a few of the words slurred but with a renewed energy, eyes sparkling with a flicker of excitement. Black realized that she'd probably done a line of coke in the bathroom to even out her buzz, and decided that spending any more time with her at that point was courting disaster. "And don't let her cripple act fool you. She could probably outrun you if there was a bottle of gin on the line."

"I've got to go talk to the security chief before the showing starts. If you'll forgive me…"

She pouted, then shrugged. "Suit yourself."

The announcement came over the public address system as he was crossing the room, and he lost his chance to talk with his friend, who sprang into action marshaling the other security men in preparation for the screening. Black hung back as the throng entered the mini-theater and made sure he was the last one in, his thoughts roiling over the interactions he'd just seen.

The film was terrible, almost a parody of a Bruckheimer action romp, and Black nearly bolted from the theater when the credits rolled two hours later. If this was the "game changer" that Hunter had bet the farm on, he was about to lose everything, Black could see that. The lackluster polite applause confirmed his take, and he hurried from the screening area before anyone would miss him, anxious to be rid of the whole scene, with its pretensions, ugliness, and the toxic environment Hunter and his wife managed to create within seconds of being in each other's company.

He stopped at Valentino's in Hollywood on the way home and asked around about Preacher and his partner, but got nowhere, and after an hour of overpriced watery drinks and too-loud music, he decided to call it a night and head back to his dump, secure in the knowledge that as rough as he had it, Hunter probably had it worse.

CHAPTER 19

"There's a gentleman here to see you," Daniela announced to Freddie over the intercom.

Freddie glanced at the speaker. "That's nice. Who is it?"

"A Mr. Black. He said that he's involved in the murder investigation."

Freddie rolled his eyes, then closed his browser. The truth was he'd been surfing the web, looking at his competitors' sites, watching how they treated the same stories he was featuring, so it wasn't like he was particularly busy at the moment. Still, he'd already spent a half hour with two detectives the prior day, and his time was valuable.

"Fine. Show him back."

When Black appeared with Daniela, Freddie appraised him briefly and then indicated one of the two chairs in front of his desk. Daniela closed the door behind her, and Freddie gave Black a wan smile that never reached his eyes before leaning back in his seat and exhaling noisily.

"I've already told you everything I know. I don't see how else I can help you," he started, irritation barely contained in his every word.

"Yes, well, we appreciate that. I just have a few questions, and then I'll be on my way," Black said in an officious manner. He had told the receptionist that he was investigating the latest murder, and she had assumed that he was with the police. He'd even favored one of his more modern-cut jackets and a pair of nondescript gray wool trousers, dressing in an impression of Stan that he thought would fool just about anyone. It had worked, and now he was with his client's nemesis, free to ask whatever he liked as long as he didn't blow it and tip his hand.

"Well, let's not wait for Christmas, then," Freddie said.

"We've already covered the victim's background and the events leading up to the unfortunate event. I want to discuss related elements of the case. Specifically, anything he might have been working on that could have triggered an attack."

"What, you think this wasn't random?"

"I didn't say that. But you have to admit that working for your company has become a singularly dangerous occupation lately. We need to consider all possibilities, that's all."

"Then you think it could be related to the other attacks?"

"We don't have enough information to draw any conclusions, sir. But it's certainly something we're looking at."

"Fine. For the record, there wasn't anything inflammatory he was working on that I know of."

"I see. Tell me, Mr. Sypes. How does your organization get its information?"

"Well, that's kind of a trade secret."

"I'm sure it is. But humor me. I'm not planning to set up a competitive site anytime soon." Black favored Freddie with an empty smile of his own.

"To answer your question, we have a host of ways. People call us with tips. We pay service people at a wide variety of restaurants and clubs where celebrities are known to hang out. Sometimes we get contacted by PR people trying to create buzz for their clients. EMT techs, firemen, even cops give us tips. There are a hundred different ways we stay plugged in."

"I was looking at your site, and I noticed a couple of pieces that caught my eye. Can we use those as examples?"

"I'm not sure how that's going to help catch Lorenzo's murderer…"

"There's a method to my madness. Play along with me," Black said in a decidedly unplayful tone. "You've got one about Terry Hollens. Going into rehab for the, what, fifth time?"

"Yes. Poor Terry. Seems like she just can't stay off the hillbilly heroin. A shame. Let's see…" Freddie tapped at his computer keyboard and then squinted at the information on the screen. "We got that tidbit from the cab driver who took her there. Called us right after she gave him the address. We paid a hundred dollars for that."

"Wow. I'm in the wrong business. A hundred bucks for a phone call. Who knew?"

"Of course, depending upon the celebrity, it can be less, or a lot more. Terry's battles with her demons are sort of old news these days, so it's just not worth what it might have been, say, three years ago when she still had her TV show."

"I see. All right, what about the one with Hunter getting into that brawl? Seems like having a photographer at a biker bar was awfully serendipitous."

This time Freddie typed more slowly. "Ah. That was an anonymous tip. Phone call."

"Anonymous? Wouldn't most of your tipsters want to get paid? Isn't that a little unusual?"

"Not as much as you might think. Sometimes people just call in because they've seen someone famous and want to feel like they're part of the process. It's a strange world. We get them all the time."

"I see. Do you tape the inbound calls?"

Freddie's eyes shifted to the side with a momentary look of cunning, then returned to Black with the steady gaze of the innocent. "Tape?"

"Record. Do you record your inbound tip calls?"

Freddie nodded. "We have a policy of doing so."

"So, for instance, you would have the anonymous tipster's voice recorded?"

"You've now completely lost me. What would that have to do with a murder investigation?"

"Two of your staff were killed at one of Hunter's press conferences, were they not?"

"Yes."

"And you received an anonymous tip alerting you to Hunter's whereabouts only a day later. I'm wondering whether they might be connected."

"How?"

"I don't know. I'm not paid to solve the whole crime, just put together miscellaneous puzzle pieces and collect information. Tell me – would it be possible to pull that call and hear it?"

Freddie studied him like a lab specimen, and then nodded slowly. "Absolutely. Just get a warrant and I'd be happy to."

Black's composure slipped just a little. "I was hoping that we could work together on these things with less formality…"

"Yes, but when cops start asking for sources, it changes everything. And frankly, I see nothing remotely useful in this line of questioning. It feels like a pure fishing expedition, and while I'm trying to be helpful, there are limits. You just reached one."

Black did a quick about-face and asked a series of innocuous questions related to building security, personnel background checks, company policies and working hours, and then extricated himself before he could get into real trouble. He thanked Freddie for his time with a cursory handshake and beat a swift path for the exit, the foray having been worth it. Someone had known about the meeting, or someone from the restaurant had called when they'd spotted Hunter; the only problem with that theory being that Hunter had only been inside for all of fifteen minutes, and Black doubted that Freddie had roving gangs of paparazzi patrolling the streets of the San Fernando Valley on a Tuesday morning. Which led him straight back to a leak having tipped FSA off in advance.

There were several possibilities: someone from the distributor's side – there was no way of ruling that out – or someone from Hunter's team.

A niggle of acidic anxiety tickled his stomach as he returned to his car. He'd had a feeling all along that Hunter wasn't leveling with him, and this sort of minor mystery wasn't doing anything for improving his faith in the man. Whether it actually mattered was a different story – the money was in the bank, and whoever had alerted Freddie, there was no harm done. That was about the only time the paparazzi had been around Hunter lately when one of them didn't wind up dead.

Back on the road, top down, the sun blinding as it reflected off the ocean of motorized metal and glass around him, he called Stan.

"Black. What's shaking?"

"Not much. Just got finished running some errands out in Santa Monica. How's your case going?"

"The skewered FSA guy? No breaks. Nobody saw anything, and there's nothing from forensics to give us a direction. I still like your client for it, but that's probably because I think he's a douchebag."

"God knows there are enough of them in this town. But if they were all murderers, we'd have a quarter of the population."

"There you go with your sunny rays of optimism."

"So is it safe to say that Hunter's no longer a suspect?"

"In that one. But on the two that went kaboom? I still have unanswered questions there. Apparently the trigger on that device was a burner cell phone. If he was smart enough to set that up, he also would have been smart enough to use a second one to avoid any link on his."

"Assuming he did it. But for what reason?"

"I honestly haven't figured that one out. Which doesn't mean he didn't do it. It just means that there are all kinds of whack jobs out there up to no good, and I can't get into all their heads. Maybe he just likes killing them?"

"We both know that's unlikely. I think he's clean," Black said.

"Yeah, I know. He's an innocent man. That's all I ever deal with, seems like. Just once I'd like one of these guilty creeps to just pull a Seven and turn himself in with a full confession."

"Tell me that wasn't a great movie."

Stan hesitated. "Not that I don't enjoy your sassy talk, but is there anything else?"

"No. I'll probably be out tonight, trying to run down a guy who ripped my neighbor off for five grand."

"Nice. I'll call you if I'm up for some wading in the sewers, then."

"One little drinky never hurt anyone."

"Too true, amigo. Catch you later."

Black's next call was to Colleen.

"Hey, gorgeous. You out and about?" she answered.

"How did you know?"

"I can hear that car of yours from here."

"Listen, Colleen, I need to talk to you some more about Hunter. I'm not sure he's completely on the level."

"Who is in this town, darling? What did he do now?"

Black told her about his doubts and about the anonymous phone call.

"Your gut's still golden, Black. That's one of the oldest tricks in the book. It sounds like a setup. He probably tipped them himself. And then had a ready-made media circus for when he took on two bikers, right before his movie premiere, to defend the honor of a young beauty."

Black was speechless. It all fell into place. "Are you for real?"

"This is Hollywood, sugar. Land of make believe. I'd give you five to one odds that he planned the whole thing. He even got Freddie to cover it, if with a negative spin. Pure manipulation, and brilliant at that. I gotta buy the man a drink next time I see him."

"Huh. While you're being so free and easy with the booze, tell me about the wife."

"Meagan? They've been married for, I don't know, a dozen years. He booted his ex for her. Caused a big stink at the time. Meagan was barely out of diapers. Maybe twenty? Twenty-one?"

"What's your impression of how they're doing these days?"

"I don't talk to her much. She doesn't like me. Feeling's mutual."

"Right. But at the sneak preview party, they didn't seem to be getting along very well."

"Maybe she found out he was banging everything in town. A man like Hunter's not going to change much. Twenty looked great to him when he was fifty, and probably looks even better to him now that he's sixty-whatever. I mean, you know he was humping his co-star, right?"

"Melody. Yeah, I kind of read between the lines there."

"And Meagan's got the appetites of an alley cat, from what I can tell."

"Do you know that for sure?"

"You mean do I have footage of her and the pool boy? No. But a woman can just tell these things, my boy. Rrowr."

"She's been coming on to me pretty strong."

"There you go. Although I also get the sense she's a calculating bitch. Might want to ask yourself what else besides your impressive physique she wants out of you."

"Fortunately for me, I don't have anything else."

"Everyone has something else, darling. You just need to figure out what you have that she has designs on. Not that you're not *muy caliente*."

"Maybe I'm just in the right place at the wrong time?"

"That could be. Damn. Hang on." Colleen had a short conversation with someone. "Sorry. Seth is painting the place, so it's mayhem over here."

"No problem. I've kept you long enough. Say hey to Seth for me – I gather you two are more than friends."

"I can't afford a pool boy, but Seth, for all his issues, manages to drive my car just fine. Why, you wanna bump ahead of him in line?"

"Maybe another time, Colleen. Thanks for the info."

"Always a pleasure, babe."

Black navigated his way back to the office, wondering what he'd gotten himself into with Hunter, and then dismissed his misgivings. The money was good, and God knew he could use more of that. Who was he to judge his fellow man, or woman, especially at two hundred per hour? One had to be flexible. Not jump to hasty conclusions.

He stopped by Preacher's apartment building again on his way back, but met with the same shrieking invective from the old Vietnamese man, and no response to his repeated knocking. Maybe the scumbag had blown town after ripping enough people off. It wouldn't be the first time, and the girl had already flown the coop. He was getting the feeling that it was a dead end, but he owed it to Gracie to put in at least a token effort. Plus, he'd been young and stupid once, and had certainly gotten tricked out of more than a few measly grand.

Black hated to admit it, but Jared reminded him just a little of himself when he'd first arrived in L.A. The timeline had just accelerated since back in his day. It had taken almost two years for the town to crush his spirit. With Jared, it had only been a week.

Everything was more efficient now.

Probably the damned internet's fault.

CHAPTER 20

Spotlights played through the night air outside of TCL Chinese Theater for the premiere of Hunter's epic, *Nine Hard Lives*, which the promo posters warned would be shocking – and that this time, it was personal. Every variety of kook and Hollywood nutcase was out in force, thronging the sidewalks on either side of the barricades that had been set up to keep the undesirables at bay, vying for attention in the way that only the certifiably insane could.

A man dressed as Stan Laurel of Laurel and Hardy, inexplicably painted head to toe in silver paint, stood next to his counterpart, an all-gold Pirate of the Caribbean who looked like he'd polished off a few too many cocktails before coming to work for the evening. Roller-skating Rastafarians for Jesus, a few holdout Hari Krishnas, three paunchy men in sombreros and gaucho suits with guitars and a sign proclaiming them as the Polish Mariachis (*Polka Con Dios!*), a juggling midget in a threadbare jester's outfit, an eighty-year-old woman screaming Biblical prophecies in between serenading passers-by with off-key show tunes…anything you wanted, and plenty you didn't, was at the spectacle, drawn to the glitter as surely as moths to a bug zapper.

Near the far barrier, the paparazzi hung in a clump, like bluebottles around a camp latrine, waiting for the big show to finish so they could get photos. They'd already disrupted the proceedings while the stars had been arriving on the red carpet, and several from FSA had made a point of yelling inflammatory questions when Hunter arrived. Hunter had barely restrained himself from lunging at the men, who taunted him with the glib assurance of children pestering zoo animals from behind the safety of shatterproof glass.

An espresso cart was set up, and the photographers were eagerly sipping the hot brew, their work hours having just begun. Many would be up until dawn, chasing down the inebriated and the unlucky who also happened to be newsworthy, and they relished a good caffeine jolt in addition to any other stimulants they could get their hands on. The film had started almost two hours before, and the air of expectation in the remaining crowd was palpable, a buzz of excitement at being in the proximity of the famous, if not the great. Young women in short skirts worked the area, their lean features already brittle in spite of their tender years, ignored by the uniformed policemen lounging together inside the barrier, safeguarding those who really mattered from those who clearly didn't.

Suddenly one of the FSA photographers by the barrier dropped his camera with a loud crash, followed immediately by his paper cup of steaming coffee, and then collapsed on the filthy concrete sidewalk and began to convulse. A nearby woman screamed as the remaining paparazzi alternated between stepping away from their colleague and drawing nearer in horrified fascination. His partner knelt next to him and began to loosen his button-up shirt collar, but pulled away when the fallen man started to foam from his mouth and nose, tiny flecks of blood coloring the froth pink.

Two policemen hopped the barrier and jogged over, hands on their holstered pistols. When they saw the commotion, the first radioed for help while the other signaled to their remaining colleagues, who rushed to join them and see what the fuss was all about.

Nine minutes later an ambulance rolled to the curb. Two paramedics leapt out and ran to examine the fallen man. One took the photog's vitals while the other removed a medical kit from the rear of the ambulance, and then stopped when his partner looked up at him from his position next to the victim and shook his head.

Ten minutes after that, the film ended. By then the area in front of the theater was chaos, with additional uniforms arriving and the crowd in a flux of slow motion pandemonium as more of the local eccentrics congregated to add their own special brand of magic to the tragedy. A legless saxophone player sat oblivious to the scene, propped against a lamppost down the block, playing a long, soulful solo as the police did their best to contain the area. A line of limousines waited at the curb like a funeral procession, yellow crime scene tape now cordoning off the espresso cart and the spot where the victim had dropped. When the theater doors swung open, the exiting audience was shocked by the unexpected display, police milling around trying to implement crowd control with marginal success.

Black was one of the first out the door and quickly sized up the situation when he saw the squad cars and the ambulance. His phone went off as he stepped backward and leaned against one of the building façade's oversized red columns, next to a highly stylized Chinese imperial lion, and he looked down at the screen to see a text message from Stan, warning him that he'd be there in two minutes and to stay put, along with his client. Black hadn't seen Hunter since everyone had entered the theater, so he was unsure how to go about alerting him that the police wanted to have yet another chat, but he figured that eventually the star would have to exit, and then Black could corral him.

The departing crowd had stopped to gawk at the scene, creating a bottleneck inside the theater that quickly developed an angry hum from the important people inside who were being blocked – something they were unaccustomed to and resented on principle. Jostling ensued, adding to the mayhem and carnival-like atmosphere on the sidewalk, the spotlights still sweeping the night sky as if nothing had happened. Traffic froze to gridlock as rubberneckers slowed to get a better look. An old Nova collided with a new Audi on the opposite side of Hollywood Boulevard, stopping the flow as the drivers inspected the damage.

Stan's unmarked sedan screeched to the curb twenty yards from the red carpet, a flashing emergency light stuck on the roof, and he hopped out from behind the wheel as his partner, Carl Field, swung the passenger door open and heaved his considerable bulk out. Stan spotted Black and gave him a dark look before quickly taking stock of the situation and assuming control. The corpse's inert form still lay on the sidewalk beneath a blanket provided by a thoughtful paramedic. The forensics van pulled to a halt shortly afterward, and three technicians emerged lugging dark blue toolboxes and started collecting prints and evidence from the coffee cart while Stan organized the onlookers into groups of potential witnesses.

Inside, the manager of the theater finally got on the public address system and announced that there had been an incident outside that would be cleared up shortly, and that he appreciated everyone's cooperation in being patient – that it was a police matter, and they were doing everything in their power to speed things along. The murmur of displeasure increased to a steady roar, and Black watched as Stan and some more detectives organized things and began allowing people out. All he could think was that he was glad he was outside and not in the room with a theater full of people who had just sat through one of the most astonishingly bad and sophomoric cinematic efforts in recent memory.

Stan saved Black the trouble of detaining Hunter, beelining toward him when he emerged, a look of fury on the star's face because his big event had been ruined. Stan told him to stay put while he finished with preliminary questioning of the paparazzi, and Black could hear the outrage in Hunter's voice over the tops of a hundred heads. In truth, Stan was overstepping, because Hunter had been inside when whatever had happened had taken place, and had about a thousand witnesses who could attest to it. Black saw Stan brushing past a group of women in sequined evening dresses and moved toward him.

"What happened, Stan?"

"Someone poisoned one of the photographers. And get this – with more cameras here than a Japanese pawn shop, there's not one shot of the espresso vendor. Not one. All anyone remembers is that it was a Caucasian or Hispanic male with a black baseball cap and a beard. Which would be really helpful if there were only five adult males living in Los Angeles. So let's just say I'm having a really bad night."

"Not as bad as Hunter is. Why are you holding him?"

"I'm not. I just asked him to wait a few minutes so I can take his statement."

"Which looks to everyone, including the press, like he's a suspect."

Stan leaned in to him and spoke so softly it was barely a whisper. "Yup. And you know why? Because I can."

"Remind me not to get on your bad side," Black said.

"I just did."

They were both startled by a commotion at the edge of the crowd where Hunter was standing. Someone screamed, and by the time Black and Stan had made it to the area, all hell had broken loose. Black was straining to get a look at what had happened when he saw Hunter being restrained by two police officers, a look of pure rage in his eyes. He pushed closer and saw a familiar figure spread-eagled on the sidewalk, blood streaming from his ruined face.

Freddie.

"What the hell is going on?" Black yelled over the shouting voices. A man next to him, in his sixties, dignified and obviously wealthy, turned toward him.

"The guy on the ground showed up and started taunting Hunter. Said his premiere was going to be the running joke of the decade. Hunter lost it when the guy said someone inside had called to tell him that the movie was worse than *Ishtar*," he said, his voice gravelly with an east coast accent, seasoned by decades of good Scotch.

"Damn."

"That's when Hunter started swinging. The other guy went down like a welterweight. Glass jaw. I guess the man can hit, even if his acting's not so great." The man paused. "I think kicking him was over the line, though."

Black edged away, his heart sinking – his meal ticket had committed assault on the world stage against one of the most powerful media figures in town. *Probably not time to be shopping for a condo*, he thought, and winced as a collective intake of breath rose from Hunter's entourage, accompanying the *snick* of handcuffs being locked into place.

Black watched as another ambulance arrived for Freddie and hauled him off. Hunter was definitely in trouble this time. Even with provocation, he was going to get collared for battery and aggravated assault, at the very least. And even in L.A. that was considered a no-no.

Not to mention that his movie sucked, and his wife was ready to jump in the sack with the hired help and maybe anyone else she happened across, when she wasn't guzzling tequila and popping pills like they were Pez.

For once in his life, he wasn't envious of the rich and famous.

Not one bit.

CHAPTER 21

Black waited by his car, smoking his fifth cigarette in the last hour as he contemplated excuses for buying a bottle of Jack and drinking it straight to his head – not that he particularly needed an excuse. A tapestry of stars glimmered overhead through the haze of smog that accumulated nightly east of L.A., the beige residue of the rush hour into Riverside. The freeway had been quiet on his night drive east, for which he was grateful. Since watching the debacle at the theater, a small part of him had died as he realized that Hunter had just shot his entire career down the toilet due to an inability to control his anger. Ground that was all too familiar to Black.

He flicked the cigarette butt away like it had stung him and turned when the front door of Colleen's trailer opened.

Colleen stepped out wearing a fuzzy pink terrycloth robe that had seen better days. She studied Black's face in silence and then wordlessly approached him and hugged him in an oddly maternal way. They stood together like that for an endless moment and then she pulled away.

"Sorry to impose. I just couldn't think of anyone else to talk to about the case."

She nodded.

"You look like a guy who could use a drink."

"I'm an open book to you."

"Come on inside before you scare the neighbors."

He hesitated. "I'm kind of afraid if I start tonight, I might not stop."

She shook her head. "If you were the guy who couldn't stop, you wouldn't be afraid. Just one. Then I throw your ass out."

"That's the best offer I've had all night."

"I'll bet. Wanna tell me about it?"

"Absolutely."

As they entered the trailer, Colleen frowned at all the newspaper and plastic taped down and shrugged. "Sorry about the mess. Seth's painting and doing some updating."

"No worries. He's pretty handy, then?"

"Yeah. You could say that."

"How did a director wind up…"

"…like this? It's okay, sweetie. I know what I am. I don't mind. The answer is, life happens. And when it does, sometimes you find yourself in places that surprise you."

She poured two glasses three fingers each of bourbon and handed him one.

"I know that feeling," Black confirmed.

"Nobody gets the life they want. Sometimes, not even the life they deserve. So you make the best of it. Cheers."

They each took contemplative swallows and Black began pacing. Colleen sat on a plastic-covered easy chair and let him be. He looked at the little collection of photographs on her bookshelf and smiled.

"You were a lot younger in these. So was Seth, in that one." He motioned to a shot of Seth standing in front of a gangplank in Newport harbor, a festive sign announcing 'Newport Beach New Years, 2000' mounted on the archway leading up to the harbor cruiser. He tapped another one. "And look at you here. What were you, fifteen?"

"Hardly. Let's just say it was a while ago. Time has a way of running away from you if you're not careful. One day you wake up and you're inhabiting your mother's body. And it's always a shock. Just as it probably was for her."

"There's something to look forward to," he said, then took another swallow.

"It happens to everyone, darling. There's no shame in it. Just…it is what it is."

"You haven't seen my parents. Where is your handyman, anyway?"

"He's out. He's a night owl. I give him his space. He gives me what he can. It works. For now."

Black didn't have anything to add, and silence settled over them like a heavy blanket.

"Tell me everything that happened, Black," she said softly.

He stopped delaying, sat down, and did.

When he finished, she whistled and downed the rest of her drink. "God, I'm sorry I got you into this. What a disaster. Although I would have paid money to watch Freddie get the crap kicked out of him."

"I'm pretty sure it will be on YouTube by tomorrow, if it isn't already. There's no place to hide anymore when every phone's a camera." He rubbed his face, tired. "Don't worry about me and Hunter. It's not your fault. Oh, and by the way, his movie blows goats. It's a total dog."

She shook her head. "Poor bastard."

"I'll say. Don't ask me how I know this, but he's up to his ears in debt."

"That doesn't entirely surprise me. I heard rumors."

"Still plugged in, are you?"

"Old habits."

Black finished his drink. The amber fluid seared a punishment down his throat before spreading welcome warmth through his body. A part of him wanted to finish the bottle with her, but a bigger part of him refused to go down that road. She was right. By now, if he was going to choose that path, he would have. After his marriage had cratered and his career had hit a wall, he'd certainly had the chance. And he'd flirted with climbing into a bottle, no doubt, but it had never happened.

And it certainly wouldn't tonight.

He looked at his watch. Three a.m. A long night by any measure.

Colleen watched him walk into the kitchen with his glass and set it next to the bourbon bottle, hesitating briefly before walking to the door.

"You live in a dark place, don't you, Black?"

"At least the rent's cheap. It's the only neighborhood I can afford."

"You're a good man. Don't ever forget that. It counts for a lot."

Black twisted the knob and pushed the scarred plastic-coated door open. "Thanks for the drink, Col. You're the best."

"One day you might be lucky enough to find out," she said, but her heart wasn't in it. "Drive safe. I'll lock up behind you."

A hot breeze off the nearby desert stirred the oleanders around the trailer as he approached his car, the liquid courage still strong in his veins. An orange moon sneered down at him as he felt in his pockets for a smoke, and he was inwardly uttering a lunar curse when his phone rang, the sound jarring in the night's stillness.

He looked at the display and spat next to his tire before answering. "I gather you made bail," Black said as he climbed into his car.

"Good guess. I could use a ride," Hunter said, his voice defeated and tired.

"I'll be there in half an hour. Maybe less."

CHAPTER 22

An ambulance rumbled into the emergency entrance bay at Hollywood Methodist Hospital with the third gunshot wound of the night – Fridays were big ones for trauma physicians all over town, as drug deals went south and passions ran hot ahead of Saturdays, which always set records for man's inhumanity to his fellow man. Something about weekends brought out the killer instinct, the desire to rob that liquor store, jack that car, teach that bitch a lesson. The emergency room was the province of the uneducated, the stupid, and the desperate at that late hour, and the staff had the air of combat medics doing triage after a particularly bloody assault.

Sick babies hacked their colicky coughs at the ceiling as immigrant mothers who spoke no English tried to comfort them. Drunks held broken arms and bloody faces while waiting their turn, and the aged and dying did so in quiet misery seated in uncomfortable plastic seats, attended to by indifferent receptionists who would gladly have been doing anything else in the world for a living – and soon would be the second they got a chance to update their resumes. The harsh glare of cheap fluorescent lighting gave even the healthy a sallow, sickly look, accenting shadows under tired eyes and flesh tugged earthward by gravity's unforgiving pull.

Upstairs in the critical care ward the graveyard shift was on duty, only two harried nurses to mind the forty-six rooms. Every night on that floor at least two, and sometimes more, patients would go to their final reward, requiring reports be filed and relatives notified and rooms cleaned and cleared for the next unlucky winner. It was an unending grind that wore the nurses down over time, and required nerves of steel and an incredibly positive disposition that could withstand the corrosive effect of watching people die every day.

Freddie Sypes was in a private room, hooked up to an array of monitors, having been CT scanned and MRI'd before having his jaw wired and his broken wrist put in a cast, an appointment already made with a cosmetic dentist who could repair the damage from the beating. There was no intracranial bleeding that the doctors had been able to detect, but he was due for another MRI in the morning to confirm, and had a concussion, the extent of which was currently unknown. He'd regained consciousness only briefly and had been incoherent, and was now on high-dosage pain medication as he dozed fitfully, the staff stopping by regularly to try to keep him awake as was routine with concussions.

The door of his private room eased open on silent hinges, the only sound the beeping of the monitors and the hiss of the air conditioning from the overhead vent. A figure in hospital greens approached his bedside, a surgical mask in place, and after a long glance at Freddie's bruised face, produced a syringe and swiftly emptied the contents into the IV line. The figure hesitated for a second, then reached out with a trembling hand and smoothed Freddie's hair before retreating back to the door and slipping out as quietly as a wraith.

Four minutes later Freddie slipped into a coma. Alarms sounded on his monitors as well as at the nurse's station, and the staff sprang into action. The ward physician came running from the employee lounge, and after a quick evaluation, ordered another scan.

Within half an hour Freddie was dead.

Nobody saw the intruder.

An autopsy would reveal in forty-eight hours that he hadn't died from the blows, but rather from lethal injection.

By which point, none of it would matter.

Not that it did anymore for Freddie.

∂∾⊰

Black pulled up outside of the Hollywood Community Police Station and lowered his passenger window, ignoring the various shifty lowlifes that were loitering in the vicinity as he searched for Hunter.

He almost jumped out of his seat when Hunter slammed his hand on the fabric roof and appeared at his driver's side window.

"Jesus. You scared the crap out of me. Don't do shit like that in this neighborhood," Black said.

"What? We're in front of a frigging police station."

"Which is about as safe as being in front of an embassy in Benghazi. Hop in."

Hunter rounded the hood of the car, gave it a pat, and then slid in next to Black. "Pimping ride there, homeboy."

"Thanks. You got out fast."

"I pulled strings at the studio. Whether they like it or not, they're pregnant with my movie, so they need me out and promoting it while this gets sorted out."

"You're a lucky man," Black said, putting the car in gear and pulling away. "I presume you want to go home?"

"You got it. Thanks for the pick-up."

"All part of the service I provide." Black gave him a sidelong glance. "I also do windows."

"Good to know."

They drove west in silence, traffic sparse at the early hour, and then Hunter cursed under his breath. "The bitch wouldn't even try to bail me out. She wouldn't answer her cell phone. Let them take me in and left me for dead."

"Your wife? She might be upset because you beat Freddie into snot at your movie premiere."

"Which you were supposed to make sure went off without a hitch," Hunter fired back, his temper flaring.

"No, that wasn't the deal. I was supposed to figure out who's killing the paparazzi, and why. You hired a security chief to watch your back and take care of the premiere."

"Who you recommended."

"Who's one of the best in the business. But he can't stop some whack job who decides to poison someone in the crowd. Nobody could do that."

"I pay, I expect results."

"Then you need to expect results that are achievable."

Hunter glared at him. "You've got quite a mouth on you, don't you?"

"You mean the only person who answered his phone when you called for a ride in the middle of the night? Is that who you mean?"

"You still have a bad attitude."

"Maybe you should try to beat it out of me," Black said, his own temper flaring from the combination of the hour, the alcohol, and his client's insolent tone. "That's worked well for you so far, right?"

Hunter seethed next to him but didn't say anything.

The ride into Bel Air was tense, and Black turned the stereo on at low volume so he didn't have to listen to Hunter breathe. When he made the turn to head up the hill, he switched it off again.

"You played me on the fight at Stubbs, didn't you?"

"Played you? How?"

"You contacted Freddie yourself."

"Wow. Sherlock frigging Holmes, at your service. Of course I did. I needed a PR moment. That's how you do it. It got coverage everywhere. And even with the spin Freddie put on it, that built credibility – nobody questioned it was genuine."

"Makes me wonder what else you've been lying about."

"I've been seeing other PIs. I'm sorry. It's not your fault…it's me."

"Maybe you can work on the comedy act while you're in the joint."

"Never gonna happen. I'll do community service, kiss some babies, haul some trash. I'm contrite. Maybe take an anger management class. Get therapy. They don't put guys like me in jail."

"Wrong."

"Maybe. But famous is famous. Look at Beretta. No way the DA is going to want another one of those nightmares. No, this will fade away."

"The civil suit won't. You'll lose that."

"You know what? You're right. But by then it won't matter. The movie will be a hit, all my financial worries will be behind me, and I'll have to cut a big check to the little prick to make it go away. In this town, that's how it rolls. Meanwhile, I'll have three more scripts in development and studios begging me to work with them."

They approached Hunter's street and Black twisted the wheel, sending the Eldorado screeching around the corner, annoyed by Hunter's assured tone.

"It's not your lucky day. The film's a turd. Probably nobody would tell you the truth, but it is. It's going nowhere."

Hunter clenched and unclenched his fingers, and for an instant, Black actually thought he was going to attack him. The moment passed, and then they were rolling up to Hunter's estate, the gate open.

"You know about as much about the movie business as you do about fashion, huh, Black?"

"I know a bad movie when I see one."

"Yeah. Everyone's a critic," Hunter said as he swung the door open and stepped out.

"It's going to bomb. Sorry. There it is."

"Thanks for the ride, tough guy." Hunter took two paces from the car, and then turned, almost as an afterthought. "Oh, by the way. You're fired."

"I guessed that. I'll be by to pick up my check tomorrow. You still owe me another fifteen grand. You already burned through the deposit."

"Sure thing. Although if you're right about the movie, you may have to sue me for it."

Black didn't respond; instead, he took it out on the accelerator and roared off, leaving a plume of blue exhaust in his wake.

CHAPTER 23

The phone rang like a fire alarm and Black turned to grope for it, the light peeking through his bedroom curtains the only clue to the time. He looked at the screen and then punched it on.

"What are you doing calling me at this ungodly hour? It's Saturday," he demanded.

"It's ten a.m., sunshine. Your client's got a big problem. He's going down," Stan greeted.

"What are you talking about? He made bail."

"Freddie died last night. So now it's murder. With about a dozen different video feeds of bully boy beating Freddie to a pulp as exhibit A."

"He's not my client anymore. We parted ways last night. This morning. Whatever."

"Probably a wise move."

"I think so."

"I was just giving you a heads up in case you wanted to be there when he got taken into custody."

"Nope. Not me. My work there is done."

"Fair enough, buddy. Go back to sleep. Sounds like you've earned it."

"Trust me. I have."

Black hung up and then stumbled to the bathroom, still groggy. He was flushing the toilet when his cell rang again.

"Black."

"Hey, boss."

"Roxie. Good morning." Roxie worked a half day on Saturdays and a floating weekday, assuming she hadn't played a gig the prior night.

"Whatever. Listen, you just got a call. Hunter's wife. She's freaking out. Wants you to call her."

"Why?"

"Sounds like Hunter's gone off the reservation."

"What do you mean?"

"Apparently he's drunk, high, and waving a gun around."

Black swallowed hard. "A gun?"

"Some movie prop. Whatever. You want her number?"

"Sure."

"I just texted you. Should be there."

"Thanks."

"Lot of drama in your life all of a sudden, Black. Just saying."

"*Gracias* for the wise observations. I have to make a call."

"Whatever. Mugsy says hello."

"What does that mean?"

"It means he made a hobby out of your chair when I wasn't looking."

"No."

"See you later, boss. Gotta run."

"Roxie—"

Black found himself talking to a dial tone. His phone vibrated, and he thumbed the cursor to the phone number Roxie had relayed and pushed send as he hurriedly pulled on a pair of gray herringbone trousers.

"Thank God you called. He's gone nuts."

"Meagan. Are you okay?"

"I'm fine. But he's lost his mind. You need to come out here and help me."

"Call the cops."

"They're already on their way."

"Then what do you need me for?"

"Black. Please. I'm afraid he's going to hurt someone." She paused. "Or me."

Damn. "Fine. I'll be there as soon as I can."

"Please hurry."

The line went dead, and Black scrambled for a shirt and some shoes. He snagged a vintage navy blue Hawaiian shirt with stylized red hula girls dancing across the fabric, slipped on a pair of loafers, and made for the door, grabbing a black fedora and Ray Bans along with his holstered gun and keys on the way out. His phone rang yet again, and he answered as he took the stairs two at a time.

Colleen's agitated voice sounded tight. "Black. It's Colleen. We've got an emergency."

"I know. I just spoke with Mea – with Mrs. Hunter."

"She called me looking for you. Sounds like the fecal material's hitting the fan."

"I'll say. I'm on my way over there right now."

"Good luck."

The Cadillac started with a throaty burble and he revved the engine until the idle smoothed out, thinking that perhaps today would finally be the day when he took it in for a tune up. Then he pointed the big white hood toward Bel Air, where his former client was on a drunken rampage. Maybe he should have stayed in bed, but he'd always been a sucker for a girl in trouble, and you couldn't get much more troubled than, "Help, he's trying to kill me," or words to that effect.

When Black arrived at Hunter's estate, police cars were parked at angles around the outer gate, the officers taking cover behind their vehicles, weapons drawn and pointing at Hunter, who was standing on his front steps in a bright orange silk bathrobe brandishing a three-quarters-empty Scotch bottle in one hand and what looked like an 1800-era long-barreled revolver in the other, his hair askew and a crazed look in his eye. Several of the statues near the front of the house had bullet scars from where Hunter had fired at them, and he looked like a madman with his robe hanging open and his star power hanging in the wind. A uniform stopped Black as he approached and told him that there was a situation so he couldn't go any farther, and then he spotted Stan, standing by his car.

Stan saw him and waved; and then all hell broke loose as a gunshot rang out and a red blossom stained the breast of Hunter's robe, followed closely by a volley of shots. Slugs slammed into the aging film star and he jerked like a demented marionette before tumbling face forward onto the bloody marble steps, his body still twitching as the police continued shooting.

"Hold your fire! Everyone. Hold. Your. Fire," Stan yelled, and then repeated the command over his car's PA system.

The gunfire stopped and relative tranquility returned to the area. Black's ears were ringing as he instinctively edged closer to Hunter, and he regarded the downed actor sadly as three of the officers approached through the open gate, weapons still trained on the motionless form. One kicked the ancient revolver away and nudged Hunter with his foot. Stan shook his head and faced Black.

"What are you doing here?" he asked, speaking louder than usual because of the tinnitus.

"Just out for a drive."

Stan gave him a hard look.

"Mrs. Hunter called. She said that Hunter had gone berserk. I'd say that was pretty accurate," Black explained.

"She called us, too. Said the same thing."

They both regarded Hunter's inert body, and then Stan shrugged.

"Looks like he just saved the taxpayers a really long, expensive trial."

"Yup." They continued to watch the officers as they holstered their weapons. "I should have stayed in bed," Black said.

"I've found that the days I say that to myself when I wake up, I always should have."

"Then again, that's most days for you, isn't it?" Black asked.

"True dat. So I'd basically just become a five-hundred-pound shut-in."

"I'm working on not judging."

"Let me know how that goes for you. I gotta go scrape up my latest problem off the steps."

"And comfort the distraught widow, don't forget."

"I'll leave that to you."

"Not interested, thanks."

"This is your big chance. You can call her, tell her all's well, and then she'll melt into your arms."

"I'm going back to sleep," Black said, walking slowly back to his car, his shoulders slumped.

Stan's voice trailed after him.

"Never a bad idea."

CHAPTER 24

The following Monday morning, Roxie looked up from her screen as Black entered the office. Mugsy was in her lap, purring contentedly, his plump face transfixed with a look of bliss as she stroked him. Black had a momentary vision of himself exchanging places with the cat, and then shook it off.

"Isn't that sweet. How was your weekend?" Black asked.

"Not bad, other than our only client getting gunned down on his front porch on Saturday. Kind of puts a damper on things, doesn't it?"

"Sure does. Especially since I never got my final payment from him."

"Bummer. Does that mean I have to go back to hooking for a living?"

Black raised one eyebrow.

"A joke," Roxie said.

"I got it. I have a richly evolved sense of humor, you know."

"I know. I see your outfits every day, remember?"

"Why all the grief over my fashion choices, Roxie?"

"Um, because they make you look kind of like a retard. And nobody's going to hire the retard PI. Which has me back on the street turning tricks with a pimp named Huggy backhanding me whenever I get out of line."

"You've been watching reruns again, haven't you?"

"Damned Seventies Channel. Curse you, Seventies Channel!" Roxie said, shaking her fist theatrically.

"How bad is the chair?"

"Don't freak out. It's only a material possession."

"Very enlightened of you, Roxie. But why is it always *my* material possessions that get trashed by that fat bastard?" he asked as he moved past her desk, throwing a wholly ignored black glare at Mugsy.

"Maybe it's because he hears you ragging on him. So he acts out."

"Roxie. He's a cat. He has no idea what I'm saying."

"How do you know?"

"That he's a cat? Let's just say I'm confident on that one. I've seen photos on the web."

"No, that he doesn't understand you."

"Animals can't speak English."

"Neither can half of Los Angeles. That doesn't prove anything."

"Fair point. But let's just say that the overwhelming proof is that cats don't *understand* English, either. There. Happy with the clarification?"

"You're wrong. I think they do. And that explains everything. Why he's always hurt and afraid of you. He's heard us discussing your rage issues, and how fat you think he is."

"I don't think he's fat. Fat would be a goal for him to slim down to. I think he's obese. Morbidly obese. Because he's lazy and shiftless and eats way too much."

"See? That's what I'm talking about."

"And 'we' don't discuss my rage issues. You do. I haven't said a word about them. Assuming I had any. Which I don't."

"Well, this is productive. Remind me about how you don't have anger problems after you see your chair." Roxie smiled sweetly and then returned to Mugsy, dismissing Black.

Black entered his office, steeled for virtually anything, and studied his seat cushion, which had been torn open, with some of the foam padding shredded. He sighed and returned to Roxie's desk.

"See? No rage. Come on. Let's see if Mugsy will fit in the microwave."

"That's such bad karma. I can't believe you would even say that."

"The damage isn't as bad as I thought it would be."

"I know. I made it sound worse than it was."

"Why?" Black asked.

"Because that way, you'd be expecting the whole thing to be ruined – basically gutted. And then you'd see that it was only partially destroyed and would be relieved. Psychology 101."

"I wasn't aware you'd been to college."

"I read a book. Or maybe it was a magazine. What's the difference between them again?"

"One has pictures."

"Oooh, pictures! Like of ponies?"

"Probably not if it was a psychology magazine."

"I thought Freund was big on phallic symbols. Aren't stallions phallic?"

"I think you mean Freud."

"That's what I said."

"No, you said 'Freund.'"

She studied his face and then shrugged. "You have to win every argument, don't you? Maybe you should think about why that is."

"I don't have to. You said 'Freund.'"

"There. That. See what I mean?"

Black exhaled loudly with exasperation.

"So did you quit smoking this weekend, boss?" she asked.

"Sort of. I quit yesterday."

"That's kind of like you ran out of cigarettes on Saturday and didn't get out to buy any on Sunday, isn't it?"

"I prefer to think of it as the first small step in building my future."

Roxie rolled her eyes. "Did you need something?"

"Why? Am I keeping you from important stuff?"

"I was getting ready to feed Mugsy."

"That's also a joke, right? See, I'm catching on."

"He hasn't eaten today."

"Look at him. His fat has fat."

"He knows what you're saying, you know. Can I get back to what I was doing?"

Black understood he would never win with Roxie, so he shook his head. "Do we have any duct tape?"

"Oh, sure, wait, let me get our air duct emergency repair kit." She kept staring at him. "Hmm. That's right. We don't have one."

"Let me rephrase the question. Do you have any kind of tape I could use to repair the perfectly good, rather expensive executive lounger that the fat bastard in your lap tore to shreds?"

Roxie slid her middle drawer open and removed a small roll of Scotch tape. She placed it on her desk and regarded it. "You might want to consider running out to Office Depot," she said.

"Yeah. That's definitely not going to do it."

"I'd go, but then who would feed Mugsy? And of course, greet all the customers that will be showing up to hire us after your marquis client went down shooting?"

"I was there, you know."

Her expression softened, and the usual mockery vanished from her eyes. Rather nice-looking violet eyes, Black thought, even with the overdone mascara. "Oh my God. No. I mean, how could I know that? How was it?" she asked.

"It started strong, but I thought the end left something to be desired."

"I'm serious."

"It was a lot like watching your client get shot to pieces within rock-throwing distance of you. I'm not sure I have a word for that."

"Are...are you okay?"

"They shot him, not me."

"You know what I mean."

"So does Mugsy, apparently. Do you let him use my computer while I'm gone, too? Does he have his own email account?"

"Mainly he watches porn."

"That figures. Another business I'll never make millions at. Kitty porn."

"I think it's a tough gig. No credit cards or opposable thumbs."

"I knew there was a catch."

"So you're okay?"

He sighed. "Yeah. It was ugly. Not like the movies. Just...brutal and ugly and...shitty. A man died. As far as I can tell, for no reason."

She turned away from him and resumed stroking Mugsy, who shut his eyes and purred again. "I can go to Office Depot if you want."

"Nah. I don't have much to do. I'd hate to think of poor Mugsy starving while I selfishly used your business hours to do things related to the business."

"Don't forget to call your mom this week. You asked me to remind you."

"No, I didn't."

"I could have sworn you did."

"No, that would have been all in your head."

"Huh. You sure?"

"Positive."

"But don't forget."

"Thank you, Roxie," Black said as he moved back to the door, the little cat entryway she'd coerced him into mounting at its base worn from Mugsy's considerable bulk squeezing through it.

"It's never too late for a chai. Just saying," she hinted.

"We're creatures of habit, aren't we?"

"You always say that."

CHAPTER 25

The aroma of wildly overpriced coffee filled the chilly atmosphere of the franchise café, its walls dutifully veneered with chrome and green lacquer, the furniture selected to create the illusory experience of a cozy, prosperous sitting room. *That figures. The shop can afford eight-hundred-dollar lounge chairs, given what they charge for a simple cup of java,* Black thought bitterly as he languished in the tortuous, crawling line, along with a hatful of other lost souls. His brooding reverie was interrupted by the ringtone of his phone. The spirited antipodean wailing of AC/DC drew stares from his fellow customers as Bon Scott shrieked "Highway to Hell." Black fumbled in his pocket before his fingers found the talk button.

"Black."

"Let me ask you a hypothetical question," Stan asked. No hello.

"Shoot."

"Let's say you had this famous movie star who went psycho, so you had to gun him down."

"I see this is really reaching."

"And let's say that thirty or so shots were fired from ten guns. Are you with me so far?"

"I know the answer. That's roughly three apiece. I'd have to get my calculator, but it's close."

"Thanks. No, the weird part is that none of the officers involved in the shooting will 'fess up to firing the first bullet."

Black thought about it. "Nobody wants to be the one who started a massacre. Especially since Hunter never fired a shot."

"I said this was hypothetical, remember?"

"Oh. Right."

"We'll get to the bottom of it, but it's just kind of weird. You were there. What do you remember happening?"

"A shitload of shooting." The woman ahead of Black in line turned and gave him an alarmed look. Black ignored her.

"Right. But do you remember where the first shot came from?"

"I thought it was off to the right of the house. One of the cops over there. You had enough of them."

"That's what I thought, too. But nobody on that side fired first. At least that's the claim."

"Won't ballistics figure that out?"

"Sure. But there are about eighteen rounds in your man. It'll take time to do matching on all of them."

"Your guys need target practice. Eighteen out of thirty? Yikes. What happened to shooting the gun out of the bad guy's hand?"

"We tend to focus more on shooting the bad guy."

"A sound approach. Roughly sixty percent of the time, if my math is right."

"You should have been an accountant."

"I should have been anything but this. At least the pay's lousy and the hours suck."

"Welcome to my world. Never mind. I was hoping you could narrow it down for me, but I guess not."

"All I can say for sure was that the first shot came from the right side of the house, if you're facing it."

"That's my take, too. Oh well. What's on your agenda today?"

"I was thinking about dumpster-diving for food."

"Well, good luck, then. I hear El Pollo is always a good bet. *Muy picante.*"

"Thanks."

The woman in front of him approached the counter and issued an elaborate order involving Italian adjectives, sugar-free chocolate, an admonishment against fat of any sort, and a precise specification of the sort and amount of foam with which she wished her concoction crowned, before moving further down the line to pay, again eyeing Black like he was going to try to steal her purse. The aloof barista, a young man with plentiful tattoos, the jaundiced skin of a junkie, and a way of repeating back orders while managing to make them sound like an insult and simultaneously seeming disapproving of the choice, greeted him with a company-issued courtesy nod that conveyed a heady mixture of contempt, anger, and apathy.

"May I take your order, sir?" he asked, in a tone that made it clear he'd rather teabag a hobo.

"Medium cup of coffee and a small chai."

"Mmmmmmedium cup of daily roast and a short chai. Would you prefer Guatemalan New Year or Ethiopian Splendor?"

"Whichever is better."

"They're both excellent."

"Then give me whichever is more popular," Black said.

"The Guatemalan is a darker, richer roast, whereas the Ethiopian has more interesting secondary flavors."

"Guatemalan, then."

"Very well. Would you like room for milk or cream?"

"Sure."

It was all Cliff, per his nametag, could do not to roll his eyes. Cliff paused for a moment, radiating ennui, and Black could sympathize with him after listening to the woman's order, a passive-aggressive cosmic minuet, a stylized choreography more intricate than a ceremonial kabuki dance, this ordering of coffee and desire to create a designer-beverage experience, the instructions as precise as the assembly of a thermonuclear warhead or the splicing of DNA.

"How much, sir?"

Black had lost the thread. The people behind him shuffled impatiently. He was now guilty of the most despised offense: the wasting of other people's time, important people with places to go.

"I'm sorry..."

This time the barista couldn't help himself, and allowed one eyebrow to cock a quarter inch, signaling that he understood he was dealing with someone of sub-custodial intellect, or perhaps an unfortunate who'd suffered a childhood brain trauma that prevented him from processing normally.

"How much room, sir? For cream. Or milk, if you like."

The elevated eyebrow had aroused within Black an irresistible urge to make the young man's life more difficult. The beverage-ordering equivalent of meeting his ante and raising him two seemed an appropriate gambit.

"Do you have soy milk?" Black asked, not the slightest trace of mockery evident in either his tone or his inflection.

"Of course, sir."

"Because I'm lactose intolerant."

"I'm sorry to hear that, sir."

"I also suffer from low-level celiac issues," he confessed, as though sharing an intimacy with a lover.

"So you'd like soy milk, sir? In your *drip* coffee?" the server asked, spitting out the final two words like a curse, Black's frugality now established for all to despise in a land of abundant plenty.

"It's not that vanilla or flavored soy milk, is it? I'm not inclined that way, if you know what I mean. Not that there's anything wrong with that." Black resisted the urge to wink.

"No, sir. It's just soy milk."

"Well then. I'll take it with soy milk, but I'd like you to warm it up if possible."

"Warm..." The young man repeated the request without a hint of disbelief.

"Yes, but not hot. Just warm. Like in a toddler's sippy cup." Black's countenance could have been carved from alabaster, his brow's ability to convey emotion botoxed away, his expression that of an inscrutable Easter Island monolith, lacking the capacity for humor, much less duplicity.

The barista understood it was game, set, and match, and merely nodded before calling the order to the next employee in a staccato jargon that sounded like a foreign language or a technical description of impossible complexity.

"Will that be all, sir?"

"Do you accept traveler's checks?"

"Mmm, no sir. I'm afraid not."

"Personal checks with no ID?"

"Only cash or credit cards."

"Not debit cards?" Black asked in disbelief.

"Yes, sir. Of course. And debit cards."

"Because you only said credit cards."

"I realize that could be confusing, sir. That's why I amended it."

"Well, how much is it, then? I'm in a hurry, if you don't mind."

"Six twenty-five, sir. You pay over there, at the register."

"Remember. Warm like mother's milk. Not scalding. I break out in hives if you burn the soy milk."

"We'll be very careful, sir."

Black detected a final flicker of rebellion in the young man's studied stoicism, and went in for the kill.

"Can I get a complimentary glass of water?"

The barista's gaze hardened, his eyes black as a shark's as he realized he'd been bested; spanked like a bitch by a master.

"Certainly, sir. Paper or plastic?" For all the scuffling, Cliff was resilient – Black would give him that.

"I don't want to do anything harmful for the environment. Is the paper recycled?"

"Of course, sir."

"Never mind, then. Recycling consumes far more energy than milling new cardboard," Black announced in triumph, having played not only the politically correct card, but also swooping to snatch the young man's ability to snipe further interrogatives from him with the alacrity of a rocket-fueled hawk.

The line behind him exhaled an audible groan of relief when Black moved to the next register and paid the perky and always friendly Asian cashier with a ten-dollar bill. The drinks arrived without delay, and he juggled them as he moved to one of the overstuffed seating areas to savor his victory drink.

As he replayed the discussion with Stan in his mind, mulling over the ramifications, a small kernel of anxiety tickled his gut. He was missing something. Stan was puzzled, which was a rarity; the man ate bullets for breakfast and tackled the most brutal killers for dessert, and Black had never seen him confused. But the shooting had him rattled – that's what he'd heard in his voice. Something was off. Wrong.

Black tried to focus, but the thought that played on the periphery of his consciousness flitted away the more he tried to corner it. He knew that there was no point in trying to force or coax it into being. It would arrive fully formed when it was good and ready, and not before.

The coffee was actually pretty good, and Black was happy with the open kitchen approach that prevented Cliff from urinating in it, which he had no doubt the humbled server had developed an almost compulsive urge to do. He sympathized with the kid. Sometimes the world dropped trou and violated you, and you had to take it. Story of Black's life. Even as he savored his petty victory, Black felt cheapened by it, and resolved to do his best to avoid abusing anyone else he came into contact with that day. He could attribute his mood to having quit smoking. It was that rough period that lasted from the final puff until you died, he thought.

The Cadillac started grudgingly and sputtered like a politician caught in a lie, and Black decided that he couldn't put off further the simple maintenance he'd been avoiding for months. His Bluetooth earpiece in place, he dialed his mechanic – a heavyset Mexican man who lived two buildings down from the Paradise Palms.

"Yo, Cesar. It's Black here."

"That so? Maybe it's gonna rain."

"No...I mean it's Black, Jim Black, the guy from up the street with the Caddy."

"Eldorado. Red leather, am I right?" Cesar replied – he wasn't great with names, but he remembered cars.

"Correct. It's time to figure out what's wrong with the engine. It's running rough."

"Didn't you tell me you haven't had a tune-up since The Beatles played the Hollywood Bowl?"

"Something like that. I was wondering if you could cruise by tomorrow and give it a look."

"Sure. What time?"

"Nine. I can borrow a car if you need it all day."

"That's a given, *esse*. You can't put this kind of thing off forever. You'll need new plugs, probably a carburetor rebuild, and some belts. Minimum. You got cash?"

"I wouldn't be calling if I didn't."

"You want I should swing by your place?"

"Yeah, if you could. You remember my apartment?"

"Upstairs. Fourth one from the stairs."

"Bingo. I'll see you at nine."

"*Mañana.*"

Satisfied that he'd done the responsible thing for the first time in forever, he finished his coffee and tossed the cup in the passenger foot well, taking care that Roxie's chai was secure in his aftermarket cup-holder before he lurched into traffic, a roll of silver duct tape gleaming at his side like a lucky talisman. As he wheeled along, he twisted on the stereo and the car filled with a Silversun Pickups single he'd downloaded from iTunes without telling Roxie for fear of mockery. Kind of catchy, he conceded, and sang along with the tune, which he'd been listening to off and on for the last few days:

If we stay here long enough
We can play with Bloody Mary
Say her name into the dark

He passed a super pet store and debated getting Mugsy another toy so he'd stop destroying everything in the office, but decided it was pointless – maybe Roxie was right and he was holding a grudge. Still feeling somewhat pious, Black made a mental note to stop insulting the cat, at least within earshot, as part of his new spirit of non-judgmental change, and to bite back any reflexive urge to refer to him as 'that fat bastard.'

The Eldorado coughed like an emphysemic during a dust storm, then settled into a truculent putter, as if to warn Black that it was running on borrowed time.

A feeling he knew all too well.

CHAPTER 26

Black's feeling of unease intensified as the afternoon shadows lengthened across his office walls, until at four o'clock he resolved to do something to put his apprehension to rest. He dialed Meagan's number with a heavy hand, and was surprised at how upbeat her voice was when she answered the phone.

"Meagan. It's Black. I hope I'm not disturbing you…"

"No, not at all. What can I do for you?"

"How are you holding up?"

"It's…it's been hard, as you might expect."

"I'm sure of it. Let me know if there's anything I can do."

"I will. It's just a bad time, is all."

"No doubt. Listen, I just wanted to check with you before I stop by. I have a few loose ends I'm tying up on the case."

"Oh. Are you making any progress? I'd have thought you'd dropped it now that Hunter's…gone."

"Not really. I'm about ready to put it to bed. This is more like crossing a few housekeeping chores off the list. Nothing more."

"Do you need to get into the house?"

"No, that can wait for a better time. I mostly just want to stop in and make sure you're okay."

"That's so sweet. And unnecessary."

"I'm in the neighborhood. It won't take more than a few minutes."

"I suppose that's fine, then."

"How's…Nicole doing?"

"I have no idea. She left the day after Hunter was killed. She wasn't here when it happened, thank God. I guess she was out with friends."

"It's got to be hard for her."

"I'm sure of it. I think she's staying with her mom. That will be good. Maybe she'll move in with her, once and for all."

Black could pick up a trace of animosity, even after everything that had happened.

"You'll figure it out, Meagan. Tell you what, I'll be by within a half hour. I just need to finish up an errand. I'll be in and out in no time."

Any other time, he was sure she would have latched onto the double entendre, but her spirit wasn't in it, and she sounded preoccupied.

"I'll be here. See you when I see you."

Black shifted on the uncomfortable makeshift seat cover he'd fashioned from tape and then rose, his pants pulling free of the silver patch with a sound like ripping fabric. He pulled on his black double-breasted jacket and cocked a black fedora on his head at a jaunty angle and emerged from his office to find Roxie actually doing what appeared to be legitimate work – paying bills with their bookkeeping software.

"I'm headed out."

"I got that. Is there a costume party tonight?"

"Another jab about my sartorial splendor, I presume."

"It's just that normal people don't dress like extras out of a Zoot Suit musical."

"I appreciate the candor. But I like this look."

"Why not try Robin Hood next? The green tights and the little vest might work nicely. And I think he wore a funny hat, too."

"I'll be on my cell."

"Good to know."

"In case anyone calls."

"Like they haven't all day. Oh, wait. We did have one wrong number. Looking for a dry cleaner. I'm guessing you don't want it forwarded."

"What would I do without you?"

"Probably starve Mugsy."

"Given that he's eaten about half my chair, I'm guessing he'd find a way to make do." Black glowered at the cat, who was lying on his back on the couch, fast asleep, all four paws in the air, soft snoring emanating from his untroubled face. "No wonder he's tired."

Black made it to Bel Air in twenty minutes, the car sounding ominous as it strained up the hills, and he congratulated himself again on his decision to finally get it attended to. When he pulled up to Hunter's estate, there was a squad car parked in front with two bored uniforms in it, and beyond it, a green pickup truck with utility boxes on either side of the bed and an indecipherable logo on either door. He parked behind the vehicles and approached the squad car's open driver-side window and stopped well clear of it – there had been enough shooting in the exclusive neighborhood already, and he didn't want a cop with the jitters to add to his woes.

"Officers. I'm here to see Meagan Hunter. I'm a friend."

The driver, the older of the pair, a well-fed Hispanic man with a neatly trimmed mustache, met his gaze. "It's a free country."

"What are you fellas doing here?"

"We were told to stop by every couple of hours and make sure nobody was loitering around."

"I imagine pretty soon they'll be loitering in greener pastures, now it's becoming old news."

"You got that right."

"All right, then. I'm going in. Have a good one."

Black paused at the front of the expansive front wall – three-foot-high mortar and cement topped with five feet of black wrought iron – and studied the house façade. The blood had been cleaned off the steps, and a handyman was perched on a ladder, repairing a window that had been damaged by the hail of bullets. Stan's question still burning in his ears, Black closed his eyes and tried to recreate the shooting. Stan had been standing next to him, cop cars spread out along the street, uniforms ducked behind their vehicles waiting for the SWAT team to show up, Hunter waving the hogleg around while swigging from the bottle...

And then a shot, followed almost immediately by more. But the first shot had definitely come from the right side. A loud, sharp report.

Black walked to the far right side by the gate and peered into the grounds. A long row of dense hedges ran along both sides, with elegantly coiffed trees lining the perimeter. He edged to the neighbor's lot line wall and squinted. There was about a two-foot space between the wall and the plants. Not a lot of space.

He had no idea what he was looking for, but something was nagging at him, and it hadn't subsided over time. He tried the heavy brass handle for the pedestrian gate and was surprised to find that it was unlocked. Then again, the maintenance men had likely been in and out. Black pushed it open and stepped across the metal threshold onto the smooth cobblestones, likely imported from Europe, and moved to the hedges, his hawk-like gaze looking for something – anything.

Unfortunately, all he saw was grass in need of mowing that extended to the neighbor's wall and rich, coffee-toned soil beneath the bushes. A faint suspicion took shape as he studied the area – there was certainly enough room for an assailant to hide, and he would have been out of sight from the street because of the way the hedges ran to the full perimeter at the front of the lot.

But not at the back. He followed the lot line until he arrived at the rear of the property, where there was a brick wall separating Hunter's estate from the one behind it – a contemporary masterpiece with a lavish pool and spa area done in symmetrical sandstone. Black studied the rear brickwork, and even in the late afternoon light, picked up a rust-colored smudge near the union where the side wall met the rear.

Which could have been anything.

Anything at all. Paint. Crap. Bird poop.

Or blood.

Hunter inched along the rear wall until his nose was only a few inches from the smear, but that perspective didn't improve his appreciation of it. It was a smudge on red brick. Hard to make out.

But it was there.

His gaze roamed along the side wall, and then he edged along it, scanning for anything out of the ordinary. Like more blood.

No such luck. It was probably just some neighborhood animal that had cut its paw. Nothing nefarious. Sometimes, just because you were paranoid, it didn't mean anyone was out to get you. It just meant you were a nutcase.

He was nearing the front of the lot again, when he saw it.

There.

On the grass.

Faint. But unmistakable.

More of the rust-colored splotch. This time, what looked like dried drops of it.

Black's awareness focused to tunnel-vision as his pulse pounded in his ears, the effect heightened by the narrow corridor effect of the hedges on one side and the wall on the other. His mind grappled for possible explanations. Perhaps a gardener had cut himself. A maintenance worker. A prowling pet.

But that's not what his gut told him.

He fished his phone out of his jacket and called Stan.

"You need to get a forensics team up to Hunter's house. Now."

"Why? Where are you?"

"I'm at his house. Just do as I ask. I'll wait for them."

"What's up, Black? You been boozing early?"

"I wish. You might want to get your tired old ass up here as well."

"Want to tell me what's going on?"

"I think I figured out where the first shot came from."

CHAPTER 27

The forensics van's lights flashed in the deepening dusk, the sky all purple and crimson smoke trails. A cool breeze rustled the hedges as the technicians gathered samples, the yellow crime scene tape lending an almost festive feeling to the area. Stan stood by watching impassively as the techs went about their task, scraping and sorting and clipping and shooting photos. Black stood next to him, with Meagan hanging off his arm like she was afraid she'd blow away, her face drawn from the events of the last few days but still undeniably beautiful by any measure.

"I don't understand any of this," she whispered for the twentieth time in the past hour and a half, after Black had knocked on the door and advised her that the police were on their way. "What does it mean?"

"It means that your husband might have been shot by someone other than the police," Black said softly. Stan's eyes shifted sideways toward them, lending a reptilian quality to his somber expression, like one of the humanoid robot warriors that Hunter had spent four sequels battling as they attempted to conquer the earth.

God, those movies stank, Black thought. *No wonder the guy's career tanked. Who greenlit that kind of garbage and sank a hundred million into it? Some committee of clueless yes-men who'd never read a script in their life?*

He realized that his mind was wandering and returned to the present.

"It's too early to draw any conclusions, ma'am. All we know is that there's some unexplained evidence here that may or may not have anything to do with your husband's death. Any speculation, especially by amateurs" – Stan glared at Black – "is premature."

"That's true," Black said, trying to backpedal. Meagan's sweet fragrance drifted from her blouse, which looked about ready to pop a button as it struggled to contain her full breasts, which he couldn't help but notice she'd been rubbing against him like she was hoping a genie would pop out of his hat.

"Can I have a word with you?" Stan asked, his gaze icy.

"Absolutely. Meagan, would you excuse me?"

"Sure," she said in a heart-melting, little girl lost voice.

Stan and Black walked together to the front gate, where two squad cars waited with the forensics van and Stan's unmarked sedan. Stan stopped and looked up at the trees across the street as though they contained the answer to a riddle he'd been worrying at with no progress.

"What the hell do you think you're doing?" he hissed through clenched teeth.

"Nothing. The woman asked a question. I gave her my best guess."

Stan shook his head. "It looks like she wants you to give her more than that."

"You picked up on that, did you?"

"She's on you like a stripper on a pole."

"You have a way with words. Like Stephen King or something."

Stan rubbed his face with a resigned hand. "Black. Cut me a break here, would you? Don't get her all riled up."

"Look, Stan, she's not stupid. She wants to know why the cops are back at her house. She deserves more than the runaround."

"And you're just the man to give it to her, huh?"

"It's not like that. She's distraught."

"Why is it that whenever I get a distraught widow she's either a crack fiend or eighty-nine?"

"Can't she be both?"

They watched as a black Bentley coupe drove by, its windows tinted dark, a vanity plate proclaiming "Frowsy" as its owner.

"I just don't need the specter of a lawsuit hanging over my head, Black. You should know that people will sue over anything."

"Dog eat dog world, ain't it?"

"Sure 'nuff," Stan agreed.

"So what's your take?"

"I think *if*, and that's obviously a huge if, there was a shooter hiding in the bushes, we might have gotten lucky and a ricochet hit him. That's what I think."

"Or the gardener got careless with the trimmer."

"Nah. The distraught hottie gave us their number. I talked to the supervisor. Nobody gashed themselves here," Stan said.

"She is hot, isn't she?"

"No offense, my friend, but she's way out of your league. She'd eat you alive. High maintenance doesn't start to cover that."

"I know. I just wish she'd stop rubbing on me. I'm starting to chafe."

"You're not just a boy toy."

"I have feelings. I think things, and shit."

"But she was all over you like that when Hunter was alive too, right?"

"Yup. I mean, not in front of him, but when he wasn't there, she just about tore my pants off."

"I'm reconsidering the PI thing, you know. You need a partner?"

"When she was married, there was no way. But now…"

"Don't tell me you're even thinking about it."

"I'm not. What do you take me for?" Black insisted, the lie obvious in his voice.

"You look snappy today. You in a tango show or something?"

"Why does everyone F with me over my clothes?"

"Jealousy."

"That's what I thought."

"Dude. Just do me a favor. Cut the crime chat with the babe, all right? Ix-nay on the ead-day usband-hay."

"You got it. I wasn't thinking clearly. Her breasts cast some kind of a spell."

"Maybe she has mini-syringes in them and she drugged you."

"She tried that with a margarita the last time I was here."

"Second to last," Stan corrected. "Last time her husband played piñata on the front steps."

"Oh. That."

"So how was it?"

"What?"

"The margarita?"

"Kind of like her. Sweet, but high octane. Packed a wallop."

"I'm definitely reconsidering the PI thing."

"It's not all sex-starved temptresses and boozing and solving crimes."

"I'm okay with the no solving crimes part. Listen. Seriously. Can you keep your pie hole shut about something if I tell you?"

"Of course. My lips are sealed. What's up?"

"When you called me? I was just reading over the forensics report on our buddy Freddie."

"Mister Paparazzi. The punching bag."

"That's him. Turns out Hunter didn't kill him."

Black suddenly craved a cigarette more than he would have thought possible. "Come again?"

"He was poisoned. Somebody gave him a hot shot in the hospital."

"You're kidding."

"Right. I'm working on my comedy act. Which is why I want to know where you get your suits."

"But why?"

"Why would I want to dress like you?"

"No, why would someone knock Freddie off in the hospital?"

"My hunch is, because they could. Probably the same perp who's been whacking the photogs. It fits. Opportunistic."

"I'll say." Black cleared his throat. "You think this is related?"

"What do I know? I liked Hunter for the killings."

"But what's the motive? Why kill them both?"

"That, my friend, is the question of the day. Assuming that the same wing nut knocked them both off. We're still a long way from that."

They turned and meandered back to where Meagan was waiting. The evening was now almost upon them as the technicians continued their work, basking in the high-voltage glare of the portable work lights.

Black took Meagan's hands in his and faced her. "Meagan, I've got to get going. Detective Colt here is the best. He'll take good care of you."

Worry flickered across her face. "Do you have to?"

"I'm afraid so. I have another case I'm working." Black didn't want to tell her the real reason he thought it was a good idea to leave.

"Okay, then…thanks…I guess. For all of this…"

"No problem. The police can handle it from here."

She seemed about to say something, and then reconsidered and instead, nodded.

He could feel both her and Stan's eyes following him as he made his way back to the Cadillac, his head spinning at the ramifications of what he'd discovered.

Hunter had been murdered.

As had Freddie.

And none of it made the slightest sense.

CHAPTER 28

The evening reeked of uncombusted fuel and desperation as Black wheeled down the Sunset Strip on his way home. Lifted trucks with gawping country boys blared twangy redneck boot-stomping anthems as they prowled by defiantly parading rocker chicks in lacquered micro-skirts, their hair a riotous rainbow of individuality. Low-riders crept along filled with gangsta wannabes looking for any excuse to prove how tough they were by squeezing a trigger, the police presence slim deterrent to a sixteen-year old hell-bent on making his bones. Traffic moved along in fits and starts, the evening flow coagulating at major arteries before dispersing once past the center of the action.

The city of angels had caught Black in its tractor beam twenty-three years ago – an oasis where infinite dreams and the restless young came to party and die. Little had changed over time other than the price of heroin and the music pulsing out at those who paid homage to the glitter gods. It had all seemed so vital and possible back then, but the corrosive effect of hindsight had eroded the cozy mirage, revealing a house of mirrors filled with hollow promises. But each generation had to live for its moment, and Los Angeles' seeming perpetual possibility was a powerful lure for those who believed that appearances were more important than dismal reality.

He turned onto Normandie and followed a beaten Volvo down the grade, then made a left on his street. Graffiti adorned the dumpsters next to the construction site four buildings from the Paradise Palms, proclaiming the block to be the turf of contentious warlords still in high school. As absurd as it seemed, lives were regularly lost over one group of teens disrespecting the others' block, the permanence of their poor choices a testament to the frailty of what passed for civilization in the shadows of the Hollywood sign.

Black slid from behind the wheel and checked to ensure his top was secure before slipping the anti-theft club on and fixing it in place with a secure *thunk*. He locked his door, considered whether this was really the week he wanted to give up smoking, and moved resignedly to his fate. The lights were on in Gracie's unit, a reflected television's image illuminating the blinds with colored flashes of meaningless imagery, and Black had to knock twice before she came to the door, the stale stink of nicotine and rotgut wafting behind her.

"Well, look who's here! The prodigal returns," she said with a cackle, and then her face grew serious. "I'm guessing you aren't here for a social call."

"I have a favor to ask you, Gracie," he said, trying to keep the bone tiredness out of his voice.

"Anything, Angel. Anything at all."

"I'm going to have Cesar work on the Cadillac tomorrow, and I need to borrow your car."

"You want to drive *La Bomba*? *No problema*, Angel. She still runs like a scared rabbit. Don't let her aging looks fool you. She's a thoroughbred. They don't build 'em like that anymore."

Gracie was right about that. The ancient Mercedes was as solid as the Matterhorn and with a little TLC would outlive them all.

"No, they don't. And they don't make them like you, either. You're a lifesaver."

"Flattery will get you everywhere, you silver-tongued devil. You wanna come in for a drink?"

"I don't know, Gracie. I'm kind of beat."

"Come on. Just one. I'll even break out the good stuff." An obvious lie. Gracie didn't have anything but glorified grain alcohol that came in plastic drugstore jugs. Black fixed on her slightly glazed eyes, hungry for any kind of company, her skin so translucent he could see the web of blue veins at her temples, and felt a surge of compassion. For Gracie, the days just blended together, some a little better than others, her life but one long bout of inebriation and hangovers, the Paradise Palms her paradise lost.

"You know me too well. I could never turn down a lady and a drink," he said, and followed her into her unit.

"Jared. Turn the damned TV down, would you?" she yelled over inane eighties sitcom music, and her nephew obligingly complied. Blackjack glowered at him from beside an obviously artificial fern in an off-color plastic pot, and Black absently wondered what it was about him and cats.

"You find the guys that ripped me off?" Jared asked, his belligerence no better squelched than the prior week.

"I'm working on it. You get a job?" Black replied, swatting the ball back over the net to him.

"I'm so proud of him. He got a position at a shop on Melrose. A high-end electronics store," Gracie answered for him. "You want soda and ice, or straight up?" she asked Black.

"Ice and soda, Gracie. And a light pour tonight, okay?" he answered, then returned to Jared. "I found where one of them lives, and I staked it out for a night. He never came home. I've been by a couple of times, but no go. So I'm going out tonight to see if he's at any of the usual haunts."

"How are you going to recognize him?" Jared asked, distrustful of Black's facile explanation.

As well he should be. Given that Black had no idea.

"I'll spread some cash around with the bartenders. A guy like this Preacher is going to be known. A regular. Probably does a little dealing on the side to support his con game. Or vice versa. Someone's going to have seen him recently, unless he left town."

"With my luck he already spent the cash," Jared said sullenly, his eyes returning to the *Married with Children* rerun.

"Could be. But I made you a promise, and I intend to keep it."

"Don't sweat it. At the rate I'm going I'll have made it all back by the time I'm your age," Jared said, the eventuality of him ever advancing to the far reaches of decrepitude Black represented clearly unimaginable.

"I see you've been working on your retail courtesy. It's infectious. Keep up the good work."

"Don't you look handsome tonight, honey! I swear, you're as smooth as a baboon's backside. Love the hat. Men don't know how to wear a hat anymore. It's a shame," she announced as she tottered toward him clutching two overflowing plastic glasses, hers amber with two ice cubes, his pale yellow with four. He moved to meet her halfway and made a show of taking his drink and sipping it appreciatively. As always, it tasted like a combination of battery acid and lye, and he closed his eyes and feigned delighted surprise as it burned its way down his esophagus.

"Mmm. This is exceptional tonight, Gracie. You've outdone yourself again," he declared, his gag reflex threatening as he exhaled slowly, fighting to keep from choking, tears welling as his eyes stung.

"I know. I won't even tell you what I paid for this. Highway robbery. I thought they made everything in China nowadays?"

"Everything but the good stuff."

"Hear, hear."

Black stood, trying not to sink into depression at Gracie's squalid surroundings, for all their shabbiness still better than anything he'd managed to assemble for his life, and took another pull on the liquid fire she'd concocted. He could only imagine what hers tasted like. The fumes alone could strip paint.

"So what are you going to do if you find him?" Gracie asked, then drained a quarter of her glass without blinking.

"Downbeat him with a pipe until he coughs up the money."

"And if he doesn't have it?"

"I'll make finding it his life's biggest problem. That's how I deal with deadbeats and thieves. They'll gladly go steal it from someone else if you become a large enough irritant."

"Back in the day, the bookies would send out a couple of goons with baseball bats and a blow torch. Which one they'd use depended on whether it was their first or second visit. Nobody wanted to owe them money for long."

"Ah, the good ol' *hang 'em upside down and take the torch to 'em* days. Gets me all choked up to think about 'em."

"Like Archie Bunker used to say, right?"

"In fewer words, certainly."

Jared scowled like Black had just drowned his puppy. "That's it? That's the plan? Intimidate or beat the cash out of them?"

"Do you have a better suggestion? I'm always interested in input from a high-roller producer type," Black said.

Jared crossed his arms and sank deeper into the couch. Blackjack seemed to match his mood, and displayed solidarity by going to sleep.

"That's what I thought. How about this? I do the job I'm paid to, and you pray I'm successful so you don't have to sell beepers for the rest of the year," Black suggested.

"They don't sell beepers anymore."

Black's expression didn't change. "They don't?"

Jared rolled his eyes and returned his attention to the TV.

Gracie took up her usual position on a stool at the breakfast bar and took another mammoth swig of her libation. "What's a beeper?"

By the time Black left he was already buzzing, the cheap alcohol having gone straight to his head on an empty stomach. He resolved to grab another health burger at the Hawaiian place to straighten out his attitude, and mounted the stairs to his place to change into something lower-key for prowling the clubs. The truth was that he'd had no intention of going out that night, but after a day like he'd had, a few drinks might be just the ticket, and who knew? Maybe he'd run across the Preacher boy and put the fear of Jaysus into him. Stranger things had happened.

He recycled his Hawaiian shirt and slicked his hair back with a comb, Elvis style, avoiding careful scrutiny of his reflection in favor of a general optimistic impression. Screw everyone that thought he looked like a douche. He had style. Panache. Something that had passed into a bygone era, but that he aspired to. And what of it? Where was the harm in that? He could do a lot worse than to let a little *Maltese Falcon* slip into his life. At least Gracie got it. Which chilled him and depressed him even more.

One cocktail at the first club turned into three, and Black began to feel like life wasn't so bad after all. No sign of anyone named Preacher, but then again, Los Angeles was a big city. Maybe he'd stop by the shitbird's place on the way home.

After three more drinks at a second nightspot, that idea took a back seat to wondering how he was going to get back to his apartment without winding up with a DUI collar.

When he made it within three blocks of his house without getting pulled over, he decided to celebrate with a half pint of Old Grandad and a pack of Marlboro reds. He was just parking down the street from the Paradise Palms when his phone rang, and he vaguely processed Stan informing him that a rush order from forensics had confirmed that the substance they'd found at Hunter's was human blood.

His soiled, beige-carpeted floor seemed to be rocking like the deck of a ship in a storm when he finally persuaded his door to unlock, and thankfully he was never far from a wall with which to steady himself. The bottle didn't last long, and the final impression he had as he collapsed onto his bed and closed his eyes, only for a second, fully clothed and huffing like he'd run a marathon, was that he might have overdone it, just a little.

CHAPTER 29

Darkness cloaked the street, the sound of traffic from the larger arteries faded now at four in the morning. The moon had already made its nightly arc across the charcoal sky, and the city was as still as it got. Rap music thumped dully from an open window of the apartment building on the corner, faint evidence of a party winding down, the celebration muted to avoid a visit from the police.

A dark brown furry form slunk along the gutter, hoping for a tidbit as it made its nightly loop around the neighborhood, lord of its domain as long as it avoided tires and the occasional loose pet. It paused by an overflowing garbage can, weighing the benefits of leaping up and gnawing the dark green trash bag open, until it stiffened, startled by a scrape from down the block.

A lone figure hugged the shadows as it made its way down the sidewalk, rubber-soled running shoes padding softly against the hard concrete. The figure stopped near a large oak tree, one of the few concessions to nature left on the street, and surveyed the area to ensure that nobody was watching. Satisfied, it moved along the seemingly endless string of cars until arriving at its objective. With a fluid motion the stealthy shape shrugged off its black backpack and disappeared from the rodent's view.

Ten minutes later the running shoes traversed the remainder of the block, continuing on until rounding the corner and disappearing into the gloom, the errand completed.

CHAPTER 30

Jackhammer pounding from Black's front door reverberated inside the cramped apartment. He sat up and his head swam. Nausea overwhelmed him, and he had to choke back the sour bile that threatened to seep out of his nose as he fought for breath. A tight band of agony had been fastened around his head, a medieval torture device fit for the Inquisition, and it was all he could do to keep from vomiting from the pain.

"Black. Yo, man, what up, homeboy? You in there? I ain't got all day. Some of us got to work for a living, you know?"

Cesar's voice sliced through the walls and into Black's brain like a lance of white-hot agony, and it all came back to him as he forced his eyes open. He was lying face down on his bed, his shirt bunched up around his chest, his slacks now wrinkled beyond salvation.

The Cadillac. Being responsible. Taking care of business.

Black sat up and swallowed the metallic taste of partially metabolized whiskey and cigarettes. He vaguely recalled the series of bad decisions that had led up to him passing out, but the knocking from his front door interrupted his quiet introspection.

"Crap. Just a second, Cesar. I'm in the can."

"Okay, homeboy, no problem. Man's gotta do what he's gotta do, an' all," Cesar answered, a man of boundless discretion.

Two minutes later Black's crusted red eyes peered through a crack in the door as he winced away the worst of the harsh morning light. The Earth must have moved nearer the sun while he'd been sleeping because the glare was blinding. Black avoided looking directly at Cesar's goateed face, two tears tattooed below his left eye, and handed him the Eldorado key on a ring with his The Club key. Cesar appraised him and nodded knowingly after taking in his matted hair, dusting of beard, and face lined and creased from the folds of the blanket.

"Sorry, man. I…I got the flu," Black said, his voice sounding phlegmy and gravelly, cracking on the final word.

"Yeah. We all been there, man. Lot a that going around, you know?"

"So I hear."

"Awright. I'll take the boat into the shop and letchou know what the damage is later on today, okay, *vato*?"

"Sure thing. Just call whenever. You know the number."

"Yeah, uh huh. And you got money, right? We straight on that?" Cesar asked.

"Sure. Of course. I'm flush this week."

"Cool. Okay, then. We good."

Black shut the door and turned to face his living room, then leaned against the door and slid until he was sitting on the floor. What the hell had he been thinking? Good God almighty. What was it? Tuesday? It wasn't his birthday or Christmas, so why had he gone out on a bender like that and gotten obliterated?

The only good news was that he had no work, no clients, and no prospects, so his phone wouldn't be ringing. He exhaled as if confirming that his pulmonary system was still functioning, then willed himself off the carpet and back into the bedroom.

He was just composing the text message to Roxie alerting her that he had an offsite meeting that day when his windows rattled from a concussive blast out on the street. Stunned, he staggered back to his front door and threw it open, stumbled out onto the second story walkway, and looked toward the front of the complex. A pillar of black smoke was pouring from a point down the block. Black barely registered the rough concrete stairs on his bare feet as he descended to the ground level. Once there he increased his pace, the whirring in his head receding as adrenaline flooded his compromised system, and by the time he passed Gracie's door, which was swinging wide as she emerged to investigate the commotion, his heart was thudding like he'd run a four-minute mile.

The Cadillac was barely recognizable, the doors blown off, flames belching from the interior and from under the hood. It looked like a giant hand had swatted it, causing the body to distend like a pregnant beetle.

There was no trace of Cesar. The force of the detonation had obliterated him as though he'd never existed, vaporized in a fireball.

Other residents were slowly shuffling to the street, and Black felt Gracie's clawlike hand on his arm as he surveyed the burning remnants of his beloved vehicle.

"Oh, my sweet lord…was that your car, Black?"

He didn't respond, so she asked the question again, her voice like the grating of metal wheels on a railroad track. He couldn't do anything but nod, and then his wits gradually returned and he raised his cell phone to his ear to call Stan.

Sirens keened in the distance while he waited on hold, and the fire department and police were rolling up when he finally reached him and explained what had happened.

Stan told him to stay put, and that he would be there in twenty minutes. Black nodded, grunting assent, and then hung up, watching his pride and joy burn to the frame. The one surviving tire popped like a rifle shot and the chassis shuddered as it dropped, the hangover now the least of his problems. Gracie eyed the car with a kind of rapt fascination as the flames licked at the branches over it, and then a powerful torrent of water streamed at the inferno and firemen were screaming instructions to one another. Black turned toward the shattered windows facing the street and dialed Colleen's number, unsure of who else to call and tell. Roxie wouldn't be in yet – she was usually at least ten minutes late most mornings, and Cesar had been early.

Cesar.

Poor bastard. Never knew what hit him. One second he'd been there, of this world, and the next, *nada*. A wave of sickness hit him and he staggered back as though he'd been gut-punched, then straightened up when Colleen's voice answered.

"Hey, babe."

"Hey."

"You don't sound so great. What are all those sirens? Black? Are you all right? Have you been in an accident?"

"Um, yeah, I guess I am. And yes, something happened. My car just blew up."

"What?"

"Exploded."

"Are you okay?"

"I am. My mechanic, though...I think he's dead, Colleen."

"Good God. I'm so sorry..."

"Yeah. So am I." Black realized that he sounded like an automaton; like he was in a daze. He forced himself to focus. "But that wasn't the reason I called..." He fought for clarity, and then remembered. "That's right. Hunter."

"What about him?"

"I was out at his place yesterday evening, and found blood."

"I'm sure that wasn't hard, given the number of bullets he took."

"No, what I mean is, I found blood of someone besides Hunter."

Colleen's voice changed, quieted, a chill in her tone. "What do you mean?"

Black was momentarily distracted by Gracie, who was pointing to him and talking to a uniform who had arrived thirty seconds earlier.

"We...the police think there was a shooter there. Who maybe got hit by a stray. A ricochet. They've got a decent amount of blood, and they're working on it..."

"Are you sure about this?"

Colleen sounded strangled. He could relate.

"Positive. It looks like Hunter was murdered. Oh, shit–" He slapped himself in the head, grimacing at the pain. "How could I forget? Freddie was murdered, too."

"Black–"

"No, listen. I don't mean by Hunter. He was murdered by someone else. The cops found poison in his system. Somebody got to him in the hospital–"

Black was interrupted by two LAPD officers, one of whom was carrying a clipboard and a pen.

"Hey, buddy. That your car?"

Black lowered the phone. "Yeah. I mean, yes, officer. It is."

"Any idea what happened?"

"Damn. Hang on a second." He returned the phone to his ear. "Col, listen, I've got to call you back." He hung up and looked over the cop's shoulder at his burning car, now mostly extinguished.

"My mechanic was going to take it into the shop today..."

Fifteen minutes later, the police had filled out the incident report. Stan called in the middle of it to apologize for not being able to get away from the office, and Black told him not to worry about it, that the police were already there.

"You were lucky that you didn't start it this morning, buddy," Stan said.

"No kidding. But Cesar…not so lucky."

There wasn't much to say to that.

"It could have happened at any time. It's a miracle you're still alive, Black."

"Doesn't feel like one."

"You're still breathing, aren't you?"

"Put that way, I can't argue."

"You need anything? I have to be here for another half hour, at least. Maybe an hour. Impromptu staff meeting. No calls, and no excuses. Completely blows."

"No. I…damn. I can't believe this. It's…"

"Just another day in La La Land. Dude. It sucks. I'm sorry your mechanic's dead. But you're not. That's the good news. I'll break away from this as soon as I can. Don't worry. Things will work out."

"My car…Cesar."

"Right. Okay. Hang in there, buddy. Keep your phone on."

Black punched the call off and found himself facing Gracie.

"You want a bracer, Black? Of any day, this would be the one," she said. He knew she was trying to be generous, her solution to everything to have another belt, but the thought of a drink made him gag.

"Um, no thanks, Gracie. Not now. I have to…I need to go find my insurance papers and deal with this."

"Offer's open, darling. Oh, and don't worry about a car. You got *La Bomba*. You can use it as much as you need."

He softened, touched by her simple words. "Thanks, Gracie. Looks like I'll take you up on that."

He followed her to her unit and waited outside while she got him the keys. The old Mercedes was parked in one of the few stalls in the rear of the building, off a driveway that was more an afterthought than an access point. He thanked her again and returned to his apartment, and had just texted Roxie with the news about the explosion when his phone vibrated, indicating he'd received a text.

Black thumbed the scroll button and opened the message, and then all the blood drained from his face as he read. He blinked to ensure he wasn't hallucinating.

He wasn't.

He slipped his shoes on, grabbed his belt holster and wallet, slammed the door behind him, and tore down the stairs as fast as his legs would carry him, dialing Stan's cell as he ran.

CHAPTER 31

The sixties-era Mercedes sulked under a bird-dropping-splattered car cover so old it had probably been woven out of papyrus. Black hurriedly unrolled it and tossed it aside, then slipped behind the wheel and felt for the seat adjustment lever – his knees were about to collide with his chin. The ancient throne slid back with a clunk and he went through the process of starting the old beast up. It sputtered, and then a billowing cloud of black exhaust issued from the rusted tail pipe before the engine settled into a steady rhythm that to Black sounded like a dozen monkeys banging on an oil drum with sticks.

He jerked the transmission into gear and eased out of the slot, then guided the car down the drive, only to find it blocked by a police cruiser. At least *La Bomba*'s horn sounded impressive, he thought as he honked to get the squad car to move while he tried his phone, frantic to reach either Stan or Colleen again.

Colleen didn't pick up and the call went directly to voicemail. Black hung up and dialed Stan again, with the same result. The police vehicle moved back just enough to allow Black to clear, and he floored the accelerator as he turned into the street. Which had approximately the same effect as flogging a sloth. The beleaguered diesel engine gave all it had, which wasn't much, and Black slammed his palm against the hard steering wheel, cursing his luck.

Once on the freeway he was able to get his speed up to seventy, which took a little longer than an oil tanker did to reach cruising speed. At that rate he estimated that he'd hit ninety around Palm Springs, or maybe Vegas.

As he pulled back into the slow lane he replayed the text message from Colleen in his head: *Can't talk. I think Seth may be involved with Hunter and Freddie. I'm in the bathroom and he can hear me. Get out here. Bring your gun.*

He had no idea how or why Seth, her boyfriend-cum-handyman, had anything to do with any of this, or why she suspected him, but it was serious enough to warrant him getting his ass to her trailer sooner than later. She'd never steered him wrong in all the years he'd known her, and he had a hard time believing she was hallucinating now.

The only problem being that while a text message from Col was enough to send Black running for his Glock, it wouldn't do much in terms of the police. Any report he filed would get put at the bottom of the pile. As far as he knew, Hunter's death was still on the books as a police shooting, and Black had no idea whether Freddie's murder had even been formally classified as such yet. LAPD could be like any other large bureaucracy and took its sweet time about moving, especially in cases where there was no perp standing over the body with an axe. Worse, from what he knew about jurisdictions, Riverside County wouldn't exactly drop everything to help LAPD.

Still, he owed it to Col to at least try. He dialed 911 and got put through to an operator almost immediately.

"Hello. What is the nature of your emergency?" the crisp female voice asked.

"It's about a homicide investigation."

"Someone's been murdered?"

"Well, yes. But not recently. It's about an open investigation."

"So there's no emergency?" the woman asked, her voice now more annoyed than anything. "What is your name, sir?"

Black cringed. "Artemus Black. And yes, it's an emergency."

"And what is the emergency, Mr. Black?"

"I got a text message from a friend who says she thinks her boyfriend is involved in a homicide. She sounded like she thinks she's in danger."

"Has she been threatened?"

"I…I don't think so."

"What is the nature of your emergency?" the operator asked again, this time robotically uninterested.

"I told you. I got a text message."

"Fine. A text message. Could you read it to me?"

175

"I'm driving. Hang on a second."

"Sir, I can't ask you to read a text message while you're driving. That's illegal. Please pull over and read it."

"I can't just pull over. I'm on the freeway. The 10, headed east."

"Then call 911 back once you're stationary. There doesn't seem to be any emergency other than a text message where nobody is in immediate danger. Is that correct?"

Black deflated, realizing how it must sound. "It was something about she thinks her boyfriend might be involved in a homicide."

"Might?"

"I don't remember the exact wording. Can't I just glance at this?"

"Sir, do not attempt to drive and read. That's a leading cause of highway fatalities."

"She said he could be involved. That she thinks he is."

"Is, or could be?"

"Look…"

"Sir, this call is being recorded. I gather you can hear the beeps. It's illegal to place a non-emergency call to 911. Are you aware of that?"

"I am."

"What is the name of the homicide investigation, do you know?"

"Hunter. The actor."

"Sir, again, we are recording this call. I saw the news. Mr. Hunter was killed by LAPD. It's not a homicide."

"It is. Or it will be soon."

"I have real emergencies to contend with, sir. I'm going to terminate this call and forward it to my superior."

"No. Wait. She also said that he was involved in Freddie Sypes' death."

"Freddie Sypes."

"Correct."

"The man Hunter beat to death on national television in front of the TCL Chinese Theater."

"He didn't beat him to death. They had a fight. Sypes was poisoned in the hospital."

"Sir, have you been drinking or taking any medication?"

"No, damn it. No. Look, my car just exploded in L.A. You can check that. My mechanic was killed. Not half an hour ago."

"I see. Did Hunter or Sypes blow up your car?"

"No. I just…"

"Did this boyfriend blow up your car?"

That stopped Black for a second. "Maybe. I don't know."

"Sir, I would advise you that policy is to prosecute crank calls."

"I understand. I tried to reach the homicide detective who's handling the investigation, but he's in a meeting."

"I see. And did you leave a message?"

"Yes. But it could be a while."

"Sir, there's nothing I can do for you. You have no emergency. You have a text message that may or may not be genuine from someone claiming her boyfriend may be involved in two homicides that are the most reported events of the last week — neither of which are actually homicides. Am I missing anything?"

"And my car blew up."

"Oh. Right. And the emergency is?"

"Damn. I knew this was going to happen. Never mind."

"I think you can expect the department to follow up on this call, sir. I'm hanging up now."

"Fine. Thanks for nothing."

By Black's reckoning, he would be at Colleen's within fifteen minutes, maybe as few as ten, assuming the Benz didn't blow a gasket first. He was grateful to Gracie for lending him the car, but it was only slightly more useful than a unicycle with a flat tire, and he was no trained bear. He tried Stan again and got his voicemail. He'd obviously turned his phone off. Which was no surprise; he'd told Black he was going to do so.

Black felt his anger mounting now at the circumstances. His car gone. His friend — okay, his acquaintance, Cesar — dead. Stan out for the duration. Colleen not answering. Her boyfriend somehow involved in the killings, but nobody willing to listen. The operator threatening him instead of helping.

His phone rang.

"Your car blew up?"

"Roxie. Yes. It did."

"So no more pimp daddy mobile."

"Correct. But this isn't a good time."

"I can see that. I got your message."

"I put that together." A thought occurred to him. "I want you to pull up everything you can on a guy named Seth…Seth…"

"Seth. Like 'Simon Seth'?"

"Just a second. I'm thinking."

"So am I."

"Seriously. Give me a minute."

"It was a second a second ago."

"Roxie."

"You want to call me back when you're done thinking?"

"That would be good."

"I'm guessing you won't be in today."

"Good bet."

"I'll tell anyone who calls you're out because your car exploded."

"Don't do that."

"I won't. But it was fun saying it."

"I hate you sometimes, Roxie."

"No you don't."

Damn. *Now what's Seth's last name? Seth…Seth Bird? Something to do with birds. Seth the birdman. Seth Birdman? Birdnest? No, that's not it.*

His head was pounding like Mr. Satan was stabbing his frontal lobes with a pitchfork. He couldn't concentrate.

Think.

Seth…birds. Seth Bird. Seth Birdhouse. Seth…Aviary! No. Not quite. Sounded like aviary…Avery! Seth Avery!

He dialed Roxie again.

"Black's Exploding Junkers," Roxie chirped.

"Not funny."

"Mugsy thought it was."

"Pull up everything you can on Seth Avery."

"Seth you."

Black blinked in annoyance. "Roxie."

"Sorry. Give me a second." He heard her fingers flying over the keys, entering in information.

"Huh. Let's see. Golfer?"

"No. I mean, I don't think so. He's about forty. Maybe younger."

"So an old dude."

"No, he's only mid-to-late thirties."

"Mick Jagger said he didn't want to live to be over thirty."

"I think he's about ninety now. And really rich."

"Who?"

"Mick Jagger."

"You want me to look up Mick Jagger? This could take a while."

"Roxie."

"I'm just trying to be thorough, Black."

"Seth Avery."

"Okay. Let's see. Ah. There's a doctor in Reseda. Hmm. His specialty is spastic color."

He held the phone away and thought about throwing it out the window, then took a calming breath. "I think that's colon."

"Oh. Spastic colon. Hey, wouldn't that be a cool band name?"

"Roxie…"

"Oh, here's one. He…well, looks like he was hot about…oh, wow. Like, the year 2000. I don't even think they had the internet back then. I was, like, twelve or so."

"Too much information."

"He was a director. Indie movie. Came in second at Sundance."

"Bingo."

"And then he…hmm. Then, nothing. That's it."

"Really? Nothing?"

"Nope. Just came and went." She paused. "Don't spastic colons do that?"

"Doesn't that strike you as strange?"

"I find anything involving colons a little weird. Even semi-colons kind of sound gross. All prolapsy or whatever."

"No, that he would rank that high in 2000, and then disappear off the scene."

"Goes to show you that winning is everything."

"I'm pretty sure coming in second at Sundance is pretty big."

"Tell that to colon boy."

"Keep digging."

"Don't go there."

By the time he took the off-ramp to Colleen's park, he was midway through the visualization exercises that he'd worked on with Dr. Kelso and had gotten his pulse back to just under trip-hammer speed. He rolled around the corner and up to the gate, which was open, and pulled up to Colleen's trailer.

Her old Mitsubishi was parked nearby, but that was the only car. No sign of Seth's pickup truck. He kept going past her place, parked in front of one of the other trailers, and shut the engine off. His ears strained for any hint of a threat, but he didn't detect anything.

Black approached Colleen's front porch and removed his pistol from the belt holster. He knocked on the door, using his shirt to cover the gun, finger on the trigger.

Nothing.

He tried again, and got no response. His hand was a centimeter away from the doorbell when he froze.

That smell.

Gas.

He tried the doorknob, but it was locked.

He could shoot it open, but that would be the last thing he did before sitting down to discuss his many shortcomings with St. Peter.

So, what to do?

He looked around the barren yard and saw nothing helpful. Increasingly frantic, he began pacing, and then a light bulb went on in his head. He ran back to the Mercedes and opened the heavy trunk. Inside was a tire iron – an old-fashioned, honest-to-goodness, five-pound steel tire iron with a long handle. He sprinted back to the trailer, wedged it into the door, and began to pry, working it carefully, wary of doing anything that would create a spark.

The crummy lightweight door gave and slammed inward. Black winced as it hit the inside wall of the trailer and bounced, but he was still alive and not blown to Judgment Day, so net positive. He held his breath and moved inside, and immediately spotted Colleen lying on the floor, immobile, a long-barreled chrome revolver by her hand.

Black crossed the room in four large steps and tried hoisting her, but his back twinged a warning at lifting her dead weight and he quickly reconsidered. He reached under her arms and dragged her to the door, keenly aware that the slightest thing could set the trailer off, even the spark of metal brushing metal. He bumped into the bookcase and two of the framed photographs fell to the floor, and he watched, horrified, as they hit the carpet and lay still – one of Colleen in better days, and the one of Seth.

Gasping once he was at the doorway, he pulled her out of the trailer and down the two stairs and kept going, grateful that she'd kept her petite figure and didn't weigh 220. Clear of the interior, he lifted her in a modified fireman's hold and staggered with her to the Mercedes and laid her on the asphalt by the rear bumper. She was cyanotic, her lips blue, and he racked his brains for a few seconds trying to remember the TV shows he'd seen where beach nymphettes gave CPR to handsome studs the sea had gotten the better of.

He began blowing into her mouth, his fingers clamped hard on her nose, and after a minute she coughed and sputtered, then gasped as her eyes popped wide. She was unfocused for a few breaths and then recognized Black.

"Wha...where..."

"The gas was on in the trailer. I carried you outside. You were unconscious," he said.

"Out..."

"Just take it easy. Breathe. Get your wind back."

She did, and the color gradually returned to her face. "That bastard. That miserable, lying, crazy bastard."

"Seth, you mean."

"He hit me. There's a bump on the back of my head the size of a baseball," she said, reaching around to dried blood caked in her hair. "Ow."

"You'll live. Why would he do that?"

"I...I'm not a very good actress, Black. That's why I went the journalist route. After your call, when I put two and two together, he could tell. I could see it in his eyes. He knew I suspected, so he had to do something."

"There's a gun inside. On the floor."

"A gun?" Colleen sounded puzzled.

"A revolver."

"I know he had a couple of guns. Two handguns and a rifle."

"What do you want to bet that's the gun he used to shoot Hunter with?"

"He was always at the range. He's a crack shot."

"Good to know. Why did you suspect he'd killed Hunter?"

"He came home that night with a bandage on his arm. Said he'd been moonlighting on a handyman job and had an accident. I was all over him about going to the doctor, but he wouldn't listen. When you said that they'd found blood at Hunter's and you thought a ricochet might have hit the shooter...with what I know about Seth's history, it just clicked."

"Seth's history?"

"He was a brilliant director. I mean, really gifted, and after he won second at Sundance, he had it made. But he ran crosswise against an industry heavyweight who put the word out, and next thing he knew he couldn't get a job as a script boy. His fledgling career took a nosedive, and it never recovered."

"And?"

"That heavyweight was Hunter."

"What? Why?"

"All he would say was that it had to do with his girlfriend. I guess Hunter took one look at her at Sundance and had to have her. You don't know what it's like with big time actors, Black. Their egos are like overgrown children. When they want a cookie, they act out until someone gets them a cookie. Apparently, Seth called him on it, there was a fight or altercation of some kind, and Seth's career took the fall. Hunter crushed him and killed his chances. Big fish eats little fish. Typical Hollywood ending."

"No wonder Seth hated his guts. But why Freddie? What did he have against him?"

"That's where it gets really weird."

"Not that being a serial killer who offs movie stars in front of half the LAPD is weird."

"When Seth hit rock bottom, he lost everything, not just his career. He was left with nothing. He told me he took up drugs, booze, you name it. And he was really, really bitter about women."

"I've been there."

"One night, I guess he was wasted, at a party that Freddie was at – you know the kind, lots of Hollywood glitz, a few minor celebrities, but mostly third-tier non-players. Anyway, one thing led to another…and Seth wound up with Freddie."

Black's eyes widened. "Seth. With Freddie Sypes."

"Hey. It happens. Don't act so shocked. Tell me you never touched another man's–"

"How about we stick to the psycho serial killer?"

"Boy, you got the psycho part right. Anyway, Seth slept with Freddie…" Colleen paused.

"…and he was furious. Felt like he'd been duped or tricked into it," Black finished.

"That's how he explained it. Made a huge point of how he wasn't gay. But…"

"But?"

"I think the problem wasn't that he slept with him. I think the problem was that Seth actually fell hard for Freddie. Bits and pieces, but from what I gathered when I put out feelers, Seth and Freddie were a thing for a short time. So it wasn't a one night deal. More like weeks."

"And…"

"And I think he fell in love with Freddie, whereas for Freddie it was just another conquest. A straight, handsome, macho heterosexual bunch of yum to amuse himself with. But the thrill didn't last very long, so Freddie moved on. That's the way it sounded to me. Remember that thirteen years ago, Freddie was handsome, powerful, rich, sexy…he knew everybody, and was on all the A-lists. He was also a miserable prick and a backstabbing user, but he was a seductive one."

"So Seth was killing paparazzi…because of unrequited love?"

"Reading between the lines, that's my bet."

"But…Col. What were *you* doing with him?"

"Black. Look at me. I don't kid myself. He was broken. Had a screw loose, too. But I'm not exactly a catch. And we had some things in common. One of which was that I hated Freddie. Another one was that I was understanding of Seth's need to prove that…that he wasn't gay. That Freddie made him do it. I played along. I gave him what he wanted and needed. Is that so strange? Two broken people finding each other and sharing each other's misery?"

"But you were also friends with Hunter."

"Not kissing friends, but he would ask my advice sometimes and suck up to me if he needed a favor – wanted dirt on someone. It was quid pro quo. And I didn't know about Hunter being the one that destroyed Seth's chances till after we were already together. But now…now I'm wondering whether that wasn't another attraction for Seth. That I would share information with him about one of the men he hated more than anything, and the other that I hated as much, or more, than he did. Freddie trashed my career as surely as Hunter trashed Seth's. In some ways, we were the perfect couple."

Just then the telephone rang in Colleen's trailer, and the gas ignited, blowing a massive fireball into the sky and flinging debris to the heavens.

Black and Colleen flinched, and then Black ducked and pulled Colleen so the back of the Mercedes protected them from falling chunks of flaming mobile home. They both watched with open mouths as debris rained around them, and Black saw tears streaming down Colleen's face as she lay on the road, bruised and battered, her future gone in one terrible instant.

CHAPTER 32

Colleen's neighbors came running from their trailers as the smoldering carcass burned, and Black was struck by the similarity to his car only an hour earlier. If he'd had any doubts before, they were gone now. Seth was out of his mind, killing anyone he thought could connect him to Freddie and Hunter. He knew that Black and Colleen were friends, so if he'd caught on to Colleen's suspicions about him…then Black would have to go, too.

Black dialed 911 and got a different operator. This time there was no disagreement that it was an emergency.

A husky man in his sixties with black suspenders holding his pants up spotted Colleen and trotted over to them.

"Col. Are you okay?"

"Not really, Stu. I think I'm in real trouble."

The expression on his face as he took in what was left of the burning trailer was akin to a bush baby caught by a nighttime flash. "Well, don't you worry about a thing. You have insurance, right?"

"Yeah. But not enough to replace the miserable pile of crap." Colleen sobbed, and Stu knelt to comfort her just as Black's phone rang.

He looked at the screen and his heart caught in his throat.

Meagan Hunter.

"Black," he answered.

"You've got to come over. Please. I think someone's trying to get in the house."

Black's mind raced. "Call the cops."

"I did. Then I called your office and your girl said your car blew up."

Good old Roxie.

"Where are you?" she asked. "Are you anywhere nearby?"

"No. Are you alone in the house?"

"Yes. It's the housekeeper's day off."

"Do you have a gun?"

"I...Andrew had one in his office, I think."

"Get the gun and call the police again. I think you're in danger. I know whose blood that was at your house. He just tried to kill my friend."

"Oh God. Someone's trying to open the back door."

The line died just as Black was going to tell her to run.

Colleen looked up at him from her position on the ground and struggled to sit up.

"No. You stay and wait for the ambulance. I've got to go. I think Seth is trying to kill Meagan. He's gone back to finish the job."

Black bolted to the Mercedes and started the engine, then roared off with the impetus of a Greyhound bus climbing a steep mountain pass.

He dialed Stan again as he was getting onto the freeway and left another frantic message before calling 911 for the third time and alerting them to the situation at Hunter's house. While he was on the line with the operator, his phone beeped.

Stan.

"Stan. Listen. You need to get everything you've got up to Hunter's, now."

"Why?"

"I know who killed Hunter. And Freddie. And the paparazzi. A guy named Seth Avery. He used to be a director. Holds a grudge against both of them. Nutty as a Christmas fruitcake, and a marksman."

"Whoa. What happened to your friend that you left the messages about?"

"Seth's her boyfriend. He tried to kill her. Left her for dead in a trailer full of gas. The trailer's history."

"Holy... Is she okay?"

"She will be. Medics are on the way. I'm headed to Hunter's. I think Seth rigged my car, too."

"I'm not going to ask why you think that."

Black's phone gave a warning tone, indicating his battery was almost dead. "I'll explain later. Just get someone up to Hunter's, now. He's armed and dangerous. You can take that—"

His phone went dead in his hand.

"...to the bank."

And his car charger had gone to cellular heaven that morning along with his red leather interior.

And Cesar.

He mashed the accelerator to the floor, which produced a sound much like playing cards stuck in bicycle spokes as the heavy car inched past seventy-five on the speedo. Black diesel exhaust belched from the back of the car, but eighty wasn't going to happen in this lifetime. At this rate, he'd be lucky if he got to Hunter's in less than forty-five minutes – by which time Meagan could have died of boredom or hunger or a glacier crushing her.

He pounded the dash in frustration, then began his visualizations again, trying to calm himself as a VW Westphalia with Canadian plates passed him in the slow lane.

If nothing else, *La Bomba* would teach him patience.

෴

When Black arrived at Hunter's, it was a familiar scene: police cars, an ambulance, Stan's cruiser all stationed out front, with the forensics van in the driveway next to the coroner's van. Black was stopped as he approached the gate, but one mention of Stan's name and title and he was escorted up the drive and into the house, where at least twenty uniforms were milling around while the forensics technicians did their thing.

Black caught Stan's eye and then relief flooded through him when he saw Meagan, sitting, crying, obviously in shock as a police officer tried to comfort her. Stan detached himself from her entourage and walked over to Black.

"What happened – didn't pay your phone bill? I tried calling back," Stan asked.

"I had a really important call from my astrologist."

"You might want to see about a refund if she didn't predict this."

"Don't make it all ugly, Stan. What happened? Is she okay?"

"She'll live. She blew a hole the size of Cleveland through this Seth chump's chest, and then blew half his head off with her second shot."

"Ouch."

"Buddy boy picked the wrong house – a .357 magnum with hollow points doesn't leave a lot of negotiating room. His little 9mm Ruger never stood a chance."

"DOA, I presume."

"He was history when he hit the ground."

Black shook his head. "How many did he kill?"

"Boy. Not that I'm counting, but…eight? Does that sound right?"

"Give or take. Either way, quite a losing streak."

"Yup. Now it's all over but the shouting."

"How's she holding up?"

"Like I said – she'll be okay. Probably need a year in therapy, but hey, that's most of L.A."

Black looked over Stan's shoulder at Meagan and caught her eye again, but she was listening to the officer's questions, giving him a statement. He realized that his hangover was still pulsing like a demon seed in his skull, but for all he'd been through, it wasn't as bad as some he'd endured.

"I'm hung over," he announced.

"You look kind of like a guy whose car blew up and who slept in his own vomit."

"Close enough on both counts." He shook his head. "Nothing left for me to do here, is there? You need anything from me? Statement?"

"Nah. Get out of here. Call me later when your phone's charged and we can have a beer or something."

"After I sleep for about thirty-six hours."

"Man's got a dream. I like that. Nice shirt."

"Thanks. I won it in a raffle in Koreatown."

"Worth every penny, too."

He took a final look at Meagan and gave her a small salute. Her face lit up for just a fraction of a second, and then fell again as she registered another in a long list of questions.

Black found his way back down the stairs and pushed past the uniforms. The Mercedes sat like a wart at the curb. Black glared at it and was reminded of Mugsy for some reason. Both were homely and terrible in their own way, and Black was stuck with them. And grateful for it, truth be told.

The two police officers by the gate watched him bent over nearly double, laughing his ass off, and shook their heads.

What a town. More like a circus.

Black was right at home.

CHAPTER 33

"So when are you going to get a car?" Roxie asked, her voice somewhat playful, which was always a dangerous sign to Black.

He was seated in his office, having grown accustomed to the way his ass stuck to the taped seat, albeit not welcoming its familiarity. Mugsy had seemingly lost interest in any further destructive binges involving his furniture, at least for the time being. He'd probably figured out he couldn't eat it, so why expend precious calories that could better be conserved for valuable pastimes like lounging and sleeping? Roxie was standing in the doorway sporting ripped jeans, a black leather choker, and what appeared to be a leotard top that highlighted her pert breasts and body art. Pert *young* breasts, he mentally corrected.

"I've got to wait for the insurance to pay out. The adjuster said it could take a week or two."

"Don't you have the company that has the commercial with the lady getting her check within forty-eight hours? I thought that was their claim to fame."

"Roxie. You might want to sit down. I don't know how to break this to you. People lie."

"That's got to piss you off."

"Do I look happy?"

"You never look happy."

"That's not true."

She grinned triumphantly. "People lie."

Touché.

Black returned to his web browsing, and then realized that Roxie was still standing in the doorway.

"What?"

"We're almost broke again. The five grand didn't last long."

"I'm working on a corporate security contract. Should get it by the end of the week. Through Bobby."

"Just in the nick of time."

She didn't move. Black leaned back in his chair, the base squeaking as he moved, and sighed.

"What?" he asked, eying her.

"Have you called your mom?"

"I tried, but her number was busy."

"Liar."

"Apparently people do that. But only if it gets them what they want."

"Ah. Good to know. Speaking of which, guess what I found?"

"What?"

"A copy of Hunter's pre-nup with your new girlfriend."

"She's not my girlfriend. I haven't even talked to her since the incident," Black said.

"A whole two days."

"Still. Not anything close to a girlfriend."

"You don't necessarily have to talk to your girlfriend."

"I'm not going to discuss this with you."

"Don't you want to know what's in the pre-nup?"

"Desperately."

She shrugged. "It's the usual."

"Which is…"

"She gets a token payout if they divorce within five years, and gets nothing if it's due to infidelity regardless of when. Pretty one-sided."

"Men are pigs."

"I'll say. But what's the alternative?"

"Girls."

"No, thanks. Just being one's enough for me. Although…is that a fantasy of yours?"

"Being a girl?"

"No. Two lipstick lesbians going at it."

"Why?"

"Just curious."

"Then, no, it's never come up."

"Because of lack of opportunity or lack of interest?"

"This is getting uncomfortable. Can we talk about something else?"

"Sure. What's it feel like to be driving the Nazi babe magnet?"

"It's very economical."

"That's good, because in case I didn't mention it, we're broke."

Black nodded. "This is becoming circular. Is there anything else besides my rich inner landscape, automotive shortcomings, and our lack of current liquidity?"

"You should really call your mom. And quit smoking."

"Thanks for the reminders."

"You're welcome," Roxie said, smiling sweetly again and pirouetting to return to her desk.

Black shook his head and picked up his cell. He'd procrastinated long enough. As much as he didn't want to disturb Meagan in her time of grief, money was money, and Hunter's estate owed him fifteen more grand, which he'd more than earned.

When she answered, her voice sounded flat. "Black. I was wondering when I'd hear from you."

"I figured I'd give you some time."

"Thanks."

"How are you doing?"

"It's been rough. So much has happened. I'm…still trying to process it all, I guess."

"It can take a while. But you're in no rush."

"That's right. Still, it's a lot to digest."

"At least you're safe and unhurt," he said.

"For which I'm grateful."

"How's the movie doing?"

"How do you think? You saw it."

"Not so great, then."

"It's never going to break even. More a question of how much it loses."

"I'm sorry to hear that. I know…I know Hunter had financial difficulties."

"That's putting it mildly. I'm still trying to wade through it all. It's a swamp."

Black stalled, wondering how to approach the subject of his fee, and decided that business was business – he'd done his part, so he shouldn't feel any shame about getting paid.

"I hate to play pile on, but there's the matter of my fee. Hunter still owed me fifteen thousand dollars for services rendered."

"Don't feel bad. That's nothing. The kinds of problems he left me with are six and seven figure problems. A few grand here or there is no big deal."

"Should I come by and get a check, or can you contact the production office?"

"I can try them, but they're not very responsive to me."

"That's…I put this off as long as I could, but I kind of really need the money."

"Why didn't you say so? If it's urgent, I'll just cut a check and sort it out with them later. No reason you should suffer because of their incompetence. Come by as soon as you can. I'm at the house."

"I really appreciate it, Meagan."

"You've done so much. You don't need to thank me."

"Still…I'll see you in a few."

"I'll be waiting."

She sounded different. Distant. After everything she'd been through, it wasn't surprising. But humans were surprisingly resilient, he knew from personal experience. She'd bounce back.

A gardening truck was parked near the entrance of Meagan's house, and Black parked *La Bomba* behind it and got out. The roar of a leaf blower from the rear pool area echoed through the estate, and Black stopped to examine the front door before ringing the doorbell. The ornate wood panels had been replaced, as had the glass surrounding the entrance area and all the off-white stone. You'd never know that a man had been gunned down where he was now standing – although Black had a feeling that it would have to be disclosed to any new buyer and would sour the deal for most.

The housekeeper answered the door and led him to Meagan, who was sitting in the kitchen, reading a magazine. She rose as he approached, and offered a cheek to kiss – a far cry from the borderline body dance she'd been throwing his way on the previous visits.

Which was fine by him. He was over his momentary infatuation. Or more accurately, lust. Although she still looked like a few hundred million, he had to admit. A heartbreaker in a city that minted them.

"Nice to see you again, Meagan," he said, taking her in. She was wearing jeans and a jade green silk blouse with strappy sandals, and still could give most centerfolds a run for their money.

"Same here, Black. What a wild ride, huh?"

"I'll say. You don't know the half of it. The killer tried to get me, too. Blew up my car. At least I think so. Not much left of it, so no way to know for sure yet."

"What? You never said anything. When did that happen?"

"The morning he came for you."

"Oh, my God. That's…that's crazy."

"That's why they call them psycho, right?"

"He was, wasn't he? Trying to kill everyone connected to Hunter. I just don't understand any of it…"

"Not sure you can ever understand how an insane person's brain works. Sometimes you just have to shrug and say, it is what it is."

"That's my approach." She stood and motioned to him. "Come on, let's get you paid. I'm sorry to seem rushed, but I've got a lunch date with some sympathetic neighbors who probably just want to hear the inside scoop on what really happened."

She led him to Hunter's teak-paneled office, bookcases lining both sides, framed photos of Hunter shaking hands with other stars, the governor, and two ex-presidents adorning the far wall. She rounded the lavish handmade desk, opened a navy blue leather oversized checkbook and selected a black Mont Blanc pen, then quickly began scribbling.

"Who do I make it out to?" she asked as she wrote.

"Black…uh, Black Investigations, LLC," he answered, coming to a snap decision to revert to the old company name as he examined the hardbound books – a few first editions, but mostly books on filmmaking and Hollywood history. His eyes roved over the photos: Hunter off-hours in the smaller framed photos, and in the larger ones, Hunter in his most famous roles – dressed as a Roman soldier, sitting in the cockpit of an F-15, astride a camel in the desert.

Meagan finished writing and signed the check with a flourish, then set the pen down.

"Here you go, Black. I threw in a little something extra to express my gratitude," she said, holding out the check. Black appeared not to have heard her, still studying the photographs. "Black? Your check."

Black turned and took it from her. He studied it as if it had been written in hieroglyphics, and still looking at it, asked a question in a soft voice.

"Thanks, Meagan. You know, we never got to talk after the shooting. Of, what was his name? Stef? Seth?"

"Something like that. Seth, I think."

"That's a pretty uncommon name, isn't it?"

"I…I don't know. Takes all kinds, right? Zander, Drake, Troy, Kendall, Chaz…you hear them all around here."

"Yeah. I guess you're right. Let me ask you a question, though. Did you know Seth?"

She looked like he'd slapped her. He raised his eyes from the check and carefully folded it as he waited for her answer.

"What? What kind of question is that?" she demanded.

"Just a question. A simple one. Did you know Seth?"

"I…I don't think so. I mean, I read about him in the paper. He was a director at one time, so anything's possible, with Hunter and all. But I met fifty people a week in the early days, when he was still…when his career was still going strong."

"So you didn't know him, or you don't remember, or anything's possible? Those are three different answers, aren't they?" Black asked, his voice still reasonable and evenly modulated. Friendly. Just two friends talking.

"Black, what's your problem? You've got your check. What else is there to talk about?"

"You know, it's strange. There have been parts of this whole thing that don't add up, but they're little things, insignificant things. I normally would just let them go."

"Maybe that's because they're insignificant."

"Maybe. But what's that saying? The devil's in the details? It just occurred to me that in this case, that holds true, in spades."

"What are you–"

Black turned toward the bookcase again and reached out to lift one of the silver-framed photographs.

"You look so young in this one. So long ago, wasn't it?"

"I…I guess so. Must have been. Lot of water under the bridge. Listen, I told you I've got a lunch thing–"

"Yes, it was a long time ago. Oh, the date's right there on the sign over the gangplank. New Year's Eve, 2000. The new millennium. I remember. Some people thought the world was going to end then. Turns out that was an overreaction. Where was this taken?"

"I don't remember. I was partying a lot back then. It was just another party," she said, her voice now matching Black's guarded tone.

"Oh, wait. Says right there. Newport Beach. Small world. Couldn't have been that big a boat. Doesn't look like it. What are the odds of two people being in the same place on New Year's Eve, 2000? Probably, what, one in a billion? Maybe a little less?"

"I have no idea, Black."

"I'd say really long odds, anyway."

Meagan's face could have been carved out of stone. "I think we're done here, Black."

"Are we? Humor me just a little. Before I go, I want to tell you a story." He held up a hand, silencing her protest. "Don't worry, it won't take long."

"Do I have a choice?"

"No, Meagan. You don't." He paused. "Meagan. That's such a beautiful name. And you were so…you were glowing back then, weren't you? I bet you stopped traffic. One in ten million. A hundred million." He hefted the photo then returned it to the bookcase, appearing to think for a moment before continuing. "I've only seen one other photo like that. Strangely enough, also from Newport, New Year's Eve, 2000. Pretty amazing coincidence, wouldn't you agree?"

She sat, her face stony, and didn't answer.

"It was at my friend Colleen's house. You know Colleen, right? Of course you do. You don't like each other much, do you? But Hunter tolerated her. Even asked her for advice now and then, isn't that right? Anyway, before her trailer blew up, I saw a photo that was this one's twin. Only it was of Seth. Probably taken with the same camera. You took his, he took yours, was that how it worked?"

"I told you. I don't remember."

"Spoken in the best tradition of Wall Street bankers and politicians. The smartest guys in the room in the seats of power never remember any of the things that made them fortunes. People are strange that way.

"But no matter. Back to my story. Seth was bugfuck crazy, all right. We know that. And we know what drove him to it – an affair with Freddie, and

Hunter blackballing him so he'd never work in this town again. Isn't that how they say it? But there's a detail to the story that's coming back to me. Hunter and Seth. They got into a fight. And it was over a girl. Seth's girl. One that Hunter put the moves on. Boy, that must have been something. One of the most popular stars in Hollywood, popular, sexy, virile…she must have been extraordinary for him to risk his marriage, and be willing to go *mano a mano* with a younger man like that, am I right? I mean, the town's full of beautiful women, and Hunter could have had any of them." Black shook his head. "But he had to have *that* one. Out of all of them, only that one would do. And it didn't matter if she was someone else's. A guy like Hunter would never let that kind of trivial obstacle get in his way, would he?"

He gazed out the window behind Meagan at the pool area, the trees softly swaying as a warm wind caressed them, blown from the hills, and then continued.

"No, of course he wouldn't. And maybe the girl didn't mind, either. Maybe she'd been given a unique chance to jump the status and celebrity ladder a dozen rungs, and move from an emerging talent to a box office sensation. That must have been an almost impossible choice. Or a really easy one. The art of that deal must have been getting past the inconvenient fact that the star was married. Probably took some doing to get him to walk away from a wife and kid – but men are strange, and sometimes they lose their way, and do anything for another bite of the apple or for a sip from the fountain of youth. It's a common story. Aging star with gray on his muzzle feels invigorated and young again with a woman half – no, less than half – his age. His wife and daughter just make him feel old. But a new, exciting mate, barely more than a girl, with that…anything's possible with a new start in life, right? Am I right?"

"You should write a screenplay. You have an incredible imagination."

Black nodded to himself. "And it ate at Seth. It must have felt like someone cut his guts out, stuck a hot poker in the hole, and burned his soul. Not only did his career go nowhere, but the man who crushed him like a walnut got his girl. It's enough to drive anyone round the bend. I'm not sure how I would react. No, actually, I am – a similar thing kind of happened to me. But that's not important. Like I said, it's a small world, and there are no new ideas. So the years pass, all the while this eating at him like a cancer, the wound festering. And the man's got issues, don't get me wrong. A gay affair gone wrong, unable to work in the career he'd proved himself a talent in…imagine it. Every day. No wonder he hated women. Only…maybe he didn't? Maybe he was still so hopelessly in love with that girl that it became an obsession. Is that how it happened? Did he come to you at some point? Want to rekindle?"

Meagan looked away, unable to meet his eyes.

"Or did you realize that it was him killing the paparazzi? You're smart. It must have occurred to you. Who would have that kind of anger against not only them, but also want to connect it to Hunter to hurt him? That couldn't have been a long list. Or maybe he came to you and asked whether there was still a chance, if Hunter wasn't in the picture? Was that what went down?"

She shrugged. "It's your story. How would I know?"

"I guess in the end it doesn't matter. Maybe you knew that Hunter was screwing everything in a skirt, still trying to feel young and vital in a world that had passed him by. Or maybe you knew about his finances, how he'd squandered his fortune, and feared that you'd lose all this. Or maybe…maybe he was going to dump you for a newer model. Wasn't that his history? You'd already seen him do it twice – and now it was your turn? So maybe with a psychopath like Seth around, there was a solution to your problem. You knew the film wouldn't save him – that was a pipe dream. His dream. But if there was no Hunter…was that how it unfolded? You would reunite with Seth if Hunter dropped out of the picture? Was that the promise? I was wondering how Seth could have known to be here to shoot him. I mean, sure, he could have been watching the house for days. Could have snapped and decided to shoot Hunter when he set foot out his door. Sort of a crescendo of crazy after killing Freddie. But what if he had help? A phone call? To alert him that his chance had come, and there was a way to make it all deniable?"

"Black, I've been patient. I've listened to this rant, and extended you incredible courtesy because of the help you gave my husband, and then me. I think you're a good and honest man in an imperfect world, and maybe the events of the last week have been too much for you. You want possibilities? Here's one that's more plausible: maybe you want to get into my pants, and that's twisted you in some fundamental way. Gotten you to invent nonsensical scenarios. When you realized I wasn't interested in you, I became the villain in your little imaginary melodrama. Black. I'm sorry. But you're way off base with this."

"You mean you don't think I can prove it. Did you tell the cops you knew Seth from before?"

"I told you. I don't remember anything from that period. It was a different era. Lots of drugs. Lots of booze. Plenty of all-nighters. Hunter had a reputation. I was no angel. Everyone was equally guilty of excess." She stopped. "I'm sorry about your friend Colleen. Sorry her trailer blew up."

"Sure you are. I wonder where Seth got the idea that she needed to go? Or that I did? Was that another phone call once you knew we'd found the blood?" Realization slowly dawned on Black and his eyes widened. "Seth wasn't trying to break in, was he? You told him to come, to be together again like you'd promised. To bring his gun so you could dispose of it, and come spend the rest of his life in your arms…And then you shot him. Like a dog, in cold blood. The trail ends there, with the crazy guy trying to finish his rampage by killing the star's wife. Who defends herself after calling everyone she knows to say she's terrified the killer's back for her. Was that how it happened, Meagan?" Black asked, ending in a whisper.

She rose and walked around the desk. "Black. Go get some sleep. You're out of it. Cash your check, take some time off, get some perspective. You're chasing ghosts. This is all a pure flight of fancy."

"Then you won't mind if I take the photo," he threatened, reaching for it. She moved like a coiled snake, so fast it startled him, and grabbed the frame before he could get his hands on it.

"Black, get out of my house. Now. Esmerelda! Esmerelda!" Meagan yelled, holding the photograph behind her, daring Black to try to get it without a fight. One where it would be her story against his – Black came, wanted to try to blackmail her out of more money with some crazy story, and then went berserk. Or maybe tried to have his way with her. Her word against his. In her own home. With the housekeeper coming.

They both heard hurried footsteps approaching down the long hall.

"What's it going to be, Black? We do this the easy way, or the hard way?" Her tone was calm, her eyes flashing with anger, but also quiet confidence. She had him. And she knew it.

Esmerelda appeared in the doorway with a worried expression. Meagan studied Black, and then nodded. "Esmerelda, *Señor* Black was just leaving. Would you show him out?"

Black shook his head and threw her a look of disgust. "You're not going to get away with this."

"Mr. Black, thanks so much for your dedicated service to both my husband and me. I'll be happy to provide you a good reference, if you need one."

"*Señor?*" Esmerelda asked, unsure of what was happening, the tension thick as a toxic fog in the room.

"You haven't heard the end of this, Meagan," Black said, but his words rang hollow, even to his tuned ear.

"It's *Mrs. Hunter*. Please, have a little respect," Meagan said, a small, playful smirk tugging at one corner of her mouth. "Good bye, Mr. Black. Take care of yourself."

The trip back to town was a blur, his mind reeling at the supernova of information that had fallen into place. Seth couldn't have been working alone. Black knew it. Was sure of it. As sure as he had been of anything in his life.

He withdrew the check from his pocket and looked at it as he sat at a red light. Twenty thousand dollars. A little going away present. Have a few crumbs, she was saying, I won this round, the insurance will pay out big time and I'm rich again, my fool husband's blunders a bad memory. Rich, the house in Bel Air paid off, and the tax lien cleared… He wondered how much a guy like Hunter would have in life insurance. Ten million? Fifty? Whatever it was, it would be enough. Better than being divorced, left with nothing – or even worse, stuck with Hunter in an apartment down the street from Black.

Some things were worse than death.

He knew.

Black stopped at Hunter's bank and cashed the check, insisting on two neat stacks of hundred dollar bills. He didn't want to give Meagan any time to reconsider. Which she would.

As he drove back to the office, he activated his phone and waited as the familiar ring sounded in his ear piece.

"Hey, big dog," Stan boomed, obviously in a better mood than of late.

"Hey. What are you doing later?"

"Rihanna's coming over to lap dance for me. What do you think?"

"You wanna get together and have a few pops after work?" Black asked.

"You buying?"

"Cheap bastard."

"Drunkard."

"Degenerate. I'm thinking The Salty Dog, say…seven?"

"Can Rihanna come?"

"You have to buy her drinks. I'm only buying yours. And tell her no entourage," Black warned.

"Cheapskate."

CHAPTER 34

The Salty Dog's interior was dark hardwood with a nautical theme, sextants and rope and pulleys and ancient barometers mounted to walls stained the color of dried blood from the decades of cigarette smoke before the citywide ban forced smokers onto the sidewalks. A tired jukebox crooned Chris Isaak's "Baja Sessions" over sub-par speakers, the singer's velvet voice lamenting lost love and heartbreak down Mexico way. A spectral bartender with an oil slick comb-over, who more resembled a mortician than drink server, stood behind the bar gazing at the entry with a vacant stare, the door a thick slab of mahogany with a porthole mounted on it. Behind him a sign warning that checks were not accepted and that no credit would be extended to patrons regardless of the circumstances hung crookedly over a blotchy mirror that had been ancient in the forties.

Stan sat at one of the crate-top tables nursing a Rolling Rock beer while Black sipped at his Red Hook pale ale and told him his theory. When he finished, Stan sat back and shook his head.

"Welcome to my life, Black. Bad people do bad things every day. A lot of the time, they get away with it. If I can catch seventy to eighty percent of the most obvious miscreants, I'm a rock star. But that means that twenty percent, at least, get away with it. Remember, in that number are the gang bangers who are caught shooting each other on security cams, domestic murders where there are witnesses, obvious drug deals gone wrong where everyone involved is so addled that they leave evidence everywhere…"

"I know. This is more sophisticated. But there's got to be a way to prove it."

"Sure. Get her to confess on camera. That would be a good start. Or have her sign and date a confession while her lawyer's present. Or better yet, have her be a complete dumbshit like her husband and carry out the crime in full view of every phone cam in L.A. Barring that, I'm just trying to tell you, there's not a lot of chance the D.A. is going to want to move forward with this – and I wouldn't blame him. What's your evidence?"

"Maybe Seth's phone has some calls from her?"

"Sure. Maybe the mastermind of the perfect crime didn't think about getting a burner for the critical calls. I'll check his records, but don't hold your breath."

"Can't you triangulate where the calls came from if you have the number?"

"You been watching *24* again? Wake up, Black. We live in an imperfect world."

"You saying you can't?"

"I'm saying that even if there's a cell tower that shows a call or two to Seth from Bel Air, that's not enough to bring a case. Not hardly. She'll just say that she has no idea what we're talking about. We make the case that she lured him there, and then her attorney trots out that the victim is a mass-murderer who killed her husband two days before. You want to pitch that one to a jury? I'm just telling you that no Los Angeles prosecuting attorney in his right mind wants another celebrity murder trial gone wrong. And if we came down on her for this, it would be front page. It's a tough case to make at the best of times. You throw in a gorgeous widow who was a victim…no, thanks."

"But she's not a victim. There's the photo."

"No, there *was* the photo. That baby caught fire before you were out of the driveway. And even if it was still there, where's its twin? Blown to kingdom come in Riverside County white trash a-go-go. Face it. You got nothing."

"I'll admit, it's circumstantial. But it's compelling. There's the pre-nup that Roxie came up with, the motive of the insurance…maybe we can find someone who knew her back in the day who would swear that she knew Seth. Maybe she was at Sundance with him. There might be photos…"

"You heard her defense. 'I don't remember any of that, it's all a blur.' By the time this went to trial, it would be fourteen or fifteen years in the past. All she has to do is say that she's slept with over a hundred men since then, and there goes your motive. I'm just telling you, it's iffy at best."

"Will you at least look into it? Do some digging?"

"I'll do it for you, Buttercup. Because you got a real purty little mouf."

"Those prison marriages never last."

"Can't we just enjoy it for what it is?"

"Why won't the world just let us be?"

They finished their beers, their third each, and Stan shook his head. "Dude. Don't let this define you. I know you. You're going to let it gnaw your guts out, inch by inch. That's a mistake. You've done everything that you could. Sometimes that's the best you can do."

"It wasn't good enough for Cesar, was it?"

"But it was for your friend Colleen. You can't make the world perfect, Black. It's always been a messy bowl of crap, and always will be. Take it from a guy who's spent his life scooping it up after the fan sprays it everywhere. Take the wins when you get 'em, because you're gonna have more losses than wins in the end. If you aren't losing, you aren't trying."

"Easy for you to say."

"Because I don't have a cleft palate." Stan pushed his empty beer away. "Go home, Black. Find someone to kiss and hug, and make them feel special. Barring that, get a dog. But don't dwell on this. I'll do what I can. I promise. But don't expect too much. This isn't a winning lottery ticket by any means."

"I have a stray cat that hates my guts and is going to have to be buried in a piano crate, he's so fat."

"So go hug him."

"He'd probably claw me. Fat little bastard."

"Don't be so sure. Cats are weird that way."

"I didn't know you liked cats."

"Of course. Especially deep fat fried."

Black paid the bill and they went their separate ways, the Mercedes ambling at its customary leisurely pace, which he was getting used to. What was everyone in such a hurry for? The ride always ended in the same destination. Why not slow down and try to enjoy it?

Stan's fatalistic attitude annoyed him, but he hadn't been expecting much more. He knew how things worked, and close wasn't the same as crossing the finish line – or as Seth had discovered, there was a world of difference between first and second place. But maybe Stan would turn something up. Black would have Roxie continue to dig as well, and between them, they might get lucky.

Although Lady Luck hadn't been dancing the fandango with him lately. But that might just mean that he was overdue.

The thought pulled him in the direction of Preacher's apartment, and twelve minutes later he was parked and walking up the sidewalk, approaching the grim little complex. The Vietnamese sentry had called it a day, and the scumbag's apartment was dark. Strike three, he thought bitterly. Still, he was already there, so he ascended the stairs and knocked on the door. Predictably, there was no answer, and he tried one last time before calling it a night.

The door to the apartment next to Preacher's popped open and a young woman, maybe early thirties, with a shaggy mop of blonde hair tied back with a bandana, stuck her head out and looked Black over.

"Nobody living there anymore," she said with a pronounced accent. Maybe German, Black thought.

"Really? When did he move?"

"Yesterday. He was only here for an hour."

"Did he leave a forwarding address, do you know?"

She reappraised him. "What are you, a bill collector?"

"Kind of."

"What does kind of mean?"

"I'm a private investigator."

"Really? Like on TV?"

"Not exactly like on TV, but close enough. I don't have a car chase every episode or slug it out with the bad guy. More like this kind of thing."

"Trying to find people?"

"Yeah. Like that. Listen, I know this is a lot to ask, but could I give you a card, and if he comes back, would you call me? There's a reward in it."

She frowned. "A reward? What did he do?"

"Took some money from the wrong guy."

"How much is the reward?"

Black thought quickly. "Two hundred dollars."

She sized him up. She had beautiful blue eyes, he noticed, and the accent was…exotic.

"Big spender. Sure. Give me your card. He was a jerk, anyway. Always hitting on me."

Which Black could completely understand, though he didn't say so. He handed her one of his cards and their fingers touched. Black felt a tingle, like a tiny electric charge had passed between them. Their gaze locked for an instant, and then she looked away.

"Okay, then. I guess that's it. Thanks. Maybe he'll come back one more time," Black said.

"You never know."

"If you don't mind, where are you from? I don't recognize the accent."

"Switzerland."

"Really? What part?" Black asked, realizing he had no inkling of anything about Switzerland beyond that it was in Europe, and famous for money laundering, chocolate, and watches.

"Basel. It's really nice there."

"What are you doing here? In L.A.?"

"I'm an artist. I had a show at a gallery in town a few months ago and sold a few paintings, so I decided to stick around for a while and see what I could put together. The owner sponsored me for a temporary visa…"

"Your English is really good."

She smiled shyly. "Thanks. I don't think so."

"No, really. It is. Wow. An artist. Like painting?"

"Exactly."

"What's your name?"

"Sylvia." She peered at the card. "I see yours is…Jim Black."

"Everyone just calls me Black."

"Ha. Like a cat. That's bad luck, right?"

"Lately it has been."

The conversation stuttered to a halt, and Black shifted nervously, preparing to leave. He backed away and was about to say good night when he was seized by an alien impulse. She regarded him, the beginning of a puzzled smile on her face, and he cleared his throat before speaking words that seemed like they were someone else's.

"Sylvia, I know this is going to sound weird, and probably really creepy, but here goes anyway. I've had a really lousy day, and you're the best thing…I mean, it's been a long one, and I don't want to go home yet. Is there any way I can get you to have a drink with me? Or a cup of coffee?"

"Are you for real?"

"I…never mind. It was a dumb idea. I'm sorry," Black said, realizing how inappropriate he was being. "Please call me if he returns. That's all I ask. Sorry for disturbing you."

He turned and was making his way back to the stairs when Sylvia called after him.

"Can you wait ten minutes? I need to put some fresh clothes on."

CHAPTER 35

Black rolled over and glared hatefully at the alarm clock shrieking like a jilted lover two feet from his head. He pawed at it and silenced the infernal contraption, then closed his eyes again, giving himself a few moments to come to. It was eight, another day in Lost Angeles, and he had the mildest trace of a hangover. Not much, and certainly nothing like a few days earlier, but still there – a worthwhile remnant of the four beers he'd had with Sylvia while she told him her story. The promised half hour in a bar a few blocks away had stretched to two, and while they weren't buying each other jewelry yet, he felt like they'd hit it off. She was smart and had a quirky sense of humor – she didn't talk a lot, but when she said something, it was usually funny. He liked that. It had been the best couple of hours he'd spent in some time, and they'd agreed to get together on Friday night for dinner.

All in all, an unexpected end to a lousy episode. He opened his eyes and spotted the two stacks of hundreds on his chest of drawers. Okay, maybe not the worst episode, but not a great one, by any means. Although it had finished on a good note. Maybe not Stan's hug and *I love you*, but still, close enough.

Black threw the sheet off and forced himself upright and into the bathroom for a vigorous shower before heading in to work.

He stopped at Gracie's at eight-forty and knocked lightly at the door.

"Who is it?" her voice called from inside.

"Black. Trick or treat."

The door swung open and she greeted him with a wrinkled smile. "Why, Black. You do look handsome this morning. What a great suit. Nothing like a well-dressed man."

"Thanks, Gracie. I'm giddy from the flattery."

"You look good, babe. Really good. If I was a hundred years younger…"

"Is Jared here?"

"He's just getting ready for work."

"Can I come in for a second? I need to talk to him."

206

"Sure. *Mi casa* and all. You want an eye opener?"

"Not today, Gracie. Duty calls."

Gracie turned from him, obviously disappointed, and called out to the walls, "Jared. Jar-red, honey, Black's here."

Jared appeared from the spare bedroom, his unruly hair still wet, and glared dully at Black. "Hey. What's up?" he asked.

"I found your guy."

"You did?" Jared perked up, and then like a battered spouse expecting the next punch, flinched at the expected bad news. "Let me guess. The money's gone. I knew it."

"Not so fast. I got your money back. I've got it right here. What was the deal? Five grand, minus twenty percent. You already gave me two hundred, so that means I owe you forty-two hundred bucks. Which I have…here," Black said, and then pulled a small roll of hundreds from his jacket pocket, bound with a red rubber band, and tossed it to him.

Jared's face lit up, and he stared at the money unbelievingly.

Gracie hugged him, and clapped him on the back. "Oh, Black! You did it. This calls for a celebration!"

"Not for me, Gracie."

Jared fidgeted, counting the money, and then looked up. "Mr. Black. Thanks so much. I figured I was screwed."

"I wouldn't quit your job just yet, and I think you've learned you have to be more careful – even if the opportunity seems impossible to turn down. Or is wearing a mini-skirt. Am I right?"

Jared nodded, clenching the bills tightly in his hand.

Black looked around. "All right. I have to run. Gracie, be good. Don't celebrate too much."

"How's *La Bomba* treating you?"

"Perfect. I appreciate you lending her to me."

"When are you getting a new car?"

"Should be any day." The insurance company owed him twenty grand for his Cadillac, which wouldn't buy a replacement, but might come close. Well worth the premiums he'd been making for years. *If they ever cut a check.* Tight-fisted bastards. Everyone was trying to get an edge, usually on his dime. "I'll have *La Bomba* back to you in no time. Thanks again. She's been great."

"Now I know you're lying to me. But since it's you, you can get away with it. You in that suit. I can't believe some lucky girl hasn't snapped you up," Gracie said.

"I'm working on it," Black said, and grinned sheepishly. "Now I have to get out of here."

"Thanks again, Mr. Black," Jared called, and Black noted how it was suddenly Mr. Black now that he'd performed.

Maybe that was the trick in all of it. Execution.

Gracie waved good-bye to him as he walked down the concrete path to the rear of the building where the old Mercedes was parked, and he continued past it to the street.

His knock on Cesar's door was answered by a middle-aged Latina woman who looked like she'd fought her share of battles, and was fighting them still.

"Yes?" she asked distrustfully.

"Are you Cesar's girlfriend?"

"Who wants to know?"

"I'm a friend of his. Jim."

"I don't know no Jim."

"Haven't seen him in a while. Are you his girlfriend?"

"I am. What's it to you?" she asked, defiance and a hint of apprehension in her tone.

"I owe Cesar some money. I heard about what happened, and I figured maybe you could use it. I'm sorry, by the way."

"How much?"

"By now, it's got to be five grand. The interest's the killer. I may be a little high, but I rounded up. Here," he said, and handed her the money he'd counted out on the way there.

Her eyes got big as softballs at the unexpected windfall – a small fortune in their neighborhood. "Wha – thank you. Thank you so much. I wasn't sure how I was going to get by this month…"

"No need to thank me. I owed him the money. He would have done the same. He was a good man."

Black was whistling as he returned to the Paradise Palms and approached the Mercedes. Doing good deeds seemed to agree with him.

When he arrived at the office, only three minutes late, Roxie wasn't there yet, and Mugsy greeted him by rubbing cat hair all over the leg of his freshly cleaned suit. Black kneeled down and spent some time petting him, marveling at his girth, and then after scratching the porky feline behind the ears, entered his office. Mugsy followed him in and managed a vault onto one of his guest chairs before curling up and promptly nodding off.

Black counted out eight banknotes from the second stack of hundreds, then folded the bills and stuffed the rest into his pocket. He was waiting for his computer to finish booting up when Roxie shuffled in.

"You here this early? What's the occasion?"

"It's Christmas every day in Black country."

Her head poked into the doorway, her mascara a little lighter than usual. "Hit the eggnog this morning?" she asked.

"Not yet. Didn't you have a show last night?"

"Yeah. But we were middle bill, so I got out earlier than when we're the headliner."

"How did it go?"

"We rocked. We rolled. And the crowd went wild."

"So not bad?"

"It was a good night. Why are you in such a good mood?"

"I just am. Is that against the law?"

"No, boss. I'm just worried that you may be having a stroke or something. It's...unexpected. Although I see you trotted out the Victorian clothing, so you must be okay."

"It's a perfectly acceptable suit, Roxie."

"You live in L.A. Even the suits don't wear suits."

"I do. I prefer a little formality sometimes. Is that a problem?"

"Nope. Always ready for a funeral."

"I've got that going for me," he conceded.

"What's with the money?" she asked, her gaze settling on the eight hundred bucks on his desk.

"I need you to find the address of the humane society and take this to them and donate it. Get a receipt for the taxes."

She didn't blink. "You're drunk. I knew it."

"I'm stone cold sober."

"Not that there's anything wrong with an elderly gentleman softening life's blows with a morning tumbler of Ballerina vodka, or anything."

"I'm not elderly."

"And no gentleman," Roxie observed.

"We agree on something. Just take the money in and put the receipt on my desk."

"But I'll have to leave the office. You hate when I'm not in the office."

"I'll risk it."

"What about all the phone calls?"

"I'll risk them going to voicemail."

She shrugged. "Okay, Mr. Moneybags. Your wish is my command." She spotted Mugsy on his chair. "What's he doing in there? You hate when he goes into your office."

"I'm making an exception today. On account of it's Christmas and all. In March."

"Now I really am worried about you. I'm not kidding."

"Worry not. I'm strong like a bull."

She stared at him and then snapped her fingers. Her eyebrows raised with dawning awareness. "Wait. Did you get lucky last night?"

"What kind of question is that?"

"You did, didn't you?"

"I don't have to answer that."

"I knew it."

"I didn't get lucky."

"Sure."

"Really."

"Actually, not if you were wearing that outfit, you didn't. I believe you."

"You do?"

"Not."

Traffic out to Colleen's trailer park was typical morning congestion, but Black found that it didn't bother him as much as it normally did. Even the Mercedes' recalcitrant performance couldn't mar his good humor, and when he arrived at the Oasis, he was whistling again.

Colleen was staying at Stu's place, and she met him at the door with a cup of coffee in her hand.

"How are you managing?" he asked, and their eyes drifted to her lot, where the charred remains of her home were all that was left to show for a life's work.

"Could be worse. Stu's been a doll."

"What's the plan?"

"Like I said on the phone, I'm waiting on the insurance company to pay out on the trailer," she said.

"How much do you have coming to you?"

"Fifteen grand. It's hard to find a trailer with furniture for that nowadays. I'll be looking for something from the sixties, I guess."

"Don't people die all the time in these places? No offense. But they're retirement communities. What happens to their trailers?"

"Usually the kids want to unload them, or a broker gets involved. But even so, they cost more than you'd think."

"What would a decent one run?"

"Twenty. Twenty-five. For a single-wide on a fire sale. I've been looking. I mean, they can go all the way to a hundred or more, but I'm not picky."

"Well, I want to make a contribution." Black withdrew a thick white envelope and handed it to her. "That's ten grand. With the insurance, you should be able to do okay."

She took the envelope from him with a look of shock. "Is this…did you rob a bank?"

"Nah. All part of the Black philanthropic foundation's good work. But be careful with those. I just printed them."

Colleen weighed the envelope and then set her coffee cup down on a nearby outdoor table and hugged him tight. "You're an angel. How can I ever thank you enough?"

"Find me some clients. Somebody's gotta pay for me being Santa Claus."

Black stayed for fifteen minutes – just long enough to tour the wreckage and wish her well, and then he got back into the Mercedes, having begged off any further visiting with the legitimate excuse of having to get back to town and try to earn his keep. He watched Colleen in his rearview mirror as he rolled slowly away, standing next to Stu, who was hovering near her protectively outside of his trailer, and a grin played across Black's face.

"You'll do just fine," he said to himself, and then twisted the knob of the old radio and began searching for a decent station for the long ride back to Hollywood.

211

CHAPTER 36

Black was surprised three weeks later when Stan rang him on a Saturday. Their occasional cocktail soirées typically took place on weekdays, to keep them both from staying out all night on a bender. If they had to work the next morning, at least there was an external imposition of discipline and order into their chaotic inner workings. Left to their own devices, they would egg each other on, and soon it would be three a.m. in an illegal after-hours casino in Chinatown drinking ten dollar paper cups of Ballentine's.

It had been a while since he'd heard from Stan. Time had flown by, and Black had been otherwise occupied with several new cases – and with Sylvia, which was developing into a good thing.

"Hey, wild man. Where you been hiding?" Black asked, upon seeing the caller ID on his cell.

"You seen the news today?"

"Why would I want to ruin my day with the news? Why, did the zombie apocalypse start and nobody told me?"

"You got time for lunch?" Stan asked.

"You buying?"

"Sure. Mickey D's or Carl's?"

"Easy one. Carl's. Up by your building?"

"Yup. Half an hour?"

"Be still my beating heart."

Stan was already there when Black arrived in *La Bomba*, wolfing down a double burger with extra everything. Black ordered the same and then carried the heaping tray to the table and unwrapped his lunch with relish.

"You haven't called. I thought it was me," Black said between bites.

"So you didn't hear about Meagan?"

"Nope. What about her? She kill anyone else lately?"

"Only herself. Yesterday. Hit a tree doing eighty in the Valley at four a.m."

Black stopped eating. "You're kidding me."

"No. She's gone to her just reward."

"Shed her mortal coil."

"Been called to heaven."

"You going to eat all your fries?" Black asked.

"That's a good way to lose a finger. Or a hand." Stan took another greasy bite.

"Wonder what happened with her?"

"Her blood alcohol was .35. Nearly blacked out. Had some valium in her system, too. And a little coke," Stan said. "Unofficially, of course."

"Sounds like someone should sue the airbag company."

"Or the tree."

"Damned trees are ruining everything. Drugs don't kill people. Trees do."

"Frigging menace, they are."

Black finished his burger and belched softly.

"Classy," Stan said.

"In China, that would be a compliment. Or maybe that's New York."

"To answer your question, she was in the Valley because she moved there. The daughter kicked her ass out of the house after the will was read."

"Really? How'd that happen?"

"Daughter got half the house, and Meagan got the other. But all that meant was that Meagan inherited the debt."

"What about the insurance?"

"Fifteen million – all to the daughter. Meagan went nuts when she found out. Hunter had changed the policy a couple of months ago without telling her. Looks like maybe your theory about a divorce was right."

"So Meagan didn't have the money to settle the liens or the debt…"

"And the daughter did. Actually, the daughter said she was selling the house. Hates it there. But in the short term, she bought Meagan's share of the debt for fifty grand – which was generous."

"Who would buy an obligation like that?"

"Someone who'd pay fifty grand to kick her stepmom's ass out of the house."

"Ah."

"So she was living in Woodland Hills. Affluent area, but not Bel Air. Wrong side of the hill. And fifty grand's nothing to a dame like that."

"She had a big rock on her finger."

"Fine. Call it a hundred. Still, a big letdown if you've been expecting fifteen million."

"She had to have other jewelry."

"Point is, it wasn't enough. No way. What would it buy her, with her lifestyle and expectations? A year?"

"Sounds like she had no plan B."

"Nope."

"So she was out, smashed, probably trying to find another meal ticket…and buh-bye, baby?"

"Either that or the tree looked like the easy way out. We'll never really know."

They sat quietly, and then Stan finished his fries and slurped the last of his full tilt Coke before standing. "Other than that, Mrs. Lincoln…"

"Wow. All that. For nothing."

"As are all our petty schemes."

"Too true, Socrates."

"Please. Call me Nietzsche if you want a piece of this." Stan pointed at his considerable waist and did a little waddle.

"Wiggle wiggle wiggle it. I heard that on the radio last week. Who buys this shit?" Black complained.

"I actually like that song. Although you're dating yourself."

"That little belly dancing routine was a horrifying display, by the way. Those kids are going to need counseling." Black indicated three gang-bangers at a table across the dining area.

"Poor things. Probably won't be able to hold their Desert Eagles steady tonight."

"It's all about the children, you selfish prick," Black confirmed.

"As it should be."

They exited the restaurant together and stood blinking in the midday glare.

"Anything else going on?" Stan asked.

"Got a girl."

Stan poked him in the ribs with his elbow. "Get out of here."

"It's true. From Switzerland. She's an ahhhtist."

"Very highbrow. You go to museums together?"

"Among other things."

"Discuss Fauvism and Impressionism and argue over the merits of Degas versus Dali?" Stan asked.

"Look at you. Mister sophisticate, speaking Latin or whatever that was."

"You like her?"

Black watched a Toyota Tacoma with a couple of surfer girls in it pull into the lot, laughing uproariously as they drove by, living the worry-free California dreamin' life that would only last the blink of an eye.

"Yeah. I do."

"Then so do I."

"We should go out sometime."

"Oh, yeah. Absolutely. I can tell crime scene jokes and show her my snapshots. The ladies love those."

"Seriously."

"Black. This is your movie. I'd just be a third wheel. Enjoy it while it lasts. I'll still be around."

Black made his way back to the car and paused before starting it. The insurance company had been promising a check for weeks now. Any day, the adjuster would lie, when he called. Fortunately, Gracie was good natured and hated to drive, so in exchange for the continued use of the *La Bomba*, Black had taken to doing a Driving Miss Daisy with her twice a week to replenish her alcohol and food stocks. For now, it worked for them both, but he was ready to move on and get his own ride again. He had his eye on a car in Nevada that only had eighty-five thousand miles on it, being sold by a little old lady, and he thought he could snag it for under twenty. If the damned insurance would ever pay out.

The engine coughed to life, polluting the surroundings with the usual black cloud of doom, and he settled back into the uncomfortable seat and belted in before swinging out onto Rampart and stomping on the throttle like he was driving a getaway car, mostly just to hear the motor clatter like microwave popcorn going off under the hood. He eased past a new AMG Mercedes driven by an immaculately groomed young man wearing a Robert Graham silk shirt, and checked his reflection in the mirror to confirm how he felt.

He looked happy.

CHAPTER 37

Dr. Kelso's eyes appeared to be glazing over, their time dwindling like a losing gambler's chips as Black finished describing his discussion with Stan and his reaction to Meagan's come-uppance.

"The thing is, I was glad when he told me. I mean, not glad that she'd killed herself. More glad in a karmic justice kind of way. It was like the universe had fallen into balance, and everything was right again. Does that make sense?"

"Mmm."

"Are you listening? Or did you fall asleep?"

"I'm listening. I just don't have an observation."

"I express satisfaction that a young, beautiful woman died, and you have no comment?"

"You mentioned that you were attracted to her."

"I did. I was. But she was married."

"Were you angry that she was married?"

"No. Of course not."

"But you're glad she's dead. Serves her right, is that it?"

"Did you miss the part where she plotted her husband's murder, as well as my friend's, before killing her accomplice?"

"I understand that's what you believe. But you also mentioned there was no proof."

"True. But I know I was right."

"It's probably not useful to debate that."

"Agreed."

"But I'd like to explore the idea that you might have been angry because you wanted her and couldn't have her."

"That's not what happened. Of course I could have had her. I took the high road on that."

"Of course. But how did that make you feel?"

"Morally superior."

"Anything else?"

"Maybe a little frustrated."

"Yes. Now we're getting somewhere. So you were frustrated, and maybe that made you angry."

"No, I don't think so."

"You don't find it strange that the first woman you'll readily admit being attracted to in a long time frustrated you, and now you're glad she's dead?"

"That's distorting what I'm saying."

"You weren't attracted to her?"

"Well, yes. I said so."

"And she frustrated you? Or rather, you were frustrated at not having sex with her?"

"I chose not to. And I felt *physically* frustrated. Not frustrated with her."

"Your distinction, not mine. And you're glad she's dead?"

"Glad is a strong word."

"Really? Your word, not mine."

"I modified that. I'm not glad she's dead…" Black said.

Kelso sighed. "Are you unhappy she's dead?"

"Not really."

"Are you neutral on her being dead?"

"Don't think I don't see what you're doing here."

"That's a deflection."

The chime sounded, indicating that the session was over. Kelso looked up, and Black could have sworn that he wore a fleeting expression of relief before his masklike demeanor returned.

"We didn't even touch on my new relationship, which is with a woman, by the way, who I'm not angry with in any way, and who doesn't make me angry or frustrated."

"It's really a shame we don't have time for that. But you know what the chime means."

"It's time to pay you."

"I see that you're still angry about that part of our relationship, too."

"Ah, so you *can* discuss things after the chime, like my anger over paying you for what feels like a total waste of my time."

"I also appreciate how you are trying to cheapen our interaction by discounting the progress you've made."

Black stood and smiled at Kelso. "I'm sorry. I'd love to discuss that, but our time's up. Maybe we can explore it next time?"

Kelso bristled, and then resumed the detached air that was his professional norm. "I'll look forward to it."

On the way to the parking lot, Black realized that he actually did feel better for having told Kelso about the whole experience. It made no sense, but there it was. Like a weight he'd been carrying had lifted, and he was in danger of floating off into space.

Once in traffic he called a number from his speed dial and listened to it ring.

"Hello?"

"Mom. It's Black."

"Hello?"

"Mom. Fiddle with your headset. Turn up the volume."

"Can you hear me?"

"I can hear you fine. You need to turn up your volume."

"I'm sorry. Whoever this is, you need to call back. We have a bad connection."

Black stared at the disconnected phone in disbelief, then pressed redial.

"Hello?"

"Mom?"

"Hello..."

Third try was a charm after she hung up on him again.

"Mom."

"Artemus! I just had the two strangest calls. I'm glad you could get through."

"That was me, Mom."

"Please. *Spring*. Remember?"

"Right. Spring. How are you and...Chakra?"

"I'm so happy to hear from you. We're good. Everything's wonderful. How about you?"

"Couldn't be better. Still got all my teeth," Black said.

"I'm so glad you find time to go to the dentist, honey."

He veered around a truck double parked in front of a bakery and received a horn toot from the Miata behind him. *Suck on it*, he thought, then continued talking.

"How did things turn out with your candle deal?"

218

"Oh, you know. It felt like such a relief to get rid of it. Although I miss being busy."

"What do you mean, you got rid of it? You shut it down?"

"No, silly. I sold it. To the nice people Trader Nick's put us in touch with."

"You sold another company?"

"Yes. I mean, sort of."

"Ah. So you didn't sell it."

"Well, I guess technically we didn't. We swapped our shares for a bunch of shares of their parent company. It's so exciting watching the price change on the exchange every day. That's my new hobby."

"You did a stock swap with a publicly traded company for your candle business? What's the name of the company?"

"I guess that's right. All I know is that it sounds like Berkeley. That seemed like a fortuitous omen. Oh, right. You father says it's Berkshire Amway."

"You're kidding."

"No, but we have to hold onto them for a while. That was part of the deal."

"Did you mean Berkshire Hathaway?"

"That sounds right. Anyway, everyone was so nice, it felt like the perfect thing to do."

Black cleared his throat. "I'm sure it was."

"Have you talked to Nina lately?"

"No. I'm kind of dating someone."

"Really! Why honey, that's marvelous!" she said, a question imbedded in her response.

"A woman. From Switzerland."

"How nice. How did you meet her?"

"I just did. Sort of one of those things."

Spring called out to her husband. "Chakra! Artemus is dating a woman! From Swaziland!"

"Switzerland, Mom. I'm pretty sure Swaziland is in Africa. Switzerland is in Europe."

"Even better. I'm so happy for you."

"I love you, Mom."

"Spring. And I love you too, Artemus."

When Black disengaged he felt drained, but he was inexplicably still in a good mood. His airhead hippy mother, who dismissed material goods and money as unimportant, had managed to sell a hobby business to Berkshire while he was struggling to make ends meet, in a great cosmic F-you, and it didn't bother him. He wondered for an instant whether he might have a tumor or something growing in his brain, then shook it off. As his mom would say, negative vibes. He considered calling Sylvia, but he was going to see her in six hours, and he didn't want to seem too clingy, so instead he turned on the radio and hummed along to Shakira's latest, which normally would have had him clawing his eardrums out.

Roxie was immersed in a video game when he entered the office, and only glanced up for a second before returning to it, at least having the decency to turn the sound down on the speakers so he didn't have to listen to the blasts and tortured screams as she fought her way to whatever the next level was. He sorted through the incoming mail and tossed the bills into her in-basket, then tore open the final one and removed a form with a check attached.

"Any calls?" he asked, eyeing Mugsy, who had struggled to lift his big fat head to look at Black before returning to his daily *siesta*, which lasted approximately sixteen hours, from what Black could tell.

"What's that?" she asked, annoyed at the interruption.

"Calls. Anyone call for me?"

"No. Nothing."

"Well then. Carry on."

She appeared to register that he was actually standing there, and paused the game.

"Oh. Wait. Somebody from the IRS called. Wanted to confirm the physical address for service."

"You're kidding."

"I didn't realize the IRS did service. On what? The office equipment? All we have is the copier. I thought that Ted dude came over and handled that once a month."

"Roxie. Please tell me you're joking."

"Anyway, I told them you were out."

"Did they leave a number?"

"You really will believe anything I say, won't you?"

"So it's a joke?" he asked, his heart having resumed beating.

She batted her big eyes at him. "Isn't everything?"

He nodded and returned the smile. "Well played. But you can't ruin my day."

"Why?"

"Because I'm headed out again."

"Really? You just got here."

"Yes, I did. And now I'm leaving."

She looked confused, and like a trout surging to the surface to bite at a spinning lure, she was compelled to ask the obvious question. He waited, watching the internal battle, and then she caved.

"Where are you going?"

He twisted the front door lever and threw Mugsy a beauty queen wave. Mugsy didn't notice. Black held the check aloft in triumph as he pulled the door open, a gleam in his eye and a spring in his step.

"Probably to hell, in the end. In the meantime, I'm buying a car."

To be alerted to new releases, sign up here:

http://russellblake.com/contact/mailing-list

ABOUT THE AUTHOR

Russell Blake lives full time on the Pacific coast of Mexico. He is the acclaimed author of the thrillers *Fatal Exchange, The Geronimo Breach, Zero Sum,* The Delphi Chronicle trilogy (*The Manuscript, The Tortoise and the Hare,* and *Phoenix Rising*), *King of Swords, Night of the Assassin, Return of the Assassin, Revenge of the Assassin, Blood of the Assassin, The Voynich Cypher, Silver Justice, JET, JET II – Betrayal, JET III – Vengeance, JET IV – Reckoning, Jet V – Legacy, Upon a Pale Horse,* and *BLACK.*

Non-fiction novels include the international bestseller *An Angel With Fur* (animal biography) and *How To Sell A Gazillion eBooks (while drunk, high or incarcerated)* – a joyfully vicious parody of all things writing and self-publishing related.

"Capt." Russell enjoys writing, fishing, playing with his dogs, collecting and sampling tequila, and waging an ongoing battle against world domination by clowns.

Visit Russell's salient website for more information

http://russellblake.com/